The Makeover Mission

MARY BUCKHAM

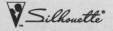

INTIMATE MOMENTS™

Published by Silhouette Books

America's Publisher of Contemporary Romance

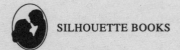 SILHOUETTE BOOKS

ISBN 0-373-27378-9

THE MAKEOVER MISSION

Visit Silhouette Books at www.eHarlequin.com

Printed in U.S.A.

Where was the legendary McConneghy control? The ability to shut off all emotions to get the mission accomplished?

Shot to hell the moment he saw this doe-eyed young woman, her look pleading with him to save her.

As if he were some angel of mercy. Hell, he was the reason she was here. And the sooner she knew it, and accepted what her role was, the better it would be for all concerned.

So far, this mission had been a disaster. If they'd had more time, they could have foregone the crudeness of a kidnapping. Avoided the emotional and physical costs the woman before him was already paying.

But if there was one thing he had accepted after years of service, there was no going back and correcting past mistakes. There was only going forward and minimizing future ones. Someone always paid. In this case—her.

Jane Richards was his responsibility now. And he would do everything in his power to keep her alive. Everything.

Dear Reader,

The weather's hot, and so are all six of this month's Silhouette Intimate Moments books. We have a real focus on miniseries this time around, starting with the last in Ruth Langan's DEVIL'S COVE quartet, *Retribution*. Mix a hero looking to heal his battered soul, a heroine who gives him a reason to smile again and a whole lot of danger, and you've got a recipe for irresistible reading.

Linda Turner's back—after *way* too long—with the first of her new miniseries, TURNING POINTS. A beautiful photographer who caught the wrong person in her lens has no choice but to ask the cops—make that *one particular cop*—for help, and now both her life and her heart are in danger of being lost. FAMILY SECRETS: THE NEXT GENERATION continues with Marie Ferrarella's *Immovable Objects,* featuring a heroine who walks the line between legal, illegal—and love. *Dangerous Deception* from Kylie Brant continues THE TREMAINE TRADITION of mixing suspense and romance—not to mention sensuality— in doses no reader will want to resist. And don't miss our stand-alone titles, either. Cindy Dees introduces you to *A Gentleman and A Soldier* in a military reunion romance that will have your heart pounding and your fingers turning the pages as fast as they can. Finally, welcome Mary Buckham, whose debut novel, *The Makeover Mission,* takes a plain Jane and turns her into a princess—literally. Problem is, this princess is in danger, and now so is Jane.

Enjoy them all—and come back next month for the best in romantic excitement, only from Silhouette Intimate Moments.

Yours,

Leslie J. Wainger
Executive Editor

Please address questions and book requests to:
Silhouette Reader Service
U.S.: 3010 Walden Ave., P.O. Box 1325, Buffalo, NY 14269
Canadian: P.O. Box 609, Fort Erie, Ont. L2A 5X3

MARY BUCKHAM

has always believed in make-believe. As a child she roped, cajoled and bullied her brothers and sisters, along with any unsuspecting neighbor child, into elaborate story productions put on in her backyard or basement. Swashbuckling pirates, damsels in distress, and heroes and heroines—this was Mary's role—who saved the day. As an adult, Mary made sure her five children had a trunk of dress-up clothes and plenty of space to create their own make-believe worlds. She married her Prince Charming, one who doesn't mind that she talks with imaginary people and who learned to cook as a self-preservation measure. She lives in a picturesque Pacific Northwest seaport community filled with writers, artists and musicians, all constantly proving that the power of make-believe can make magic happen. Mary loves hearing from readers, writers and everyone in between. You can reach her via her Web site, www.marybuckham.com.

I think one's first dedication page is the hardest to write, because there are so many to thank for their support, encouragement and help over the years.

For my mom, Joy Arsenault, and my mother-in-law, Marilyn Buckham, and Allie Burnell, who all believed. For Sandi Harbert, who was there from the first lines written. For critique partners and fellow writers, friends and believers and, especially, my husband, Jim, and my children—Lizzie, Michael, Brittany, Devon and Tyler— I couldn't have done this without any of you. Thanks!

Chapter 1

"Tell the major she's awake."

Jane Richards snapped her head back, paying for the movement with a pounding that felt like a band of fire across her temples.

Who was the major? And where was she?

She blinked, straining to see into the darkness. Nothing. Something shielded her eyes. What? Why?

Panic tightened her throat.

She attempted to rip off whatever covered her eyes. But her hands wouldn't budge. They were strapped to the blunt edges of what felt like armrests.

Blindfolded and trapped.

But why? Where?

"Who are you?" The words were hers, but the voice didn't sound like her own. It sounded weak and scared.

No one answered.

The air around her felt clammy. The darkness seemed uniform throughout. There were no traffic sounds beyond thin windows, no voices through walls. The only noise permeating the silence came from behind her. The sound of someone breathing. Slow, even breaths. The sound from a child's nightmare. The sound from a woman's worst fears.

But it was real. And it was happening to her.

She wanted to scream. The temptation to struggle against the bonds trapping her was stronger. It must be a nightmare. It had to be. People like her did not end up in dark rooms with their hands tied to the arms of chairs.

"Who are you? Why am I here?" Her voice shook; her whole body mimicked it.

No answer. The breathing continued. Evenly paced and controlled.

She had to keep calm, to regain control. Isn't that what they'd told her during library fire drills? *The person who panics is the person who's lost.* And she was ready to panic in a big way.

Jane squeezed her eyes shut, attempting to hold back the tidal wave of terror pulsating through her system. She wiggled her hands, wondering what held her in place. Tape? She could feel adhesive tugging at her bare skin with each twist of her wrists.

The fear wanted to paralyze her. If she let it, it would. She flexed her hands, the tug of the tape holding strong. Her legs too were bound. Helpless.

Scream? If she shouted would anyone hear her? Could she alert someone before the breather stopped her? Did she have any other choice?

She might have only one chance. She had to make it good. She opened her mouth to scream.

"I wouldn't do that if I were you."

The voice stopped her cold. It was male. Rough-edged and deep.

Poised on the brink of shouting, she paused. Listening. Straining against the darkness to locate the speaker. His voice had sounded in front of her, not behind. Had the breather moved? Or was there someone new in the room?

But she hadn't heard movement. Had she?

Her jaw relaxed, but not because the fear lessened. If anything it had increased. The voice was that of the hunter and she was the prey.

"Who are you? What do you want with me?" She sounded like a tape recorder stuck on one line and felt the rise of laughter bubbling through her. Hysteria? Possibly, not that she had much experience with the emotion. Hysteria happened to others. Not to her.

"Turn the light on, Elderman." The voice spoke again, ignoring her question as the sound of footsteps moved closer. Leather soles slapped against a hard floor behind and then in front of her. What sounded like at least two others stepped closer, making her want to cringe. To flee. But she couldn't. Not with her hands and legs bound.

Before she prepared herself, a light blazed forth. Not strong as much as startling behind the muffled darkness of the blindfold. She knew she was spotlighted before these strangers.

She pulled back, jerking her head with the movement, setting off the cannons pounding double-time in her head. There was no place to run, no place to hide.

She might have gasped, or flinched, because the deep voice demanded. "How much did you give her?"

"She didn't come easily, sir." Another male voice replied from behind her.

"I asked how much you gave her."

The man's voice radiated cold assurance, unrelenting authority. Jane wanted to hide from that voice. There was no doubt that voice could order men into battle and expect to be obeyed. But what did they want with her?

"Thompson handled the dosage, sir."

"Then he'll be dealt with."

This new voice jogged a fuzzy memory.

Someone had grabbed her arm from behind in the parking garage of her apartment building. The very unexpectedness of it had caused her to turn, to catch the shadow of a masked face. She felt another grab her other arm. Then the pain of a scratch near her elbow. A scratch or a poke. She'd called out. Swung away, striking the nearest man with her purse. He'd muttered an oath, or what sounded like an oath, but already things were blurring.

She'd felt herself falling. She thought she'd screamed again and knew she'd lashed out, her foot connecting with a shin, her hand tearing cloth. The jabbing sensation to her arm came again. Then the darkness.

"You were at my apartment," she whispered the words aloud, feeling anger slide in where moments ago there was only fear. "I want to know what you're doing. Why I'm here."

"Enough." Another man spoke, this one with a guttural accent she couldn't place. Eastern European maybe. That and an imperious tone to his voice; a man used to getting his way. A different kind of power than the first voice. "I cannot see what she looks like with that thing around her face."

"That *thing* is for your protection, sir." The first voice spoke, and in spite of the salutation there was no deference in his tone. "For your protection and hers."

"We are running out of time. She looks like Elena but I must be sure."

Who was Elena? And who was the first voice protecting? He'd said "her" but surely that didn't mean *her*. Why would someone drug and kidnap a person then worry about protecting them? Nothing made sense.

Before she could demand answers, someone bent down next to her. She could smell the scent of soap and feel the warmth of a hand brush against her shoulder.

She flinched, pressing as far back as the unyielding chair would allow, straining against the tape, but it was useless. There was nowhere to go.

A hand slid down her hair. A gentle touch, soothing somehow, though that made no sense. The human contact should have frightened her, but it didn't. She felt fingers tugging at the knotted fabric covering her eyes. The material bunched, catching strands of her hair before it loosened.

''You won't be hurt.'' The dark voice came like a caress in the darkness. ''Do exactly what I say and you won't be hurt.''

Now she knew it was hysteria bubbling through her. The need to laugh aloud. The wanting to believe the voice when logic told her it'd be a fool's mistake.

''Why—''

''Shhh. The less movement you make the less your head will hurt.''

The words sounded tinged with regret, as if he understood the pain slamming through her temples, the terror surging through her system. Maybe he was sorry for his part in it.

For the space of one deep breath she would have believed there were only the two of them in the room. The fear began to subside. Until the cloth gave way and slid from her eyes.

The harshness of the light felt like a thousand suns instead of the gritty wattage of a single bulb directly overhead. Two soldiers garbed in rumpled camouflage gear flanked her and a man in a pressed uniform of white and blue faced her. And next to her, instead of a dark voice, she found herself staring into a pair of gray eyes, as cold as a frozen lake, as unreadable as the ocean deep.

If she had thought she wanted to run and hide before, it was nothing compared to what she felt now. Those eyes pinning her as effectively as the straps around her wrists, searched her gaze until she felt stripped bare, exposed and more vulnerable than she'd ever felt before.

"It is true then. She *is* Elena." The uniform spoke, startling her with his words. Yet, in spite of his gold epaulets and row of medals marching across his chest, no one could doubt who held the power in this room. And it wasn't him.

She found herself licking suddenly dry lips, felt the blip in her heart rhythm when the movement caught the attention of the man kneeling before her, compelling his gaze to shift to her lips, then back to her face. His expression remained enigmatic, except for the briefest tightening of his facial muscles.

He wasn't handsome. Far from it, with unforgiving lines and a square jaw. His hair looked dark, black maybe, with a hint of gray near the temples. Not softening in its effect. There was nothing soft about this face. Not with the lines radiating from the corners of those glacial eyes, bracketing his mouth and dug deep along what looked like a scar near his right temple. His skin was tanned, like a man who lived beneath tropical rays.

It was a strong face, one as compelling as his eyes.

Jane held no doubt it could be implacable and hard when he chose. But she thought it wasn't inherently cruel or vicious, which, for the first time since she'd awakened, gave her hope.

He rose beside her, his gaze still locked with hers, as if silently assessing and measuring, though he spoke to the uniform. "There are enough similarities that she could easily pass as Elena, especially from a distance."

"Then she will do," came the immediate, and dismissive response. The uniform's accent had deepened. "It has taken too long as it is."

Who was Elena? What did it matter if she looked like her? Who were these men?

"There are still a number of obstacles," the man they referred to as the major said, leaving no doubt Jane was one of them, before he continued, ''There will be repercussions. Too much has already been badly handled.''

''That, then, is what you are here for.'' Gold epaulets flashed and the uniform shifted. ''I have heard you were the best. Fix the problems and we will be on our way.''

''It's not that easy—''

''I do not wish for excuses, Major McConneghy. I want only solutions.''

Jane watched the other man's gaze darken and shift and was thankful he was no longer looking at her. Even the uniform seemed to realize he'd taken the wrong tone with the man he called McConneghy as he stepped back and waved a hand before him. ''My fear is for Elena. This is a terrible strain on her.''

''I understand.'' The reply indicated understanding would only be extended so far and not an inch further. ''But a shoddy operation is worse than no operation. I'll take care of the details here.''

''Well then…'' the uniform glanced around the room. ''I shall be on my way and expect to see you in Dubruchek tomorrow.''

Jane did not feel relief when he turned on a booted heel and marched from the room. In spite of his commands and imperial words, it was Gray-eyes who worried her.

His stillness permeated the room, as if he were weighing options and gauging consequences. The two soldiers kept their gazes on him, their attention as ramrod straight as their stances.

''Elderman.''

''Yes, sir.''

''Tell Winters to ready the plane.''

''Yes, sir.'' The soldier closest to the door saluted and disappeared.

Two down, two to go, Jane thought, not finding an ounce

of comfort in the realization as long as one of those two was Major Gray-eyes.

She watched him, every cell in her body waiting, hoping against hope that now that the others had left he would turn toward her, tell her it was all a big mistake and unstrap the tape. But then optimism had always been one of her weaknesses.

"I won't say anything to anyone if you'll let me go." She heard the plea in her own voice.

"It's too late." The man said it as if with regret, then nodded to the soldier behind her. His gaze shifted to hers, right before he crouched beside her once again, his hand covering her own clenched fist, his eyes steady on hers. "Just do exactly as I say and I promise you'll be safe."

She believed his words, maybe because of the intensity of the gaze riveted to hers, until movement out of the corner of her eye snagged her attention.

The other man, the soldier who had been slightly behind her, moved. He stepped forward, far enough into the light that she could make out his face. One that looked too young to be dressed in fatigues. A soldier-boy she thought, then caught sight of what was in his right hand.

Light flashed off a sliver of metal. A sharp, lethal-looking slice of silver. One attached to a hypodermic syringe.

"No. No, please no." The words were automatic. And useless. As useless as struggling against the bonds holding her. But she could no more stop either reaction than the pounding of her heart. "No, I won't tell. I won't—"

"It will be all right." Gray-eyes spoke, his words like an anchor in the swirl of terror surging through her. Yet he was one of them. More than that, he led them.

Her gaze snapped to his. "Please, don't let him do this. Please...I won't—"

She could feel the other man's hand pin her arm even as

Gray-eyes raised his free hand, holding her chin so she could not look toward the needle.

"You'll be safe. This is the best way. The only way."

She tried to pull her chin away but he wouldn't let her. Cold dampness touched her lower arm. The pierce of a needle slid beneath her skin. And yet he held her. There would be bruises tomorrow. If there was a tomorrow.

He spoke again, gently murmured nonsense words. Words that in another place might have been of comfort, or compassion.

But this man held no compassion. If he did she wouldn't be there, feeling helpless. Defenseless. Terrified.

The needle receded. The fear didn't. But it took only a heartbeat to feel it muted. Her struggles slowed. Became exaggerated. Even more useless.

"Shhh. It won't be long now." Silence, then more words. "You'll be safe. Remember that, you'll be safe."

She heard what he said. And knew he lied. His words lied. The emotion in his gaze lied.

The cottony feeling thickened, but not enough to douse the realization that he was still lying. She'd never be safe around this man. Never.

And then the darkness descended.

Lucius McConneghy watched the flutter of the woman's dark eyelashes as they slowly closed, creating half circles against the paleness of her skin. She was fighting the drug Versed but it was pointless. Between the earlier dosage and the fear accelerating through her system it'd be a matter of minutes at the most, then they could move out.

"Check on the vehicle." He barked orders to Corporal Tennison, aware they sounded harsher than they needed to be. Where was the legendary McConneghy control? The ability to shut off all emotions to get the mission accomplished?

Shot to hell, he mused, watching the younger man snap to attention and all but run from the room. Shot to hell the moment he saw this doe-eyed young woman, her look pleading with him to save her.

As if he were some bleeding angel of mercy. Hell, he was the reason she was here. And the sooner she knew it, and accepted what her role was, the better it would be for all concerned.

He felt the scramble of her pulse lessen beneath his hand. Her head lolled forward, the curtain of her midnight-black hair shielding all but the curve of her chin, the paleness of her complexion. One that had turned sheet-white when she realized what Tennison was doing to her with the hypodermic. Then her gaze had consigned him to a hell with no return. Not that he blamed her.

But that was his job. Make the tough choices, get the mission accomplished. Maybe he was getting old, or stale, since the thought sat heavy on him. But he meant what he'd said. So far this mission had been a disaster. If they'd had more time, they could have foregone the crudeness of a kidnapping. Avoided the emotional and physical costs the woman before him already was paying.

But if there was one thing he had accepted after years of service, there was no going back and correcting past mistakes. There was only going forward, and minimizing future ones. Someone always paid. In this case—her.

Jane Richards was his responsibility now. And he'd do everything in his power to keep her alive. Everything.

"I will keep you safe," he whispered aloud to the woman who couldn't hear him. He squeezed her hand, knowing it was a useless gesture, surprised that he was compelled to do it at all.

Chapter 2

"Here, drink this." The voice was close to her. A male voice, like hot caramel over cold ice cream. One she thought she should know.

"Open your eyes and drink this."

She didn't want to open her eyes. Then there'd be no going back, no pretending she was safe and in Sioux Falls. But there was no avoiding it. The voice wouldn't let her.

Slowly, as if they had been glued shut, she pried her eyes open. Then shut them quickly.

Gray-eyes. Mesmerizing, compelling, lying Gray-eyes. Like the crash of a wave—it all came back to her. Her apartment building. A cramped, airless room. A man with medals strung across his chest and another man—Gray-eyes—telling her one thing, holding her still while yet another shot her full of who knew what.

"You can't ignore it. Better to face things head-on."

Easy for him to say, she wanted to snarl, surprised at the clean edge of her anger. It felt good. Better than the terror she remembered so vividly. The helplessness and confusion in the small room. The willingness to trust a man who said one thing and did another. This man.

She opened her eyes again. Cowering was for cowards. While Jane thought she was a lot of things—shy, unprepossessing, ordinary—she didn't like thinking of herself as a coward.

"Who are you and what do you want?"

The demand she heard in her voice pleased her. For a second she thought he might have felt the same way. A glimmer of a smile touched his lips, until he pushed forward a glass. It looked as if he'd been holding it, waiting for her. "Drink this. Then we'll talk."

She raised herself to a reclining position, balancing on her elbow and reaching for the glass, aware her hand shook as she grasped its cool surface. Even under ordinary circumstances it would have been difficult to appear unmoved when a man like this hovered next to her, close enough that she could smell the scent of his skin and feel the heat his body radiated. An awareness out of place with the man who had kidnapped her.

She willed herself to look away, to break the contact of his gaze pinning hers, and caught herself wondering what was in the glass he insisted she drink. More drugs? Something to keep her quiet and compliant? Until what? Or when?

"It's just water."

"Then you take a drink first." She thrust it back into his hands, surprised she dared such a thing, even more surprised when he accepted it and took a long, slow draught, his gaze never leaving hers over the edge of the glass.

"It will help with the dry mouth." He pressed it back into her hands. Obviously this man had dealt with drugged women before. Not a comforting thought. "Later, if you want, I'll get you some aspirin for your headache."

Yes, he definitely knew the aftereffects. Just who was this guy? And what did he want with her?

She watched him rise to his feet and cross to a chair several feet away. Only then did she sip from the glass, thankful for the cool sensation soothing her too-dry throat, yet wary as to why he was being so solicitous. He remained quiet until she had finished most of the water and placed the glass on a coffee table before her.

It was only then that she sat up and looked around her. Looked around and felt the flip-flop of her stomach. They were no longer in the small, cramped room. It looked like a plane, but not the passenger kind.

Instead it looked like a living room, with carpeted floors, two butternut-brown leather chairs on both sides of the couch she was sitting on, end tables and a series of oval windows on either side which showed nothing but blue, blue sky. With a feeling of detachment, or maybe it was hysteria again, she was glad to find that here at least she wasn't tied to anything.

Not that she could make a run for it thousands of feet in the air, she thought, sure it was hysteria making her want to shake her head and close her eyes again.

But Gray-eyes had his own agenda.

"We're thirty-two thousand feet above the Atlantic Ocean," he remarked, his voice calm and level. "We should be landing in a little over two hours, given our present rate of speed."

"Landing where?"

"Dubruchek."

"And Dubruchek is where?" Jane wrapped her arms around herself to keep from shaking.

"Dubruchek is the capital city of Vendari. A small, very important mountain country in the Balkans."

"Important to whom?"

"To a lot of people." He shifted in his seat, leaning forward, his fingers splayed across his knees as if they were discussing the weather. It was then she saw the gun peeping out from a shoulder holster he wore and knew, like a swift kick to the head, that this was not a dream. It was a nightmare.

"I know this is all very confusing."

That was an understatement if she'd ever heard one. But something in his look told her he'd have little patience for pithy comments.

"Vendari is a monarchy sandwiched between two larger, and unstable countries, which makes it of strategic importance to the United States."

Great, she wakes up to a strange man and a throbbing head only to get a geography lesson.

He continued. "It's a monarchy with its own history of bloodshed and violence. Its last king, Zhitomir Vassilivich Tarkioff, was assassinated twenty years ago."

"And this means what?"

"Since then they've undergone two attempted coups." He was ignoring her. "Again, not without bloodshed."

"What does this have to do with me?"

His gaze asked for patience, his voice gave nothing away.

"Today Vendari is ruled by King Viktor Stanislaus Tarkioff."

"The man with the medals?" It was a wild guess, but obviously right on target as she saw his glance narrow, his hands tighten minutely.

"Yes, the man with the medals."

"And what is his relationship to Elena?"

Instead of answering directly, Gray-eyes leaned back in his seat, his gaze shifting to scan the horizon out the row of small windows, his expression blank.

She thought he might have sighed before he turned to face her again. "Elena Illanya Rostov is the king's fiancée."

If she thought pushing for answers was going to make

things clearer, she was wrong. She was more confused now than when they had started this bizarre conversation.

"I don't get it." Ignoring the pain it caused, she shook her head, and tightened the grip of her hands wrapped around her arms. "Why does it matter that I look like this Elena Ro...Ros..."

"Rostov."

"Why does it matter that I look like her?"

"Take my word for it that it does. That's all."

Obviously she wasn't going to get any more information. At least for now. He rose from his seat, shoving his hands deep into the pockets of pressed khaki pants, uneasy about something. He walked away and she guessed it did not bode well for her.

Lucius glanced out the window, seeing nothing, buying time, even seconds worth of time. How had things unraveled so quickly? Had it been only minutes ago that he was thankful Jane Richards wasn't in hysterics or fighting him tooth and nail? Not that he'd blame either reaction. But he wasn't getting that.

His limited research had informed him she'd taken a job as a librarian straight out of college, was dependable and conscientious in her habits, didn't even have an outstanding parking ticket to her name and, if a bit boring, could be expected to behave in a rational manner.

What they had neglected to discover was that she was also a woman who had a quick and ready intelligence. One able to control herself under the most extreme circumstances, and one who was unlikely to accept pat and pretty answers about what was going on.

Things were going to hell in a hand basket.

"You're not answering my question." She sounded almost prissy.

If he didn't think it would get him into hot water he'd smile at her tone. Didn't she realize he was the one in the position of dictating—not her?

He turned to face her, wondering if he was doing it for her sake—or his own. "Elena Rostov plays a very pivotal part in the politics of Vendari. She's the daughter of one of the king's leading rivals for power."

"So her marriage to the king consolidates power in the country."

"Exactly."

"I still don't see why it's important that I look like her."

"Because early last month there was an assassination attempt against her."

Silence hung in the air. McConneghy could tell to the second when she grasped what he was saying.

"If Elena dies, the country could be plunged back into civil war?"

"Not could. Would. There's no doubt about it. Her family has a distant contention to the throne. If she's killed it will be seen as an attempt to discredit her family's future ties to the royal family."

"So you're trying to make sure that the marriage goes through."

"Once Elena and the king are married, her value as a political pawn is decreased."

"Because?"

"Before her marriage Elena is seen as much as a daughter to her father, Pavlov Rostov, as a fiancée to the king. After the marriage—"

"After the marriage, if she's killed, the king or his family will no longer be the prime suspects."

He'd definitely have to watch himself around this one, he thought, admiration—and wariness—increasing.

"So where do I come in?"

Seconds ticked past while he grappled for the right words. As if there could be "right words" in a situation like this. "We need a stand-in for Elena. Until the wedding."

"A what?" She rose to her feet now, facing him across the cabin, all color drained from her face.

"We need a volunteer to take Elena's place until the wedding."

"A volunteer?"

"Just until the wedding."

"To do what?"

It was getting sticky. "To take over her official duties. To portray her in public."

The silence thickened until he could have sworn he heard the pilots breathing in the cockpit.

"Portray her in public?"

"Just routine. At this time she has no real duties, but she's appearing among the people before the wedding so that they feel a part of the process."

"You want a guinea pig." Her voice rose an octave. So she wasn't as calm as he might originally have thought. "No. No, make that a target. A sacrificial lamb."

He could lie to her. Tell her he'd do everything in his power to protect her, which he planned to do, anyway. But there was something in her gaze that made him hesitate. He could appreciate someone who wanted the truth—the unvarnished truth—rather than platitudes.

"That's exactly what we need."

She swayed. He moved to prevent her crumpling to the floor, but at the last second she raised her hands, warding him off. He told himself he deserved her lack of trust. But that didn't mean he liked it.

She lowered herself to the couch, perching on the very edge of the leather cushions, her fingers curled into the fabric as if she was holding on for dear life. When she glanced at him he saw the confusion, the disbelief in her gaze. If he'd felt like pond scum before, he felt like bottom sludge now.

"Who are you?"

It was a fair question, just not one he had expected so soon. "My name's McConneghy. Lucius McConneghy."

"Major McConneghy."

Yes, he'd definitely have to watch himself around her.

"Major Lucius McConneghy."

"Which branch of the military?"

This is where things started to really get sticky. "It's an obscure bureau tucked in a back corner of the Pentagon."

"But it's one that allows you to abduct and drug unsuspecting civilians in broad daylight and transfer them, against their will, to small eastern European countries?"

"Something like that."

"Aren't there laws against that type of thing? Or do you think yourself above the law?"

He tried to ignore the disdain in her voice, but couldn't. Then he wondered why it didn't just slide off his back as it should.

"There are times when laws have to be bent."

"Semantics."

"Reality."

She was glaring at him now. No longer looking as though she'd crumple and fold, for which he was grateful.

"There are people who're going to notice I'm gone."

He heard the hope and knew he had no choice but to crush it. Hope might cause her to take unacceptable risks, putting both her life and the lives of his team at risk. So why did it feel as if he was destroying a child's vision of Santa Claus? Sometimes he hated his job.

"The library has been notified there's an illness in your family. That you'll be away for some time."

"You know I work at a library?" She shook her head,

obviously not comprehending the means available to some-one like him to meet a strategic objective.

"Of course you know." She slid back against the cush-ions, her shoulders slumped, her voice less forceful. "What else have you taken care of?"

"We've canceled your speaking engagement for the grant-writing seminar, asked your landlady to look after your cat until you return and have arranged to have your bills automatically paid, courtesy of Uncle Sam."

If he thought he would interject a little levity into the situation he was dead wrong. Her gaze, when she raised it to his, was as bleak as any he'd ever seen. And that was saying a lot.

"I have friends—"

"Not a lot I'm afraid. And they've received word that you're off to visit an elderly sick aunt. Aunt Dorothy."

"I don't have an aunt Dorothy."

"We know it. Fortunately, from our perspective, you do not have many close friends." He watched her shoulders slump more and felt like a heel. But she had to know where she stood. "In fact, very few know you outside of your work. Your parents are both dead. No siblings. No lovers."

She blushed, keeping her gaze averted as she mumbled, "So you've made me disappear with no one the wiser?"

"Yes."

"And what if I don't want to play stand-in for this Elena? What if I refuse?"

"You have no choice."

"Meaning what exactly?"

Time to play hardball. He sat back in the chair, making sure he enunciated each word clearly. There'd be no doubt here. Neither one of them could afford it. "You can agree to play the part of Ms. Rostov, attending functions, being seen in public, doing what any young woman would do on the eve of her marriage—"

"Or?"

"Or Elena Rostov can be devastated from her recent ordeal and need to be kept under sedation until she's feeling better."

"You'd drug me? Again?"

He couldn't be swayed by the despair he heard in her voice, nor the silent appeal he read in her gaze.

"Yes, if we had to, we'd drug you. It's up to you."

"Even if it meant that, being drugged, I'd have no chance at all against someone trying to kill me?"

She caught on quick.

"You'll have all the protection we're able to—"

"Enough." She shot to her feet, pacing to the far side of the plane as if she wanted to put as much distance as possible between them.

"I might not have a lot of experience in this sort of thing, but I'm not a total idiot, either. If you were so sure you could provide total protection you'd have no problem with Elena continuing as she has been."

No, this woman was definitely not slow on the uptake.

"I could lie to you."

She speared him a withering glance. Who'd have thought dark eyes could hold such fire?

He changed his tactics, if not his tone. "Do you want me to tell you what we're asking doesn't hold risks?"

"It'd be a lie. And you're not asking."

"You have a choice here."

"Not much of one. You've made darn good and sure of that."

"We didn't create the situation, Ms. Richards."

"But you brought me into it. Against my will. Without my knowledge." She paused, gulping air before she added. "And now you have the audacity to tell me I have a choice."

Yeah, the lady saw too clearly what she was up against.

He rose to his feet and glanced at his watch. "It might be best if you thought of it as a service to your country. A vital service. We'll be landing within an hour. I have some things to see to in the cockpit." Which was an out-and-out lie, but right then the only thing he could think to give to her was space and a little time. A very little time. "I'll need your decision when I return."

He didn't wait for her answer. As she had pointed out, there wasn't much to choose between. But for her sake, and the sake of the mission, he hoped she'd make the right choice. If she didn't, well he'd deal with that if and when the need came.

Jane watched Gray-eyes, or Major McConneghy, or whatever he wanted to call himself walk silently from the cabin space and disappear through a metal door marked Private. She waited until she heard the click of the door being closed before she gave in to what she'd wanted to do since she'd opened her eyes. With a small oath her co-workers from the library never would have suspected she knew, she sank into the nearest chair, her legs no longer capable of holding her. Her head slipped into her hands, despair finally overcoming her outrage, her fear, her confusion.

How dare some nameless government agency snatch her from her sane, comfortable world and force her to become a target in some obscure country's game of survival? And *force* was the operative word. Even the major didn't pretend there was much of an option. For that at least she was thankful. Not that she was willing to give the man points for anything else.

It didn't take a high IQ to know he was the brains behind this crazy scheme. That he was the puppet master, pulling strings and disrupting lives with as much compassion as a sponge soaked in vinegar.

She glanced at her watch, surprised to see it was a little

after ten in the morning. Which morning she wasn't sure, but she did know exactly what she'd be doing if some grim-lipped major hadn't changed everything.

She'd have been at work for a little over an hour. If it was Wednesday, the weekly staff meeting would just be finishing and she'd be rotating from the main circulation desk to the information desk. She'd handle questions, from the obvious to the esoteric, feeling as if, in her small way, she was helping others.

So what if she didn't have a large social life outside of the library? Or really any, to speak of. The stark facts the major laid out before her were pretty bleak. No family, no friends, no life. How did he phrase it? No lovers. But it still was her life. She should be the one in control of it.

She should not be sitting in a private plane being whisked half way across the world to some country she'd never heard of, to risk her life for people she didn't know, to pretend she was something she wasn't, and possibly to die in the process.

With a groan, she fought against the temptation to curl up into the chair where she sat and bury her head even deeper in her hands. But that wasn't going to solve anything. It'd be better to figure out how to tell Major Gray-eyes to take his not-so-brilliant idea and bury *it*.

But she already knew what would happen then. He'd hold her tight, tell her everything would be all right, while he shot another dose of whatever through her system, rendering her completely vulnerable.

He was right. There was a choice, a small one, but the only one as far as she could see. And while her elderly parents had raised her to be mild-mannered, they'd never raised her to be a fool. And maybe, if she kept her wits about her she might even be able to figure a way out of this nightmare. A service? Yeah, right. She knew about service, had spent a lifetime fulfilling duties and obligations to others. This did not feel like service. This felt like suicide.

She was still sitting in the chair, gazing out the far windows when she heard him return. He said nothing, just walked over and stood near her, obviously not expecting her to look at him. The man could give lessons in patience to a stone, she thought peevishly, aware of the sigh slipping from her.

"You've made your decision."

He didn't even have the grace to make it a question. "You know there's only one choice. I'll pretend I'm Elena—a functioning Elena, not a drugged target."

"Good."

"But I want to know how long this…this farce is going to last?"

He shrugged. Not a reassuring sign she thought, before his gaze slid from hers. "Until the wedding."

"Which is when?"

"There's some question about it at this time. Elena, the real Elena has not been well since—"

"The attack?"

"Yes."

"She was hurt?"

"No. But it has caused her great distress. I have been told she is under a doctor's care."

"So the wedding is postponed?"

"No. It will go on. We're working on the logistics now."

She just bet he was. But before she could press the point he moved to the opposite chair and said, "The plane will be landing soon. There are some clothes in the back room. All are appropriate to what Elena would wear, and, as you're the same size, should fit you without a problem."

Jane bit her lip, wondering what would have happened if she'd chosen option B. Would this man have stripped her from her serviceable cotton skirt and oxford blouse, something very appropriate for midsummer in Sioux Falls, but obviously out of place in Vendari? She didn't want to think such thoughts, nor feel the flash of heat warming her cheeks.

"Is there something wrong?"

"No. No, nothing." Leave it to Mister in Charge to see her blush. She turned to glance at him, catching the wariness in his gaze. "But wearing the proper clothes is not going to turn me into a king's fiancée."

For a moment she thought she saw the glimmer of a smile, quickly banked. "No, but it's not going to hurt. Why don't you change now? Then I'll give you some background on Elena."

Like an automaton, she rose, surprised her legs didn't buckle beneath her. Her stomach felt as if she'd been riding tilt-a-whirls all morning and the headache Gray-eyes had alluded to earlier was all but bringing tears to her eyes.

Yet, in spite of, or maybe because of, feeling the major's gaze monitoring her every move, she marched toward the door he indicated, her head held high, her posture rigid. She might feel like a rag doll without its stuffing but it'd be a cold day in July before she'd let him know it.

Lucius waited until she crossed into the bedroom before he let out the breath of air backed up in his lungs. He had to give Jane Richards credit; she was showing a degree of determination and bravery he rarely saw except in battle-seasoned troops.

For a second there he'd thought she was going to cave. She looked whiter than the clouds out the far windows, and about as steady as quicksand. But she'd pulled herself together, never indicating by as much as a peep that she needed or wanted help. Yeah, the woman had guts.

Brains and nerve, it was a powerful combination as far as he was concerned. In another woman, at another time, he'd be mighty drawn to such attributes. But he couldn't here. Here he had a mission to accomplish and, if it went anything like it had gone so far, he was going to have his hands full keeping Jane Richards alive.

Not that he wanted her to know that. She had enough to deal with, and more to come. With a pang of conscience he couldn't afford, he wondered: If she had really known what she was up against, would she have chosen to be drugged and unaware?

"How does this look?"

He hadn't heard the door behind him open, an unusual occurrence that clued him into how deep his thoughts had been. But when he turned he found himself pausing, amending his earlier assessment. This woman not only had brains and guts, she had beauty, too.

A strapless, ruby-red sundress cupped and molded curves he'd never guessed lay hidden beneath the librarian's plain garb. She'd let her hair fall loose, undone from the pins holding it back earlier, creating a waterfall of darkness against her pale shoulders. A waterfall a man could ache to run his fingers through.

Any other man except him. He had a job to do. End of story.

Yet this double-punch-to-the-solar-plexus kind of beauty wasn't going to make his job one iota easier.

"Well?" She fanned the skirt away from her. Its color only served to highlight the combination of sultry beauty and innocence that looked nothing like Elena Rostov. Nothing at all.

"Do I look enough like her to pass?"

"You'll do." He heard the dryness of his response, hoped he alone understood its curtness before he saw the quick flash of emotion in her eyes as she lowered her gaze.

"There's a blue dress that might work better—"

"I said you'll do."

He was acting like an idiot, a rude idiot, but he was finding it hard to recover his sense of equilibrium. Damn hard.

"Sit down." He waited until she complied, her shoulders a little more slumped than even seconds ago, and called himself a fool. She needed his support, not the sharp edge of a temper.

"The dress looks very nice on you."

As far as compliments went the words didn't seem like a lot. But he noted that her hands stopped pleating the skirt between her fingers and stilled. Her eyebrows arched, as if he'd taken her by surprise. A clue that he'd come across like a real jerk before if it took so little to reassure her.

"Tell me about Elena." She spoke first, saving him from wondering where to start. "Won't my speaking English be a problem?"

"No, English is widely spoken throughout Vendari. That and the fact the king insists on bringing Vendari into the new century. He requires English to be the primary language spoken. Having been raised in a boarding school in Switzerland, Elena's two most fluent languages are English and French."

"But the general population? What if someone asks me something in their native language? Won't they expect me to respond?"

"No. It's widely known that Elena does not speak any of the three local dialects. She has, on numerous occasions, let it be known that she believes clinging to the old customs is barbaric. English is the only language she will respond to. She follows the king's lead on this issue."

"Well, good. At least the part about the language. But it sounds like she didn't grow up in Vendari."

"No, she didn't. She left the country before her fifth birthday, coming back only for short visits."

"How old is she?"

"She turned twenty-three two months ago."

"So she's a year younger than I am."

"Yes."

"And how does she feel about this marriage?" He thought he detected a note of compassion in her voice. "Surely she can't know the king well if she has hardly been in Vendari?"

"If you're asking if this is a love match, it isn't."

"Oh." Did she have to sound wistful?

"Ms. Rostov knows exactly what she's getting out of the deal, so don't waste any pity there."

Her eyebrows arched again, making him feel like someone who routinely stole candy from children.

"We don't have much time and a lot to cover," he said.

"Of course." Damn, if she didn't sound like a prissy librarian catching him chewing gum behind the stacks. He resisted the urge to squirm. Barely.

"We'll be landing at Dubruchek's only airport where one of the king's limos will pick us up."

"Will the king be there?"

"No. He's involved in a series of high-level meetings that will occupy most of his time for the next couple of days."

He could have sworn she looked relieved at the news.

"Will I have to…to interact with him much?"

"You *are* his fiancée."

"I'm a hostage pretending that I'm a political pawn entering a loveless marriage," she threw back, blowing a stream of air that made the midnight-black strands of hair dance around her face. "I just want to know how far I'm going to have to take this farce."

"No, you will not be expected to sleep with the king if that is what you're asking, Ms. Richards." Now it was his turn to sound prissy and her look told him as much.

She released the breath she'd obviously been holding.

"We don't know the principals behind the last attempt on Ms. Rostov's life and, until we do, we have to assume any number of individuals close to the king may be involved.''

"But you do have some suspects?''

Too many to count, he silently acknowledged, including some bad customers he'd tangled with in the past. But that was his problem, not hers.

"There are suspects.'' Instead of replying with specifics he nodded his head, scanning a sheaf of papers he had extracted from a file. "You'll want to be on your guard. At all times. Trust no one. No one. Am I clear?''

When she didn't answer immediately he raised his head, catching the speculative look in her dark eyes.

"Is there a problem?''

She shrugged and looked away. "I'm assuming that includes trusting you.''

"Especially me.''

He let his words hover between them, laser-sharp and lethal. There was no point in pretending otherwise. There was too much at risk for both of them.

He watched her swallow, hard, before she pasted a shaky smile on her lips and leaned forward. "I'll keep your advice uppermost in mind.''

He could like her at that moment. Admit, if only to himself, he admired the flashes of fire she probably wasn't even aware she possessed. But there was no room for such thoughts or feelings.

Instead he glanced at the papers and continued as if the last seconds hadn't occurred. "Elena Rostov is the only daughter of Pavlov Rostov. Her mother died when she was still a baby and she's been raised almost exclusively in Switzerland.''

"Will her family know I'm impersonating her?''

He shook his head. "No.''

"Surely you can't believe her family wants her killed?''

"We can't take that chance. It's a known fact that Pavlov

Rostov would gain a lot of sympathy if his daughter is killed.''

"But—''

He rose to his feet. "Have no doubt about the matter, Ms. Richards. We have taken care to protect you from coming too close to the Rostov family. As for others, make no mistake, there are a lot of individuals who would benefit by Ms. Rostov's death.''

"You mean my death.'' She looked at him then, her gaze holding him as effectively as any set of restraints. "I think you've been honest, at least as honest as you think you can be. Let's not pretty up the picture at this point.''

"All right.'' He set down the file he'd been clutching. "You're in a very precarious position.''

He thought she mumbled something about an understatement but couldn't be sure.

"It's my job to make sure you're safe and I'm very good at my job.'' He wished she didn't look quite so skeptical at his statement. "I'm going to be right at your side as much as possible while you're in Vendari. If there's an attempt on your life, they'll have to go through me to do it.''

When she gave no response, not that there was a need for one, he glanced behind her shoulders and caught sight of the granite-studded mountains of Vendari out the plane windows.

Their time was up. Ready or not.

"Buckle up, Ms. Richards. We'll be in Dubruchek in a few moments.'' He heard the command in his tone and wished it could be otherwise. But wishes wouldn't keep Jane Richards alive.

Chapter 3

Jane's hands shook as she buckled her seat belt. How was she possibly going to get through this? Nothing in her life had prepared her for international politics, mysterious missions or heroics. Especially heroics.

She came from the heartland of America, the backbone, not the front lines. She could get through her monthly grant-writing workshop, giving a little talk that would have her sweating and wishing for oblivion. And once she'd given the welcoming speech for a visiting library dignitary, which had her stomach in knots for weeks.

Now this total stranger, of wary glances and few words, wanted her to impersonate someone who, judging by her taste in clothes alone, was more sophisticated than Jane could ever hope to be.

As if he read her thoughts, or the panic she felt welling from her very toes, the major glanced her way.

"Breathe," he ordered, as if that alone would make a difference. "The temperature in Dubruchek should be around eighty degrees."

She didn't need a tour guide. She needed a miracle. But his gaze on her remained calm, his voice low and level.

"The country is land-locked by mountains, keeping it cool in the summer months. Many think it resembles Switzerland."

Great, she was going to die in paradise. Was she supposed to take consolation in that?

"Because of the mountains, and except for Dubruchek and the smaller city of Dracula, most of the locals live in small farming villages."

"Dracula?"

He shrugged as if he didn't hear the terror in her single word. "It was a poor choice I agree, but the town's founders were told it was a well-known name in English literature."

"I guess it could have been worse. Something like *Frankenstein* definitely would have kept away tourist dollars."

"Most likely." He offered her a crooked smile that softened the harshness of his face. Making it charming, almost, though she didn't think he'd be flattered by the observation. But it was a smile.

A first, she realized, surprised to find that something as small as that was helping. The panic was still there, but so was something else. Not camaraderie, exactly. Major McConneghy didn't look like the type to indulge in camaraderie. A knowledge that she wasn't going alone into the unknown. Unwilling, maybe, but not alone.

"We're here."

She felt the thud of wheels hit the tarmac, heard the whine of engines reversing themselves.

"I don't know if I can do this."

He paused in the act of unbuckling, his movements economical, unhurried. Nothing like what she was feeling, fear freezing everything.

"Of course you can do it." He stood, moving toward where she still sat, petrified in her seat. He knelt beside her, unbuckling her seat belt as if she were a small child, extending his open palm to help her to her feet.

She placed her hand in his. An automatic response, she told herself, until she felt the heat of his fingers close around hers, comforting and commanding at the same time.

"When the door opens you'll step forward—"

Her breath hitched but he continued, pulling her to her feet.

"I'll be right beside you. If there are reporters nearby you'll wave and act as if everything is fine."

"I think I'm going to be sick."

He gave her a look that reminded her of her maiden aunt Gertrude. The one who didn't like sticky-fingered, skinned-kneed little kids.

"We'll walk down the stairs and directly to the waiting limo."

He propelled her forward, giving her no choice but to move, his hand no longer holding hers but tight around her bare arm. She swore it would leave a brand there, but wasn't sure she could blame it all on him, not when she was dragging her feet as much as he was tugging her forward.

"What if there are reporters and they want to talk?"

"They've been informed you're still a little shaken."

"I won't have to act that part."

"—and that there'll be a formal news conference."

When her knees started to buckle at that piece of information he only held on tighter and added, "Later."

"But what if—"

"You'll be fine. Just smile and wave."

"But—"

The man obviously didn't take terror as a reason not to keep plunging forward. Already the sounds of a ramp being adjusted into place sounded from the other side.

"I can't—"

"You can." Major Gray-eyes all but breathed against her

ear, his words meant for her alone. "You've made your choice."

As if she'd been slapped with cold water she felt her panic recede. Anger replaced it. She'd had no choice. Not really, and the look she gave her abductor told him as much. Right before she shrugged off his hold, straightened her shoulders and told herself that nothing, no one, especially not a gray-eyed dictator standing almost on top of her, was going to know the cost of the next few minutes.

When the door slid open, and a rush of fresh mountain air washed against her, she stepped forward. The sunlight blinded her, the air chilled her skin, creating a ridge of goose bumps along her arms. She wanted to choke. Or cry. And made herself do neither.

Just as he'd said, there was a crowd of people beyond a barricade of orange cones and yellow flapping tape. She raised a hand to her eyes to cut the glare and scan the rest of the tarmac.

A stretch limo waited at the far end of a blue-carpeted runway that began at the base of the stairs where she stood.

Once, long, long ago, when she had watched a television special about a Hollywood star, she'd wondered what it would be like to ride in a car the length of a city block. Now she was about to find out—if an assassin's bullet didn't stop her first.

"Don't think about it." The major spoke behind her. Either a remarkably astute man or a compassionate one. But that would make him human and she didn't want to think of him that way. Not when he was the reason she was in this mess in the first place. "Smile and wave."

She did. Ignoring that her arm felt like a lead weight and her jaw muscles ached after only a few seconds.

The major took her arm; from a distance it probably looked as if he was assisting, not forcing her to take the first step down the metal stairs. First one, then another.

"I can walk by myself," she muttered between stiff lips locked in a smile. "You don't have to worry I'll run away."

"There's nowhere to run."

Oh, the man was just a font of cheerful news.

"Pause before we enter the limo and give the reporters one last photo op."

She did as he asked, no, demanded, and was never as thankful as when she slid into the cool leather interior of the vehicle and heard the door slam shut behind her.

So far, so good, Lucius thought, watching the color seep back into Jane's face as she leaned against the limo's luxurious seats, her eyes closed, her breathing less shallow than it had been only moments ago. He'd give her a minute, but couldn't afford much more than that.

He watched her eyes flutter open and asked, "Feeling better now?"

"No."

He wouldn't smile. Not at her acerbic response, or the brutal honesty of it.

"Fine, we'll start, anyway."

"Don't let the grass grow under your feet do you, Major?"

"Can't afford to."

She took a deep breath and glanced out the window. Except for the way her fingers smoothed and re-smoothed the folds of her dress he'd have thought her totally under control. If she managed to keep her composure, and if his team had made progress on who was behind the attempt on Elena Rostov's life, and if there were no more attempts until they could eliminate the threat, they just might make it through this mission. But that was an awful lot of ifs.

"When we reach where we're going you'll be taken to your quarters."

"Where we're going?"

"There's a small villa outside of town where we'll remain as long as we can."

"Doing what?"

"Teaching you to be Elena." He noted her puzzled look and added, "It's wiser to ease you into your position. Cover the basics. The way Elena talks, the way she walks, who her friends are and what foods she'll eat or not eat."

He thought he could hear the air sigh from her lungs.

"And you didn't think I should know there was going to be a reprieve, even a short one, before you throw me to the wolves?"

"Listen very carefully, Miss Richards." He leaned forward, watching her eyes widen with his movement. "There is no reprieve. The mission has begun and you *are* the mission. From now on you will think, act and believe you are Elena Rostov. Your life depends on it."

She glanced at him but said nothing.

He continued. "You're Elena now." He glanced toward the smoked glass separating their seat from the driver and armed guard up front. "It's imperative that you talk about yourself as such."

"All right," she took a deep breath and looked as if she was holding back her temper. "What would *I* normally do when *I* arrive at wherever we're going? Is that better?"

He ignored the sarcasm. "You've been known to ask for a review."

"A what?"

"You like to have the household servants line up so you can review them."

"I see. A queen to her subjects."

He ducked his head to hide a grin, aware he couldn't have described the process much more succinctly. "Yes, something like that."

"That's the most archaic—" she caught herself, flattened her fingers against her skirt and started again. "Then won't the household know something is up when Ele—I mean, when I don't do that this time?''

"We're using the excuse that you're tired from your long flight and justifiably concerned about security.''

"Where am I supposed to be flying in from?''

Another good question.

"You've been in Switzerland and France, visiting old school friends.''

"And recovering from my ordeal.''

"Exactly.''

"How many people know about this scam you're running?''

"I prefer to think of it as a mission.''

"I bet you do.''

"Only the king, his head of state security, Eustace Tarkioff—''

"I thought the king's name was Tarkioff?''

"Eustace is his brother.''

"Ah, nepotism at work.''

"As I was saying, only they, my team and myself know of our mission.''

"And me.''

"And you.''

She turned away from him again, her fingers taking up their pattern among the dress folds.

"Look, Miss Richards—'' he began.

"Elena. My name is Elena. Remember?''

So maybe he shouldn't be trying to offer comfort. Not when she sounded as hard as week-old ice. But he knew from first-hand experience what bravado often hid.

"All right, Elena. I know this is difficult.''

"Try downright impossible.''

"You did fine back there.'' He nodded to indicate the airport they'd left behind. "You'll do fine again.''

Her glance held fire as she replied. "I'll do fine until I

don't recognize someone I should know, or say the wrong thing to the wrong person or pick up the wrong fork to eat with. There are a million ways I can slip up and we both know it.''

He'd be lying through his teeth if he refuted her words and he knew they both realized it, especially when she spoke again, her words pitched low, as if in speaking them aloud they might come true.

''The problem is you can't be with me twenty-four hours a day and I can't use the excuse of still being in shock for more than a day or two. You've got yourself a librarian here. That's all. Not someone who's been to a private school, who's traveled through Europe, someone who—'' she glanced down at the dress she wore, ''who wears clothes that show more skin than I do in my swimsuit. I'm going to mess up here—sooner or later.''

She glanced away, her hands curled into tight balls of misery. ''And when I do, some nameless, faceless person is going to notice and the whole thing is going to come crashing down around *my* head. If I haven't been killed in the meantime.''

''That's why we're taking what time we can to prep you for the mission.''

''And how long will I have?'' she asked.

''A week at the most.''

''And if I don't have my…'' she mumbled around the word, ''…my *role*, or part or whatever you call it… What if I don't have it down in this week or so?''

There were times, in the course of a number of missions, when Lucius had felt that he wasn't going to pull through; that the end was just around the next crumbling wall, behind the next bend in the road. But never had he felt the frustration of helplessness so keenly. Every word Jane Richards spoke was on target and there wasn't a damn thing he could do to make the problems go away.

He set the sheaf of papers he'd been holding onto the seat next to him. "There's still option two."

She glanced at him with contempt. Not that he blamed her. "You mean the one where I'm drugged and helpless?"

"The one where, if something bad was going to happen, you'd never know about it."

He thought she might have sniffed, but her eyes were dry as she replied, "No, thanks, Major. I'd rather be led to my execution with my eyes open."

"We're doing everything in our power—everything in *my* power—to protect you."

She looked away, wishing she could believe him. She believed he was serious in his declaration, but right now that didn't feel like a hill of beans. But maybe with a little time? She watched small, closely spaced stucco buildings give way to open yards and smaller homes.

Who was she kidding? A week wasn't going to make a lot of difference. What was the old saying? Silk purse out of a sow's ear. This whole scheme was ludicrous. No one in their right mind was going to mistake a midwestern librarian for a future queen. No one.

"If you're ready, I'll continue." His voice slashed through her thoughts. But this time he wasn't a mind reader. She'd never be ready. Never.

Her parents hadn't raised her to rock the boat, but neither had they raised her to back down when the going got rough. And this definitely qualified as rough.

"Fine, finish your briefing, Major." She glanced out the window as the limo slowed. "If I'm not mistaken that big, pink building on the hill must be the villa."

His gaze followed hers. "It is."

"Then you don't have much time to tell me what I need to know."

Jane waited, sensing the major wasn't happy with her

response, maybe with her whole attitude, but she didn't care. And that in itself scared her.

She had always been aware of and sensitive to the needs of those around her. She'd had little choice in the matter. The only daughter of a couple who had long before given up on ever having children, her arrival into their lives was not a blessing as much as a shock. A little like a Christmas gift delivered too late and the wrong size.

Her earliest memories had been of needing to be quiet to let her father prepare for one of the college English classes he taught, or to wait for her mother to finish editing a manuscript. Her parents were both studious, quiet people who had taught Jane, and taught her well, not to cause problems.

But right then she didn't feel accommodating or tolerant of others' needs. Not one bit, and she guessed that the major sensed it, too.

"We'll talk later. At the villa," he announced before leaning forward to push one of the buttons lining the arm of his chair. "Stefan, I'd like you to drive to the side entrance rather than through the main gates."

"Yes, sir," came the quick response.

"Slipping me in through the side door?" Jane heard herself ask in a voice she hardly recognized as her own. Did hysteria come masked as sarcasm?

"I'm trying to make this as easy for you as possible."

She found herself wanting to believe him.

"You'll have a maid who'll help you unpack your luggage."

Great. She didn't even know she had luggage.

"I'll give you about an hour before I come for you."

So she had a little over sixty minutes to pull herself together, she thought, watching as the limo slid smoothly beneath an arched entryway, into a cobblestone courtyard that might have been charming except for the barbed wire and glass spikes sprouting along the top of every wall and the absence of anything that might have served as a hiding space. Not even a pot of flowers broke the starkness.

The limo stopped too soon for her. But, between the look the major shot her and the actions of a uniformed man opening her door, it looked as if she wasn't going to be allowed to linger.

Let the show begin, she thought, sliding forward to step into the bright, unadorned courtyard.

Less than ten minutes later she found herself in a bedroom the size of her whole apartment back in Sioux Falls. Cream-colored. Silken upholstery. A bed large enough to host a slumber party dead center in the room.

It was a fairy-tale room: tasteful, ultimately feminine and so quiet Jane was tempted to tiptoe across its polished wood floors.

"Mademoiselle Rostov, welcome home." A young woman's voice interrupted her perusal. "It is good to have you back."

Jane spotted a woman standing in the doorway of an adjoining room the size of a small bedroom and froze. The woman could not have been too many years younger than Jane, but she carried herself with a quiet maturity. Maturity or wariness, Jane wondered, noting that the woman's gaze did not rise from staring at the floor, nor did the welcoming words extend to her expression. If anything she looked as though she was waiting to be rebuked.

So, Major McConneghy, Jane thought silently, what am I supposed to do now? Never having had anyone wait on her, she wasn't sure if she was supposed to know this woman, or treat her with the same degree of familiarity as one addressed a waiter in a restaurant.

With a pithy thought regarding the major's ancestors, she decided that when in doubt, do what felt right.

"I'm sorry." Her voice sounded like sandpaper, "I don't recall your name."

The woman started before quickly glancing up. "It's Ekaterina, mademoiselle. Ekaterina Tabruz."

Well, either Elena should have known this woman's name, in which case Jane had already blown things, or the king's fiancée would never have bothered to ask. Either way it was too late to go backwards.

"Thank you, Ekaterina. It seems as if I've heard so many names lately that they become jumbled in my memory." That at least was the truth. Or part of it.

"Would mademoiselle wish me to draw her a bath or turn down the bed covers for a rest?"

This having-a-maid thing was going to take some getting used to, she realized, feeling too restive for either suggestion but not wanting to cause too much suspicion on Ekaterina's part as to why her mistress was acting out of the norm.

"Actually, Ekaterina, what I'd like is to ask a few questions." At the other woman's immediate look of wariness, she added, "I'm feeling very disoriented and am sure you can help me."

"Yes, mademoiselle." Ekaterina bowed her head and folded her hands together in front of her. Not an auspicious sign for a friendly chat, Jane thought as she wandered toward the far side of the room and a set of French doors.

Opening the doors she immediately felt better, as the pine- and cedar-scented breeze drifted in. The cries of birds beyond the fortified walls sounded like a National Geographic soundtrack.

There was a small balcony, ringed by an elaborate wrought-iron railing and, Jane noted with a quick glance down its length, obviously connected to a room just beyond hers.

"Whose room is next door?" she asked the silent Ekaterina.

"It is the major's, mademoiselle."

"Major McConneghy's?" Not that the news should have surprised her, but it did.

"Yes. He asked specifically that you be given this room. For the security. If you wish to choose another room at the villa you must ask it of the major."

Like that was going to happen.

She tried a different tactic. "The villa seems different?"

"Different?" The maid's face looked confused, until she nodded. "Ah, I understand."

Jane was glad somebody did, because it sure wasn't her.

"They said it was made to look like a Swiss home but maybe not so. I can show you around the rooms to see more if the major allows it."

Jane breathed a silent sigh of relief. So she had not previously been at the villa. Which was good news. Too bad Mister I'll-Protect-You forgot to mention this little detail. He had given her explicit instructions about the location of everything, but they all seemed to be jumbling in her head. If she hadn't been here before it meant she could ask questions about the layout and not be expected to know how to find her way back through the labyrinth of halls and stairways she'd traveled earlier. At last, something was going her way.

"Who else is in residence in the villa?" She remained standing at the open doorway, listening to the sound of a heavy vehicle driving over the cobblestones below her.

"Only you and the major."

She wasn't sure why that news made her feel both safe and uneasy at the same time. Strategically she could see why it made sense, but there was something intimate about the isolation that made her hesitate. An awareness that deep in the darkness of the night it would only be she and Gray-eyes, a wall away from each other, a world away from the rest of the universe.

"Does mademoiselle wish me to tell the major she wants different rooms?" Ekaterina asked.

"No. That won't be necessary." Somehow she knew anywhere in the villa would be too close to the major. Jane kept her own concerns from her tone until she turned and noticed a door in the wall. "And where does that lead?" she asked, though she'd already guessed the answer.

"To the major's room."

She walked toward it, aware there was now even less separating her sleeping quarters from the enigmatic major's. Sort of like a lamb lying next to the lion's cage, only with removable bars, she thought, reaching for the door handle and turning it.

"It's locked."

She hadn't realized she'd spoken the words aloud until Ekaterina replied, "Yes, the lock is on the major's side."

"And do I have a lock on this side?"

The young woman shrugged. "I know of no key, but I will check if you wish."

"There's no need."

Jane whirled at the sound of the dark voice behind her, felt the triple-time pounding of her heart before she registered it was McConneghy who had spoken. He dominated the now-open doorway connecting the two rooms, either in response to her rattling of the door handle, or on his own agenda.

"Speak of the devil, Major," she said, aware of the intensity of his gaze on hers, and of how his presence dominated the room even though he remained on the threshold. "I was just wondering about a key for this door. I know I would feel much more secure." She made sure he heard the stress on the last word. "If I knew where it was."

"I have it." He nodded to the maid. "You may leave us now and finish unpacking mademoiselle's luggage while we're at dinner."

Jane waited until Ekaterina closed the door behind her before she spoke. "That's pretty presumptuous and arrogant—" she began, only to be cut off as McConneghy strode into the room, closing the door as he moved.

"It's a security issue." He ignored where she stood as he walked through the room, looking high and low. "I need to have access to protect you. You don't."

"Don't what?" She could feel the anger start to simmer inside her. Never a fan of high-handed tactics, she was even less inclined to ignore them after the day she'd already been though.

He peered beneath the lampshade on the bedside table and picked up the phone receiver. "You don't need to access my room, thus you don't need a key."

"I don't want a key to access your room," she wanted to choke on the words. "I want one to make sure you don't access mine."

He spared her a glance. Quick, appraising and heated.

"I can assure you the only reason I'd use that key was if your life was in danger."

And just what did he mean by that two-edged comment? she wanted to know, and was afraid to ask. Especially as he crossed to tower in front of her, the strength and size of him making her feel all the more vulnerable.

She checked the urge to step back and stepped forward instead. Something the old Jane Richards, the one who went to bed a librarian and expected to wake up a librarian, would never have done.

With a finger sharpened by frustration and something more, she stabbed his chest, knowing it was about as effective as howling at the moon. "Listen here, Major, if you think I can't control my primitive urges—"

"Primitive urges?"

She heard the laughter in his voice and ignored it. Easier to do if she kept her gaze level with his chest. "Yes, primitive urges. If you think I can't, then you're beyond idiotic. Not that a man who came up with this whole hare-brained scheme—''

"Mission."

"Hare-brained *mission* would know the difference between reality and fantasy.''

"Oh?" His tone snapped her gaze to his. A mistake, a big mistake she realized—too late.

There was something in his look, in the flare of his nostrils, in the tightening of the skin across his cheek bones that warned her they'd strayed far from the point she wanted to make.

The mountain breeze cooling the room only moments ago disappeared. It was the only explanation as to why it suddenly seemed harder to breath, the air thicker, heavier, her skin too sensitive, feeling goose bumps where there should be none, aware of the abrasion of her dress across her nipples.

The shifting of his gaze told her he'd noticed.

"You were saying?" His look dared her to jump deeper into the waters already threatening to take her under.

"I...I can't remember,'' she admitted truthfully, aware it gave him an advantage.

Yet, as if she'd thrown a switch, his expression changed, became banked, distant. He mentally and emotionally retreated from whatever brink they'd both teetered on.

"Everything I do is for your protection and the protection of this mission.'' She wondered which of the two protections took priority in his mind. "I give the orders. You obey them. Clear?''

As glass, she wanted to respond, but found the words stuck somewhere in her throat. She nodded instead, too worn out to fight this man on so many levels at the same time. Whatever had just happened between them had been a mistake. Her head relayed the message, his actions reinforced it, but it wasn't going to be easy to forget that for a few seconds at least, the world had slipped out of orbit.

"I'll have your maid show you the way to the dining room for dinner."

"I'm not hungry."

He looked like he wanted to argue, then stopped. "Fine. I'll have a tray sent up later. Tomorrow she can show you the way to the dining area."

"It's all right, I'm sure I can find my own way."

She heard the sharpness in her tone. It was a tone she'd never have used in her own world. She'd been taught to be better than that, gentler, more willing to please others.

"The maid will show you the way." Either he didn't hear her response, or chose to ignore it. Then before she could say more he added, "It's for your safety."

That's right, they wouldn't want to lose their pigeon at this point, she thought wryly. Her expression must have given her away, for he shrugged his shoulders and turned.

"I'd recommend you retire early this evening. We have a full agenda tomorrow."

The man could burst bubbles quicker than a pin in a balloon shop. So they were back to dictator and minion. There was no time for a snappy comeback before the connecting door snicked shut behind his silent departure.

At least she had all night to pull herself together. Enough time, she hoped, to resurrect her defenses and to remember, all too vividly, the major's words from earlier that day. His directive to trust no one. Including himself. Especially him.

Lucius wondered if he'd lost his mind. What else could account for the few moments when he'd stood over Jane and no longer thought of her as a pawn in a dangerous mission? He'd forgotten everything except for the way her dark eyes flashed fire, her ridiculous phrase about primitive urges and the white-hot stab of lust slicing through him like an inferno sweeping across dry timber.

He'd been an operative long enough to know that desire and adrenaline were twin cousins under tense situations. But that knowledge had deserted him without a qualm, to be replaced by other knowledge. The certainty that, if he'd pushed moments ago, he'd not be standing, still breathing heavily, on one side of a two-foot thick wall right now, with her on the other side.

He'd seen it in her gaze, anger giving way to wariness, wariness slipping into desire, a heartbeat away from capitulation. He'd registered the way her breath hitched a notch, her pulse escalated in the hollow of her throat. One step, one minor movement forward and he'd know if she responded with the same lightning quickness he'd observed in her thought process, if she tasted as sweet as she looked.

And it was that thought that had stopped him cold. Days ago he'd never have met Jane Richards, their paths would never have crossed, their destinies never intermingled. But she'd been right earlier when she'd accused him of forcing her into limited choices.

He'd brought her to Vendari, against his better judgment, and thrust her into a mission fraught with danger on all sides. What kind of low-life scum was he that he'd place her in more peril? The kind that came with an emotional price tag.

He was going to do everything in his power to keep her safe, but he couldn't do that if he led her into a physical relationship based on nothing more than close quarters, fear and dependence on her side, dominance and power on his. Like a lamb to slaughter, he could manipulate her total dependence on him, her vulnerability without him, until she wouldn't know the difference between her abductor and her angel.

But he would.

Maybe that few minutes was meant as a sign—a warning that for some reason this woman tugged at emotions he'd thought locked and buried away, at least as long as a mission was involved. And now that he knew, knew to tread lightly, he could save them both pain.

The mission came first and, as long as Jane was a key component of the mission, any feelings he might experience around her had either to be kept strictly under control or downright ignored. Not easy, he accepted, crossing into the room he was to occupy during the duration of this stay in Dubruchek. Not easy at all when this librarian from Sioux Falls slipped through his best defenses against personal involvement—with anyone.

But he'd handled difficult, if not impossible, tasks before. He could, and would handle this one. Both of their lives, as well as the lives of his team members depended on it.

Chapter 4

In spite of a night spent tossing and turning, Jane did find herself feeling more refreshed in the morning. She thought she could get used to sleeping between Irish linen sheets every night. But even as the thought materialized it was followed quickly by reality. The reality that this was going to be her first full day of playing Elena Rostov. Or at least trying to.

"Is Major McConneghy awake?" she asked, already guessing the answer. He didn't strike her as the kind of man who would lag around in bed.

"The major wakes with the sun." Ekaterina walked back and forth between the main bedroom and the walk-in closet, her hands busy with dresses, accessories and shoes. "He swims each morning in the pool behind the villa."

No wonder the man looked like he had abs of steel beneath khaki, she thought. Not that she'd noticed. Much.

"And do you know where he is now?"

"He waits for you in the breakfast room."

''What?'' That was the last thing she wanted. Setting aside her coffee and hopping from the bed she raced toward the bathroom and a shower. It was worse than being late for the weekly staff meeting and she hadn't done that once in her four years of employment. What must the man think? That she was a sluggard, a lazy-bones, avoiding her duty— or at least what he saw as her duty.

It might not have been an issue, as she normally didn't take much time to get ready in the morning anyway, but heading to a job as a librarian hadn't meant much in the way of makeup, finishing her hair and accessorizing her wardrobe. Being Elena might be harder than she had first thought. On the other hand, maybe Elena, being a real princess, was allowed to lie around and do nothing. Oh, why hadn't she read the *National Enquirer* more closely?

Sure Major McConneghy would be pounding on the door any minute, Jane tugged on the outfit Ekaterina had laid out for her. It looked like a jogging suit made of washed silk. Maybe that's what well dressed queens-to-be wore to eat breakfast. No one in their right mind would exercise in such a suit. At least not exercise and sweat.

Remembering all too well the major's last command to her the night before, she called for Ekaterina to accompany her and all but ran to the dining room.

Skidding around the last corner and coming to a full halt outside a room bright with early-morning sunshine she wondered why the room left little impression on her. Not with the major sitting there. He should have looked out of place amidst its cheeriness, he of the pressed chino pants and casual shirt, every crease in place. But of course, he didn't. He sat there, an elegant china cup raised partway to his lips, his dark brows arched in a V, his eyes as still as an Arctic lake.

''I'm sorry I'm late,'' she exhaled, sure she could explain, though it looked as if it might be an uphill job, considering the man's impenetrable expression.

"You're not late." He glanced at his watch and added, "In fact, you're almost two hours early by Elena time."

"Elena time?" The question came out a little breathlessly as she scooted into the closest chair, hating the fact she could feel perspiration clinging to the back of her silk shirt. "Just what is Elena time?"

"Simple. It's always two hours after everyone else has assembled."

"You mean Ele—" she quickly glanced around the room, noting Ekaterina had already left them before she lowered her voice and continued, "You mean I'm habitually late?"

"No." He reached for a croissant nestled in a basket. "Being late implies you know when a function is scheduled to begin. Elena time is an orchestrated move guaranteed to let all and sundry know that the most important person has just arrived. It's a very effective ploy."

He said it so calmly, she thought. Such slashing, cruel words would have devastated her. But she wasn't really Elena, she reminded herself, reaching for the carafe of coffee.

"I don't know if I can do that." She hadn't realized she'd voiced her thoughts aloud until the major shot her one of his enigmatic glances.

"We'll make excuses for such inconsistencies."

She spread butter on a croissant and shook her head when he offered her some jam. "I have a feeling there's going to be a lot of explaining to do."

"We'll take care of it."

All too clearly she remembered the king's cryptic comment from that small, cramped room. "Your job is to fix problems."

Major McConneghy appeared perfect for his job.

"You're wearing perfume."

Leave it to a man like McConneghy to notice, she thought, feeling the heat begin to climb into her face.

"Ekaterina said it's my favorite."

"It suits you." He looked at her over the rim of his cup. "Enticing yet innocent. Though smelling of sunshine and soap also suits you."

Not sure what he meant by his words, or if she was ready to know, she quickly changed the subject. "What's on the schedule today?"

"Drills."

"Drills?"

"A future queen must know how to walk, to talk, to address her superiors and inferiors. There is a lot to learn."

Jane wanted to groan aloud. Somehow she thought it'd all make more sense by the light of day. But it didn't.

As if he guessed her thoughts he pitched his voice lower. "The more you learn now, the less likely you'll make a mistake later."

Like she needed reminding.

"Fine." The word came out sharp. "Let's get started then."

"First, you eat something." He spoke as if talking to a child. "We have a long day ahead of us and I won't have you fainting on me."

"I've never fainted in my life."

He leaned forward. "You've never taken lessons in deportment before, either."

Jeesh. How hard could it be? she thought, picking up and biting into a ripe plum. Being a queen couldn't be that much harder than actually working for a living. Could it?

She found out several hours later.

If she'd thought the major was diabolical before, it was nothing to what she felt about him after four straight hours of "drill." The man was a sadist.

Stand. Sit. Walk straight. Curtsey. Smile. Wave. Stand up

straighter. Who'd have thought there was a way to graciously sit in a chair by approaching it backwards. Or three different kinds of waves to use when communicating from far away. Or six kinds of forks to choose from at official state dinners.

Her jaw hurt from smiling. Her fingers cramped from waving and gesturing. Her knees ached from rising and lowering herself into five different kinds of chairs.

And all through it Major Lucius McConneghy just kept saying, "Now do it again."

She wanted to throttle him.

By the time they took a break for a light lunch she felt as if running a marathon, cold turkey, would be better than being a queen-to-be.

As if he read her thoughts, a talent he was particularly adept at, McConneghy handed her a slice of cheese and said. "This morning was easy compared to what's coming."

The man was a font of good news.

"Didn't your parents ever tell you if you couldn't say something nice, not to say anything at all?" she snapped back, too tired to care about the tone of her voice.

He actually had the gall to smile. Something that made little butterflies spring to life in her stomach, fluttering around the knots already there.

But he didn't respond directly. Instead he looked at a clipboard in his hand. "This afternoon the hair stylist will be here. And the manicurist."

Without thinking Jane's hands reached for the ends of her hair. "Don't tell me Elena has one of those short, chic haircuts."

"You're Elena and no." His eyes swept over her in a way that made her want to blush and stammer before his cold, matter-of-fact voice added. "There won't be much change."

"How are you explaining the need to…" she waved her hands before her. "The need to fix me?"

"These are not Elena's regular people," he replied. "We couldn't risk them noting the differences."

The man thought of everything.

"Come on," he motioned before she'd even finished her last bite, one she didn't even taste over the exhaustion she felt. "Let's get going again."

"Sadist," she mumbled to herself.

At least she thought no one had heard, until he speared her with one of those penetrating gray-eyed glares. "Sadism would be to let you walk into a situation without any preparation. I'd prefer to think of this as protecting you."

She mulled over his words the rest of the afternoon, keeping her own opinions to herself. It was too much effort to voice them, anyway. Maybe it was still shock, or jet lag, or her mind's inclination to retreat from something so out of her control, but by the time Major McConneghy called an end to the day she was ready to sink to her knees right then and there. The only thing that kept her upright and functional was the realization that he was waiting for her to do just that.

It was in the way he watched her, the way he said little but implied much with his body language. But she wasn't going to give him the satisfaction. She'd fall apart later, in the privacy of her room. Or so she promised herself as she picked at a dinner served in the ballroom they were using as a training area.

"If you don't eat, you won't keep up your strength," he said to her when she waved off the second course.

"And if I eat I'll lose it all over your spit-and-polished shoes," she replied, wondering what had happened to the Jane who got along with everyone, who never uttered a rude word or spoke back.

All of a sudden a question that had been bothering her

resurfaced. She leaned forward and asked, "Exactly where is the other Elena? The real one, I mean."

For a moment she thought he might not answer. Not that she learned all that much when he finally did. "That's need-to-know information."

She sat back as if he'd slapped her. "And I obviously don't need to know."

"Exactly."

Well, she might not be experienced in the ways of the world, but she could translate do-not-enter signs as well as the next person. Choking down another slice of her rare roast beef, she set the rest aside, sure it would lodge in her throat. Why should it hurt that he wanted her to risk her life for this missing Elena, but didn't trust her to share all but the barest information?

"All I can tell you is that she's recovering, away from Vendari. It'll be safer for you if you don't know any more details."

His words caught her off guard and she found herself glancing up, surprised by the understanding she saw in his gaze, not trusting that it was really meant for her.

Then the implication of his words set in. If she was killed outright it wouldn't make a speck of difference if she knew the whereabouts of the real Elena. But if she was kidnapped—again—then she could be tortured in an attempt to get her to reveal information she didn't know.

Swallowing hard she pushed away the rest of her meal. Her stomach felt as if she'd taken a dive off a very high tower, knowing the ground was coming up, hard and fast.

"You can't keep skipping your meals and expect to function at top form."

Major Miss-Nothing obviously thought he could control everything. Including her stomach. She had to remember her role here. She was part of a scheme—or mission, or whatever—and that was all. Not a person who was scared right down to the soles of her feet. Not a woman who might want to be comforted instead of admonished.

She kept her voice calm when she knew it wanted to quiver as she lifted her gaze to the man across from her.

"I will do what I need to do to get through this masquerade."

"Mission."

"And you'll do what you need to do. But—" she saw she had his attention by the way the lines bracketing his eyes deepened, the color of them intensifying. "—if you criticize everything I won't be able to function at all."

He weighed her words. "That wasn't a criticism."

"I think you're used to dealing with subordinates. I'm not, nor will I be treated like one."

The old Jane would never have dared to confront another, especially one who glared at her with ice in his eyes. But a small part of her exalted.

Silence spun between them. She vowed not to give in, not on this. A man like McConneghy would eat her alive if she let him. And while that challenged her at one level, or at least evoked some pretty heated images she had no business dwelling on, she needed some sense of control. Everything else had been taken from her—her sense of security, her identity, her freedom of choice, but she refused to be treated like a non-thinking, non-feeling robot.

He reached for his drink, taking a long, slow sip, one that had her thinking about the taste of it upon his lips before she glanced away.

"I will," he uttered at last, setting down his cup, "attempt to remember not to treat you as a subordinate."

She gave him a smile, one that seemed to disconcert him, though she didn't have a clue why. "And I will remind you when you forget."

"I have no doubt about that," came his dry answer, as he rose from the chair. Dinner was obviously over.

But she had won. Not a battle perhaps, more like a skirmish. But she'd made her point, stuck to her guns and felt like skipping. Until he turned, remarking, "Gloating does not become you."

Oh yes it did, she thought, not dimming her smile one bit as she followed him out of the room. She thought she could get used to gloating. Quite used to it.

The next days passed in a blur to Jane. Rising with the sun, she repeated, over and over again, the same moves, the same comments, the same actions until she could do them in her sleep. She learned to crook one finger while sipping tea and to hold her head at an angle when listening with concentration, something the major said happened mostly when a man talked to Elena, very little when a woman did.

Jane learned to keep her eyes downcast when thinking and to eat escargots without gagging. That lesson took a whole afternoon. But since the squishy, chewy morsels were one of Elena's favorites, the major was adamant that Jane practice eating them until she could without even a grimace. He even handed her a cool washcloth after the first two times her stomach revolted and she had to run to the nearest restroom.

Protection her foot, the man was a sadist.

But somewhere along the way she found herself hearing less and less often, "do it again" and more and more often, "that's right. Just like that."

It was a little like absorbing someone else's thought patterns. Until the day that McConneghy told her to eat squid, dressed up in a fancy name and rich sauce.

Jane simply glanced at him, then at the inch-long chunks on her plate, gave him an arch look and said, "Eat it yourself, Major, because I'm not going to."

She set down her fork.

Whatever she expected, it wasn't his grin, one that did marvelous things to the planes of his face.

"I think you're there," he replied, ignoring her open-mouthed stare. "If that wasn't a queen-to-her-subject comment I don't know what is."

"Then you think I'm ready?"

He sobered immediately, his expression once again shuttered and closed. It was as if a light had been quickly extinguished and she wanted to shiver in the dark.

"You're as ready as you'll ever be."

So why didn't the words make her feel better?

She was asking herself the same question when he met her outside her room that evening for dinner. A dinner they would not be having served to them in the training room.

Jane tugged at the simple sheath of blue silk and wondered if the woman she was impersonating owned anything that didn't dip to here in front and there in back. She could swear there was less material in this dress than in the one she'd worn the day she had arrived in Vendari, and that said something. But there'd only been two choices that Ekaterina had laid out on the bed and who was Jane Richards to start pawing through that walk-in closet full of clothes to pick out something more appropriate? With her fashion sense she'd probably end up wearing pajamas and not know the difference.

But on the other hand, she thought, feeling the slide of silk against her skin, it was a bit exciting to step into another's shoes—or in this case clothes—and find herself feeling sexy and provocative instead of competent and unremarkable.

For the briefest of seconds she allowed herself to wonder if Major Gray-eyes would like this dress on her, before she ruthlessly shoved that idea away. There was no place for such thoughts, not when she knew she'd be a fool to believe the man would want someone like her—plain, everyday, ordinary Jane. That's what she was and a man like him would never look twice at her unless she was involved in one of his schemes, or missions, or whatever he wanted to call them.

It must be the long days getting to her, something had to account for that briefest of expressions she'd thought she'd seen cross his face earlier. Or maybe it was just her imagination. She'd always thought of herself as sensible and rational, but then again she'd always thought that if you woke up in Sioux Falls, South Dakota, you'd go to sleep there, too, and not on another continent in some mountain-ringed country that was ripe for revolution.

She sensed his arrival before she heard him. Not that he made a lot of noise when he moved. The man walked like a cat. A sleek, predator kind of cat.

If she thought she was going to receive a compliment from him, she was wrong. There was a quick scan that lingered overlong exactly where she felt most exposed, a tightening of his already stoic expression and a harsh, "Let's go."

So much for wowing the opposite sex, she thought wryly, making a quick two-step to catch up with his long-legged stride down the hallway. The click of her heels across wooden then marble floors was the only sound between them until they descended down a waterfall of a stairway that looked as if it should be on a movie set. The kind of movie where the princess glided forward into the arms of the handsome prince.

But not for her. All she did was catch her heel in one of the runners while she was busy gawking. She kept herself from pitching head-first over the rail by grabbing for it and felt the bite of the major's hand around her arm as he stabilized her, with a glacial glare from those gray eyes ordering her to behave herself.

Nothing like an unspoken rebuke to put a little starch in one's backbone, she thought, waiting until she reached the bottom step and stability to tug her arm free, square her shoulders until she thought they might snap and ask with a frosty tone she was sure the wife-to-be of a king would use when necessary, "Which way?"

They were in a part of the villa she'd never seen.

"Straight ahead and to the left."

Obviously hauteur didn't dent the man one bit. Neither did the fact that when they reached a room with a table large enough to seat a sea of dignitaries, it was empty, except for a ramrod-straight gentleman dressed in what looked like a tux standing just inside the door.

She hesitated to proceed into the room lit with tapered candles, their flickering lights tossed here and there by two walls of mirrors, a half-dozen crystal chandeliers overhead and furniture polished until it gave off its own light.

"Will there be others coming?" she asked, hearing the small echo of her own voice in the room.

"We'll be dining alone tonight." He tucked his hand around her elbow and propelled her forward. She might have thought it a gesture of courtesy but dismissed the idea. The man no doubt guessed she was ready to bolt and was just making sure she had no choice. Again.

When he pulled out her chair and she slid into it, her "thank you" sounded like a cross between a hoarse croak and a hairball. Then she forgot all about it as she caught his smile reflected from a dozen of the mirrors. A smile she doubted he even knew he used. Charming. Inviting. The kind of smile that made women forget about security, stability and thinking with their heads. A big-time-trouble smile.

"There will be other dinners with many more guests." He took a place opposite her and snapped open a damask linen napkin which should have looked out of place in his strong hands, but didn't. "Tonight I thought you might enjoy a quieter setting."

There was no enjoyment in it, she silently acknowledged, sliding her own napkin from beside the china place setting to her lap. How could she enjoy anything when everywhere she looked there was a reflection of her, but not her. There was nothing plain or ordinary about the woman she saw mirrored over and over again, exposed skin looking luminescent in the candlelight, eyes too large in her face, her hair left free around her shoulders. This was not the same woman who normally ate at a dinette table in the kitchen, a book propped on the table before her, her cat twining himself around her ankles.

Maybe it was all a nightmare, and any moment now she'd wake up and be where she should be, which wasn't in the formal setting of a baroque villa, watching a servant fill her crystal glass with red wine.

But if it was a dream, where did Major McConneghy come from? There was nothing in her wildest imaginings that could have manufactured the man across from her. He'd changed from his khaki clothes into more formal wear, but not a stuffy suit. He should have looked different, which he did, but not in the way she expected.

Leave it to the man to look as at-home and competent in a collarless shirt and unstructured suit jacket as he had in his earlier casual outfit. The way he sat in his chair, calm, relaxed, tasting the wine and nodding his approval to the servant as if he did this often—well, as often as he arranged to abduct small-town librarians from their ordinary worlds.

"Don't you enjoy Bordeaux?" His question startled her enough that she glanced at the fragile stemmed glass he held in his hands, glanced at the touch, delicate but strong, rough against smooth, by which he held it. An image that had her wondering if he'd hold a woman as carefully, as gently, before she felt the heat steal into her cheeks and through her body.

With a deep swallow she reached for her own glass.

"I don't know if I've ever had a Bordeaux," she admitted, making sure first there was no servant to overhear her statement. For all she knew, Elena drank the stuff like water, so she didn't want to slip up there. She raised the glass to her lips, and with a sip, part apprehensive, part daring, she tasted, delighted to find it wasn't just one taste but a whole range of tastes dancing across her tongue.

"Oh, this is good." The words came out as a whisper as she traced her tongue where the wine had been. "I didn't think it'd be like this at all."

Then she looked up, caught by the expression on the face of the man opposite her. She might have thought she'd imagined the tense moments between them before, but this time it wasn't an overactive imagination or a long day. Not when the image was reflected back, again and again, by the mirrors around her. As if in a kaleidoscope she saw his gaze lock on her lips then slide lower, causing the wine she'd just sipped to feel like liquid fire scorching her throat.

He looked like a man waging a war with himself, skin stretched taut over his cheekbones, eyes narrowed, gaze hidden. She could feel her own immediate response, one that nothing in her years as a librarian had prepared her for. The fluttery feeling in her stomach, the sudden aching heaviness of her breasts, the rasp of silk against sensitized skin with every breath she inhaled. She felt hot and chilled at the same time, caught in a no-time space that seemed to stretch out forever, but that must have lasted only seconds.

It was broken, like glass against a marble floor when, with a sound that rivaled a cannon blast, a servant cleared his throat before entering the room, a covered silver tray in his outstretched arms.

Jane very carefully set her glass down, thankful she managed it without spilling its contents across the pearl-white tablecloth. She felt as if she'd been caught in an indecent act and didn't know where to look, what to do while her cheeks flamed and a trio of servants rustled around her, serving food she neither saw nor smelled.

Automatically she thanked each and every one of them, surprised when her dinner companion remarked, ''You'll have them talking in the kitchen for a week.''

Her gaze shot up to lock with his, sure he was referring to the servant catching her staring at him like an infatuated teenager, appalled that she'd given herself away so easily. Until he added, ''They're not used to being publicly thanked for doing their job.''

''Oh.'' She glanced toward the far doorway, feeling as if she'd failed her first exam in the art of impersonating the rich and sophisticated. ''I didn't know.''

''An error we can remedy. Tomorrow we'll focus on more of the details to your position.'' He gave her a sharp-eyed look, not like the earlier one, but said nothing more.

How was she ever supposed to impersonate Elena if she couldn't even get through a simple meal? Not that the meal before them was simple. It wasn't. It was exquisite, with a cold tomato-red soup, a salad of a dozen different greens, a poached white fish sautéed in what smelled like a mango and papaya sauce and more. And it all could have been sawdust as much as she was able to taste any of it.

Each bite stuck in her throat, like a lump of ineptitude that wouldn't go down no matter how much she swallowed. She'd taken to just moving piles around on her plate when one of the women servers asked her, ''It does not meet with mademoiselle's approval?''

Before she could reply, the woman continued, ''I will have the cook prepare something new. Something better.''

''Oh, no please.'' Jane reached her hand to the one removing her half-eaten meal. "Please, it's a wonderful meal. It's just been a long day."

When the woman looked at her as if she'd sprouted horns, Jane glanced toward the major, who regarded them both. "Do something. I don't want the cook to feel insulted."

He glanced from her to the servant and nodded his head. "Tell the cook the meal was exquisite. As usual. Mademoiselle has had a long day so we'll skip the dessert."

The woman nodded and silently retreated, still looking befuddled, but before Jane could ask why, another person walked into the room. A man she recognized only too well though she'd seen him only briefly, through a haze of drugs and fear.

"It really is remarkable," Viktor Stanislaus Tarkioff, King of Vendari, remarked, striding into the room, his medals shooting spears of light with every step he took. "Simply remarkable."

He moved to stand across from her, placing himself behind and to the left of the major, silently watching Jane as if gauging her reaction to his nearness.

That alone kept her from revealing it. At least she hoped it did, because she didn't think the king would appreciate knowing his pretend fiancée loathed him right about then. Like a magnet for all the turmoil this man had caused in her life, she fought twin needs. One to hurl something at him, preferably something heavy, the other to run from the room, screaming at him to find another way to fix his country's problem.

It wasn't helping matters that he was looking at her not as a person, one unwillingly abducted from her home to travel half way across the world to become a pawn in a dangerous political game, but as a tool. Nothing more, nothing less.

Goose bumps crawled up her skin as his gaze raked over her, impersonal enough, but leaving her feeling as if she was less than human. Nothing like the way the major had made her feel with his look. Nothing.

"You have little to say?" His voice mocked, in spite of its soft tone, lyrical with the accent of his country.

"Nothing appropriate for mixed company."

"That is good." He laughed, a sound rolling around the room like an empty can. "I like a woman who looks like ice while she spits fire."

Well, he'd gotten the wrong woman. There was no fire in her and never had been. What he'd gotten instead was a small-town librarian who could blow this crazy plan at any minute, who just wanted to live long enough to sleep in her own bed once again and wear her own clothes.

As if the weight of the last days slammed against her all at once, she knew couldn't stay in the room with either of these men for one more moment. They each demanded something from her, something she did not want to give.

"Excuse me." She rose to her feet, ignoring both the king's surprised look and the major's wary one. "I'm sure you'll understand when I say it's been a long day."

The king tried to interrupt, but she wouldn't let him. "I'd like to go to my room. Now."

"I thought we would have a glass of cognac in the library. I have come a ways to visit with you tonight," he pouted, but she did not glance his way. She knew it was the major who would make the final decision. She held his gray-eyed glance until he rose to his feet, crumpling his napkin into a snowy mound on the table.

"Your Highness," he began, though he, too, did not look at the man. "I think your fiancée is right. I shall escort her to her room, then return to join you in the library."

"See that you do," came the king's snapped answer. One that told her she'd made no brownie points with her supposed intended. Not that she cared.

In silence she walked from the room, aware of Mc-

Conneghy's silent presence shadowing her, up the stairway
and down the long hallways. Only when they reached her
room did he speak.

"Wait here."

"But, I'm—"

"Do as I say. Wait here."

Did she have any choice? She assumed not as she
watched him step in front of her, slide into the room, turn
on the light and inspect every corner before he gave her an
all-clear nod.

The man missed nothing. Which was probably a good
thing, she realized, because all she noticed was the thin
scrap of sheer pale peach lace that must have been meant
as a nightgown draped across the turned-down covers of the
bed. Never, in all her life, had she dreamed of owning such
a garment. Nightgowns like that belonged to seductresses,
to women who reveled in their power over men, to bank
accounts that didn't need to be constantly balanced.

The major's gaze followed hers before he came to stand
beside her. Obviously in his world such garments were not
out of place because his look wasn't heated now, but worried. He gazed down at her, standing so close she could
watch the pulse beating in the hollow of his throat. He raised
one hand, tentatively, a move that looked out of place for
him, then let it slip back to his side.

"Sleep will help." He sounded as if they weren't the
words he'd originally intended, but was at a loss for others.

She could find no energy for an answer.

He was almost at the door before he spoke again. "This
is an important thing that you're doing."

"If you say so."

Silence descended, a tense, awkward pause thick with
tension. Until he broke it. "You'll feel better in the morning."

She waited until she heard the door click shut behind his

departure before she allowed the sigh she was holding to escape. She might feel better in the morning, but she'd still be an impostor in Vendari. She'd still be everyday Jane Richards playing a life-or-death part with no script.

Lucius waited outside the door, feeling as frustrated and powerless as a raw recruit on his first mission. Part of him wanted to turn back, tell the hollow-eyed exhausted woman he'd left on the other side of the door that there'd been a mistake, that tomorrow he would put her on a plane for home and make her nightmare disappear.

But he couldn't do that.

He started down the hallway, seeing all too clearly in his mind the way she'd walked it earlier. Who'd have thought a librarian could wear silk with the grace of a duchess? They'd lucked out there. She fit the part of a king's intended better than the real thing, though he figured he'd be keeping that observation to himself—if he wanted to retain his role as peacekeeper to Tarkioff.

But there were other issues he'd be addressing with the king and, though he felt like day-old dog meat, chewed up and spat out, there was no time like the present to get a few things straightened out.

Tarkioff sat behind the desk as Lucius entered the library. A room so called because a former owner had enjoyed literature and had filled this room with the thick dark wood paneling, shelf after shelf of books, and plush red carpet he felt befitted a man of literature.

The fact that those who had followed never cracked open one of the handsomely bound books didn't seem to matter. They too enjoyed the aura the room exuded and kept it virtually intact. Like a lot in Vendari, there was power in appearance alone.

"Ah, Major," Tarkioff hailed him as he looked up. "Come in. I think we have much to discuss."

Since McConneghy agreed and knew the room had already been swept for listening devices by his men, he didn't hesitate to speak his mind once he closed the door.

"You should never have authorized the abduction of Miss Richards," he spoke bluntly, knowing the best way to deal with the man before him was head-on. Tarkioff listened to little else. "Or at the least you should have allowed me to handle it differently."

"You were moving too slowly." The king waved away objections like fireflies in the night.

"We are asking her to risk her life." He'd moved far enough into the room to splay his hands across the highly polished surface of the desk. "You might have given her a choice."

"And if she had said no?" Tarkioff rolled an unlit cigar between his stocky fingers. "You and I both know there is too much at stake to have allowed that."

"I could have persuaded her." At the other man's look, he added, "A willing individual is much easier to work with than an unwilling one."

"I still think you can use your powers of persuasion," came the casual reply as Tarkioff continued to study his cigar, rolling it back and forth. One eyebrow arched.

"We're not talking about a seduction here," Lucius bit back, surprised at the anger rolling through him. "We're talking about a young woman who could lose her life for your country. She deserves better treatment than she has received thus far."

The cigar snapped between the king's fingers. "It is of no consequence. *She* is of no consequence." The man's voice no longer sounded modulated and even; his face was as flushed as the pile carpet. "She has a purpose. As you do, Major, or have you forgotten your own role?"

"I may have found the girl for you, but I certainly did not authorize her being drugged and kidnapped."

"And yet you brought her to Vendari."

He knew he'd have to live with that knowledge for a long, long time. "I had my orders."

The king leaned forward. "And is not one of those orders to make sure that I am kept content? That my goodwill continues to be extended toward your country?"

Lucius wanted to wipe the smug look off the bastard's face with one punch. But it would serve no good. He'd worked with men like Tarkioff before, some worse, a few better, but all of them aware of the see-saw game of international politics, a game that had innocent casualties all too often.

"I will keep Miss Richards safe." He enunciated each word so that they both understood where he was coming from. "She is under my protection while she is in Vendari."

The other man shrugged and smiled. "And who is going to protect the young lady from you, Major?"

Chapter 5

Jane joined the major for breakfast the following morning. She had barely slid into the straight-backed chair and grabbed a cup of coffee before he announced, "We've arranged two events for you today. We're using your long trip as an excuse not to overtire you."

"Today?"

"You're ready."

Wrong. She'd never be ready for this. Never.

"But what if I—"

"You're ready. The limo will be here in less than half an hour to take us into the city. Eat your croissant and we'll be on our way."

McConneghy was sure if the croissant was a lethal weapon it'd be lobbed his way in a heartbeat.

But he couldn't afford to pretty up what wasn't pretty. It'd been a long week but he'd been honest with her. She was ready. As ready as she'd ever be, and they could no longer afford this time in seclusion. The rumors were already circulating and rumors in an unstable country were too dangerous to go unchecked.

The rest of the brief breakfast was spent in silence. She still wasn't eating enough to feed a bird but he'd let it go this time. One skirmish at a time and he held no doubts there would be more skirmishes ahead.

"Eustace Tarkioff will be joining us in the limo," he said and watched her pale.

"The king's brother?"

"Yes."

"Why is he coming?"

"He wants to make sure all is well." He could have lied. Should have when he noted the way her hands moved to her lap, pleating her skirt. "He's the Head of Security. It's his job."

He wondered what she was thinking as silence descended, until she squared her shoulders, looked him straight in the eye and asked, "Can he nix your mission?"

"It's too late—"

"No, I mean, does he have the power or authority or whatever to force the second option? The one I didn't choose."

No wonder she looked as if she was preparing to meet the firing squad.

"No. The choice has been made. The mission goes forward as planned."

Less than twenty minutes later, he wondered if he should have made Jane more wary of the king's brother. Eustace Tarkioff possessed several attributes his royal brother did not, secrecy and control being two. There had been many times Lucius had wished Eustace had been the ruling brother rather than the more volatile and unstable Viktor.

This was not one of those times, Lucius thought, as he watched the cool way Eustace introduced himself to Jane and her response.

Was it only days ago he'd been dealing with a woman on the verge of snapping? Where was that woman? He'd all but swallowed his tongue earlier when he'd seen her standing in the open doorway of the breakfast room, the color of her suit enhancing the golden tones of her skin, darkening her eyes, highlighting every inch of luscious, satin-smooth skin. It was all he could do not to choke on the sip of coffee clogging his throat.

And then she'd slid into the chair across from him, the movement hitching up her skirt to expose one creamy thigh, the V-neck slipping until he thought he'd drool. The scent of her skin-warmed perfume kicked him dead center. On the real Elena Rostov he'd have thought the move calculated, or practiced overkill. But Jane Richards didn't seem to have a clue what she was doing to him.

She had him by his windpipe and was tightening her hold by the second. Hell, even the way she spread butter on a croissant had him imagining how her long, slender fingers would feel stroking him—touching, caressing, memorizing. It was a miracle he hadn't poured hot coffee all over himself.

Now Eustace was taking her at face value. With her attention focused on the city rushing past outside the window, her posture that of any elegant woman, at ease, in command, sure of herself, Lucius himself might have been fooled into thinking the hardest part of this mission was behind them.

It'd be a dangerous mistake to make. Especially as they were even now moving toward a possible trap. One with Jane Richards as the bait.

He wouldn't think about it. Couldn't or he'd scrap the mission. Hadn't his team been over and over the area already? They were in place now and he'd be there, too, determined to make sure nothing happened to her.

"You look very serious." Her voice washed over him. Calm. Almost too calm, as if she was exerting every ounce of energy to keep her tone even. Not that he blamed her. He felt the same way himself.

He listened as she continued, "I don't know if that frown you're wearing bodes well for where we're going."

He forced his features into a calmness he didn't feel, knowing Eustace Tarkioff was weighing every word. "It's an elementary school. A couple of songs from the kids, a speech or two from the administration."

"And do I have to make a speech, also?"

He found himself reacting to the near panic in her eyes. "No. A few words of thanks, shake everybody's hand that you can, smile constantly and you'll be fine."

He watched her tug at her skirt and wished he hadn't. It didn't take much to imagine tugging at it himself, but for a whole different reason.

"You're frowning again."

"Occupational hazard."

"How did you get into what you do?" she asked, quickly glancing at the king's brother and adding, "I mean, if it won't reveal any secrets for you to talk about it."

"I was recruited in college." Lord, that was a lifetime ago.

"I didn't know they recruited for stuff like that." She leaned forward, her blouse gaping slightly, his throat going dry. "It's not like there are college courses in abduction and international troubleshooting."

He couldn't help the wince.

"I'm sorry," she immediately offered, her smile small but genuine. "I didn't mean it to sound like that. I just meant how could college have prepared you for this." She waved her hand toward the front of the car, the guard riding there, the bulletproof glass, the escort of uniformed soldiers on motorcycles beside the vehicle.

"It didn't." This time he could smile back. "I showed an aptitude for languages and history." And the ability to absorb, understand and synthesize vast quantities of information quickly and easily.

"And the next thing you knew you were in an obscure room in an obscure corner of the Pentagon?"

"Something like that."

"What exactly is your job title?"

He glanced at Eustace before replying. "Advisor to the king."

"Advisor on?"

"Security. Politics. International Relations."

"But you're not an ambassador or with the State Department?"

"No. At this time Dubruchek does not have official diplomatic relations with the United States. A situation we are hoping to rectify."

"By my being here. Quid pro quo?"

The woman caught on quickly and Eustace was now the one frowning.

"We'd been talking about my career path. A very mundane subject, I'm afraid."

She leaned back against the leather seat, her expression thoughtful. "I think you're leaving a few details out."

He couldn't help but grin at her wry tone, and look of disappointment. "Look, I'd love to tell you some wild and exciting story, something that makes me sound larger than life and out of the ordinary, but it wouldn't be true."

"No?" One elegant brow arched upwards.

"I'm just a guy trying to do a job the best way I can."

"Some job."

Since he didn't know if she meant it as an accusation, or in admiration, he let her words slide. After all he had a few questions of his own. "How did you decide to be a librarian?"

She glanced at him as if looking for a hidden agenda before giving a silent shrug. "I always enjoyed books and research.'' She paused, as if hesitant to continue before adding, ''And helping people.''

He sensed there was more to her answer so he waited. It didn't take long.

''I know it's not in the same league as helping troubled countries, but in my own way I do help people. Not to change the world, or save lives, but I try to make a difference.''

''Are you justifying what you do to me, or to yourself?''

He heard her quick intake of breath and regretted his observation, no matter how accurate it might have been.

''I'm not—oh, maybe I am, just a little.'' She started to pleat her skirt through her fingers. ''But I never wanted to be in some glamorous occupation.''

Lucius thought of all the hellholes he'd been in through the years, the jungles and inner-city slums, the all-night meetings making choices that left bile in his gut and emptiness in his soul, the decisions made, lives sacrificed and people scarred by actions he did and did not take, and he thought the word *glamorous* as far from the truth as the woman before him was from the real Elena Rostov.

''I think the world needs a lot more librarians,'' he remarked, as surprised as she that he'd said the words aloud.

She appeared to want to respond, but time had run out; the car swung down a street that was swept daily and pulled into an open paved area. He quickly picked out several of his men, stationed where they could see the most, offer the most protection. The setting was still vulnerable to attack from a number of points, but he'd stationed men to watch them too.

It was show time.

''Miss Rostov,'' he offered his arm, aware a member of the school staff had opened the limo door and was both watching and listening. Jane glanced at Eustace Tarkioff, who gave a silent nod.

"Major McConneghy." She placed her hand in his, her eyes suddenly hesitant and unsure. But her voice betrayed nothing as she slid along the seat toward him.

Atta girl, he wanted to tell her. Just as he wanted to let her know he'd be right there with her. Right beside her. Protecting her in every way he knew how.

He'd made his promise and meant to keep it. As long as it took to get her back to her world, the quiet, normal world of a small-town library, he'd be there for her. No matter what the cost to him.

Jane gazed out across the semi-circular courtyard, aware of the chant-like tones of the third—or was it fourth?—speaker extolling the need for a stronger educational program for Vendari, the sounds of deep-throated birds warbling from cone-shaped trees in the background, the soft gurgle of a fountain somewhere out of sight.

The school behind where she sat on a platform rose like a grand old dame, its stucco pockmarked and crumbling, its paint faded tones of gold and cream. Before her a small sea of faces stood and sat, the older ones on folded metal chairs, the younger ones cross-legged down in front, hopping from one foot to the other in the back rows.

Though she wasn't a parent herself, had never even allowed herself to think along those lines because they seemed so impossible, she'd worked with enough kids to recognize their feelings as being akin to hers—impatience, boredom, with maybe a tinge of anticipation thrown in for good measure.

Soon she'd have to stand, walk before the collection of dignitaries flanking her, feel McConneghy and the king's brother judge and weigh her every move, waiting for her to mess up or stumble her way through, nod and say a few thank yous and then they'd be done. Thank heavens.

Her lips felt stretched into an impossible smile, except

when she looked at the children. They watched her, not because they expected anything from her, but out of undiluted curiosity. When she thought no one was looking she'd wiggle her fingers at them, watch their grins widen, and listen to McConneghy smother a cough next to her.

At least she thought it was a cough, yet when she'd glance his way his expression was as blank as ever. His concentration never wavered from scanning the rooftops around them, the blank windows in the buildings across the street. The man never relaxed, except for that rare moment in the car when not only had he offered up a smile, he'd followed it with a grin. A look that did funny things to her sense of equilibrium.

"...and I give you Miss Elena Rostov," she heard the speaker say, jerking her back to reality with a thud.

Show time, she thought, smoothing down her skirt as she stood, wishing she was anywhere but where she was, reminding herself that the old Jane might not have been able to pull this off, but that the new one would at least give it a try. Her first step wobbled, her second didn't. She kept her gaze on the children's faces, strengthened by their smiles and continued until she stood at the mike, one hand waving, the other grasping a huge bouquet someone had shoved into her hands when she first arrived.

The next seconds took all the nerve she'd ever possessed, but just as McConneghy had said, a few words, a few more waves and a never-ending smile and she finished. Before she knew it there were people on their feet, applauding, McConneghy at her side, his hand strong and reassuring as it cupped her elbow, his voice pitched low for her alone.

"Good job. Now it's time to go."

They'd obviously have to work on the dictator-to-subordinate thing some more. Couldn't she savor her own personal victory a few seconds longer? But it was clear the major had his own agenda. Like a pro dancing instructor he waltzed her off the stage, through a crowd of well-wishers and almost into the limousine before she could grab a deep breath.

But when she did, she halted, caught by two things. One was the sight of a small girl, stick-thin but with a smile as large as her face, and the other, a drooping flower, scarlet-red, wilting in her hands.

"Wait," Jane whispered, pulling away from the major, ignoring his look of outrage as she stepped forward. The girl stood on the other side of a roped barrier, almost obscured by a row of fatigue-covered soldiers and adults in suits.

How long had she waited there? Jane wondered, touched by the gesture, determined that it would not go unrewarded.

"Hello," she offered, once she'd reached the girl, bending over until they were eye to eye. "Is this for me?"

The child offered a shy smile and a nod as she extended her clenched hand and the sad-looking flower. Jane reached for it, never as touched by anything. The moment passed as a strong, male hand bit into her arm, a familiar terse voice ordered, "It's time to leave, Miss Rostov. Now."

She could have sworn the humid temperature chilled by several degrees. But she held her ground, a difficult feat with a fire-breathing dragon tugging at her arm.

"Thank you for the beautiful flower." She spoke only to the little girl. "Did you pick it for me?"

Another nod.

"Then I'll treasure it forever." She wanted to brush her hand across the child's bangs, give her something in return, acknowledge her in some way.

The hand tugged again.

"Here, do something useful," she snapped, straightening and thrusting the elaborate bouquet she'd been holding into the face of a man who looked as frustrated, as put out by her actions, as she was by his.

"Miss Rostov—" His words sounded like the rumble of a freight train bearing down on her before she turned her back on him. The little girl had been joined by others, many holding single flowers held in hot, grimy hands for who knew how long, all of them extended in her direction.

Without waiting for approval from the man she could all but feel steaming at her side, she reached for them, offering genuine smiles and thank yous, unaware of how much time had passed until the major spoke again, only this time not to her.

"Miss Rostov thanks you all but she must leave. *Now*." She knew the last word was stressed expressly for her benefit. "Or she'll be late for another important meeting."

This time it wasn't a tug but a command as she fell into step beside him, aware of the ring of soldiers closing in around her, blocking the children, bringing her back to reality with their impassive faces. Did they learn blank looks in military school? she thought peevishly as she was all but shoved into the limo, the door closed behind her with a resounding thwack. This time they were alone. The king's brother had obviously found another ride. No doubt the man knew enough to stay out of the lion's den when the lion was mad.

The limo hadn't even begun to move before McConneghy leaned toward her, his words as cold and controlled as his eyes were heated, "If you ever pull such a stupid stunt again—"

"It wasn't a stunt." Her own voice rose, an unheard of thing in librarian-Jane. "Can you imagine how long that little girl waited there? And for what? For me to ignore her? For me to walk past as though she didn't even exist?"

He ran a hand through his hair, a movement that spoke even louder than his voice. "This isn't about that little girl."

"It is too about that little girl." She leaned forward herself. "It's about her worth as a human being. Have you ever been ignored by an adult? Treated like you didn't quite count because you had no power? Kids can't fight back, they have no choice but to give way.''

He gave her a sharp look, but held his tongue. Suddenly Jane found all the energy, all the anger pumping through her evaporate. She leaned back against her seat, her voice calmer now, her gaze locked unseeing out the window.

''I know exactly how that little girl felt. How it is to be invisible in a world of adults too busy, too preoccupied to notice. I've felt like that.'' She wished the words didn't sound so whisper-thin. ''There was no way I could walk past that child and ignore the look on her face.''

''How in the world am I supposed to keep you safe if you march right into a crowd of potential killers?''

She heard the frustration in his voice and answered with her own. ''They were children. Not killers, or assassins, or revolutionaries. They were simply children. Is everything in your life so black and white? Either you know them and they are thus okay or you don't know them which mean they are a threat? Are there no gray zones? No people who might be just what they seem—ordinary, everyday people?''

She heard him shift, sensed he'd leaned forward, felt the brush of his pant leg against her skirt, a move that was hard to ignore, but she was going to try.

''Do you know how the last attempt on Elena Rostov's life was made?''

She looked at him then, surprised he didn't freeze from it. ''As a matter of fact I don't know. I figured it was on a need-to-know basis.''

He didn't look away, though his expression tightened, his hands came together in a tight ball. ''It was a bomb, strapped to the underside of a baby's carriage.''

''There wasn't—''

''No, the carriage was empty, but we still lost seven people. Seven.'' His voice sounded calm, but his expression was not. Especially his eyes. Windows to a soul. A tormented soul. "The assassin, three of my men and four bystanders, all because no one thought to look beneath the bloody carriage. Nobody wanted to believe something so innocent could be deadly. And if you think they're not beyond using a child, you're wrong."

If she thought she felt deflated before, it was nothing to what she felt like then. She could hear the pain in McConneghy's voice. The pain and the cost to him.

"You feel responsible for their deaths." Her words whispered against the hum of air conditioning in the car. "You think it's your fault they died."

"It *was* my fault." He glanced away, but not before she saw the bleakness in his eyes deepen. "Just like it's my responsibility if anything happens to you."

Wrong button to push.

If there was one thing she couldn't tolerate it was being a responsibility, an obligation to someone. Her parents had never let her forget that she was an obligation to them. Being in that position with this man was no better. But then he was the type of man to assume obligations, to accept duty and responsibilities, and then to live with the aftermath when things didn't go right. How could a man like that ever understand a woman like her? Worlds apart and no common ground.

She leaned her head against the seat, closing her eyes. "I didn't accept the flowers to make your job harder."

"I know you didn't, but the end result was the same."

She wondered if he knew he'd sworn aloud. "It doesn't change the fact that I can't ignore those people. I won't purposefully put you or your men at risk but you can't expect me to change what I am inside just because I look like someone else on the outside."

"I can't protect you if you won't follow orders."

Trains on one-way tracks were hard to change. But research librarians did not give up if they didn't find what
they wanted in the first place they looked.

"You're treating me like a subordinate. Again." She
opened her eyes, glad to see the signs of strain on his face
lessening. "Isn't there a way we can compromise?"

"I won't compromise with your life."

She told herself he'd say the same thing, feel the same
way with any of his responsibilities, but that didn't seem to
stop the warmth spreading through her at his words.

She closed her eyes again, feeling the emotional drain of
the last few hours. "I have great faith in your ability to find
a solution to our dilemma, Major."

He made a sound that might have been a snort. His tone
was dry as he remarked, "Now you have faith in me?"

"Of course." She couldn't help the yawn. "The king said
you fixed problems. This is your area of expertise."

Lucius didn't know if he wanted to lose his legendary
sense of control, or applaud the woman before him for
neatly boxing him into a corner, a very tight corner.

She sat before him, her eyes closed, creating half moons
of dark lashes against her satin skin, her breathing even and
deep, while he churned inside like an ocean beneath a ty-
phoon's wind.

Part of it was residual fear. The minute she'd broken pattern and approached the crowd he'd aged ten years. Logi-
cally he knew she didn't have a clue what she was up
against. Why should she? Librarians from the midwest
didn't have to fear crowds and the threats so easily hidden
in their midst. But logic had nothing to do with the riot of
emotions erupting within him when she'd made her instinctive move toward the small child.

He'd heard it in her voice. That need to make another
feel good, to make sure they were acknowledged, that their

gesture did not go unrecognized. It was a move worthy of a country's ruler, and Tarkioff would be blessed if he had such a mate at his side.

That was part of the problem. She was *not* Elena Rostov. Her role was *not* to make the future queen beloved by the people, it was to make sure there was going to be a future queen. And to do that she needed to stay alive. He had to make sure she stayed alive.

But there was more than that, and he knew it. Not that he liked accepting it, his job was challenging enough without emotions clouding issues, but damn if he was going to let her get hurt—at all—in this mission. She'd had no choice but to be a part, and he couldn't go back and fix that, though in his final report he was going to make darn good and sure heads would roll because of it. But he could do everything in his power to make sure she came out in one piece. If she let him do his job.

Now she wanted him to allow her to be accessible while keeping her safe. Impossible. It wouldn't work. There was no way.

So why couldn't he ignore the way she'd looked when she'd reached for that bloody wilted flower? There was a softness about her face, a smile in her eyes, the kind of look that the children automatically responded to and that made grown men want to slay dragons. Or do whatever was within their power to see that look again. Even if it meant twice as much work for his men and thrice as much for him.

"Damn," he uttered the word aloud, but softly and without heat. She looked so relaxed at last that he hated to disturb her. He was glad someone could relax because it sure as hell wouldn't be him or his team. Not until they got one stubborn, independent-minded woman who looked soft as fluff and smelled like sin, out of Vendari and back to where she belonged.

Punching in the number of his second-in-command on his cell phone he wondered if she had raised this much trouble in the library.

Jane opened her eyes slowly, aware that the limo had stopped, but not sure why or where she was. The feeling increased as she glanced across to the opposite seat, her gaze locking with McConneghy's.

Maybe she felt so disoriented because she'd fallen asleep in front of him—a move that left her feeling exposed and vulnerable. It was an instinctive response, an age-old one, a silent admission that she'd been willing to let her guard down, had been helpless while he was there, just across the car, watching her while she'd been unaware.

She couldn't believe she'd done that. Or that it implied a measure of trust and sense of security she wasn't aware she possessed around him. He'd said he'd protect her, but that was his job and she accepted it as that—nothing more. She knew instinctively that around a man like him, a woman's best defense was constant wariness. And she'd dozed off like a lamb with a wolf on guard.

"Where are we?" she asked, sitting up straighter, wishing there was more of her skirt to pull over her knees.

"We're at the Ministry of Industry and Commerce. You're expected inside in a few minutes."

"I'm sorry, I must have fallen asleep."

"You needed it." He sounded so cool, so controlled, she must have dreamed their earlier argument, the emotions reflected in his face. The man before her would never have unwittingly exposed so much of his soul.

"Do you want a glass of juice or something before we head inside?" he asked.

She glanced at the small bar to one side of where they sat. "No, nothing."

He sat still, his gaze steady, his posture relaxed, but she

wasn't fooled for a moment. There was a lot going on behind those gray eyes.

She glanced out the window, still feeling disoriented. "I've forgotten who I'm supposed to be meeting." It wasn't quite true, but as long as they were discussing logistics she could have a few minutes to regain her sense of composure, what little she ever had around this man.

"It's a consortium of agricultural interests, farmers, land policy makers, mining interests."

"A few tree huggers?" She didn't know why she asked, but was secretly thrilled when he smiled, even if it looked a little tired and haggard. It happened so rarely.

"Tree-huggers only exist in a climate of free speech and civil liberties."

How could she have forgotten so soon? A country scarred by back-to-back attempted coups was still a child struggling with ideas and concepts she had always taken for granted.

She brushed a strand of hair from her face, aware of McConneghy's gaze following her movement, sensitive to the conflicting feelings it aroused. "I'm supposed to smile and wave again?"

"Yes. Though it'll be a smaller group, more smiling, less waving."

"Got it." She swallowed, surprised to find she wasn't as frightened this time as she had been earlier. She'd done this once already and McConneghy had been there the whole time, at her side, lending her silent support when she needed it most.

"Ready?" he asked, the expression in his eyes telling her they'd wait where they were, in the safety and obscurity of the car, for as long as she needed.

"Yeah, I'm ready."

"Good. I'll lead. You'll follow."

That she could do. And he didn't think she could take orders.

A little over two hours later she found she'd survived. More than that, she'd actually enjoyed herself. That and the fact that, at the very end, when she was getting her hand squeezed by a number of dignitaries who all looked alike, McConneghy had taken her aside, gesturing to a line of ordinary-looking people waiting to meet her.

"A compromise?" she asked, touched that he'd actually listened, and maybe even understood, a little.

"A compromise." He nodded toward where a half dozen men stood, controlling the line by the positioning of their bodies. "Watch them. They're here to protect you."

Risking themselves, she realized, even as she stepped forward to accept the first handshake from a man who looked as if he'd spent every day toiling in the fields, his skin weathered, his hands roughened by calluses. One after another they came, their smiles tentative, their manner wary. And yet they came, judging her silently. Not her, but their future queen, Jane thought, greeting them all, until her hand felt like putty and her legs quaked.

It was McConneghy who came to her rescue. Again.

"Time to go," he murmured as she smiled into the face of a woman who must have been a hundred if she was a day.

"Did I meet everyone on Vendari?" she asked as he escorted her out of the hall and into the blazing afternoon sun.

He gave her a skeptical glance as he opened the limo door. "Rethinking your position?"

"No." She laughed, surprised at how good it felt to sink into the leather seats. "Not at all. I just hadn't realized how much work is involved in shaking hands. I always thought dignitaries and movie stars were spoiled and lazy."

"And now?" He'd opened a bottle of orange juice, poured it into a crystal glass and handed it to her; its taste was ambrosia on her tongue.

"And now I take back every petty, envious, unjustified thought I had about them."

"You did a good job back there."

The words both surprised her and pleased her, she realized, shoving away the feeling that it was much like being a child seeking approval. A feeling she knew only too well. Instead she changed the subject.

"Thank you for making it possible for me to meet those people."

This time he was the one who looked surprised.

"You mean for Elena to meet them."

She knew the smile on her face wavered, but she kept it there, even as she turned her gaze away. It was silly that his words should hurt, especially following a compliment she knew was sincere. But they did. It was as though he was reminding her she was a fake. None of this was real and she was only doing a job.

"You never told me how long I'd be here," she found herself remarking, knowing she'd meant to ask the question earlier, surprised at the conflicting feelings it aroused in her. On the one hand she'd be able to get back to her real life, the one where she belonged, not walking around in silks and pretending she was somebody important. On the other hand it would mean never seeing Lucius McConneghy again, a man, who by all rights, she should despise. But the anger wouldn't come, nor the bitterness. No matter how hard she tried.

"The wedding is back on schedule. It will happen three weeks from yesterday."

"Three weeks?" The words came out as a squeak. "I'm supposed to keep this up for three weeks?"

"You've had no problem with it so far."

"It's been one day." She knew she sounded slightly hysterical. She felt that, but darn if she could pinpoint exactly why. "There's no way I can fool Elena's real family for long and they're bound to show up here sooner or later."

"I told you when we first arrived, it's being taken care of."

"How?"

"Pavlov Rostov is having some difficulty with his overseas investments. They're requiring him to handle them personally."

"Oh." What more could she say? If she'd had doubts about the power behind the obscure government agency he worked for before, there were none now. "You can manipulate something like that?"

One of his brows arched. "I'd prefer another term than *manipulate*."

"You know what I mean. Why do you bother with this elaborate hoax? Why don't you just dictate to Tarkioff and Rostov what they will and won't do and be done with it?"

"We don't work that way." He gave her a long, all-too-seeing look. "We've also sidestepped the real issue here."

She felt like a petulant, unreasonable child being called to task. "The real issue is that three weeks is too long. I can't possibly not make a mistake in that time."

"That's a double negative."

She wanted to toss her juice over his head. "That's reality. There's no way I can go on pretending I'm somebody I'm not for three weeks."

"You're doing fine so far."

"You're not listening to me." She wondered if he was taught obstinacy or if it just came naturally. "We're talking about three weeks of dinners, and functions and…" She waved her free hand. "…and things."

"Things?" She could have sworn his lips twitched.

"You know what I mean. Who's off the subject now?"

He reached for her glass, probably afraid she'd either drop

it or bean him with it. "I'm sure you're still tired and not thinking clearly."

"Don't you dare do that dictator-to-subordinate thing with me here," she warned him. Not that it fazed him in the least.

"We'll take this one day at a time."

"And if I say no to something, is it still a go?"

His face registered nothing. A very neat trick to avoid commitment, she realized, wishing she could do the same.

"We'll take this one day at a time."

"You sound like a parrot." She turned to stare out the window, not caring if it was a juvenile move.

"You have no other meetings today. You can spend the afternoon resting in your room at the villa."

She held back the inclination to snap him a salute— barely, but didn't bother to respond. She knew he wasn't waiting for one. It wasn't a suggestion as much as an order, one he'd give to a balky child who was not behaving.

But maybe some time alone was exactly what she needed—time when she wasn't being watched, weighed and analyzed by this man or anyone else. Time to deal with the fact she'd be almost in his hip pocket for another three weeks. Time to figure out if that was bad news—or good news.

Chapter 6

Jane had barely waved off Ekaterina's solicitous offers of a warm bath or back massage when they'd returned to the villa when there was a knock at the door.

It shouldn't have surprised her to see McConneghy there, but it did. Obviously the man's idea of some time alone was different than hers. And here she'd thought she was going to have communication problems with the people of Vendari.

"Yes?" She had hardly got the door open before he brushed past her.

"Good. You're not busy."

"Define busy." If he thought she was ready to head out to another reception or dedication they really were going to have to work on a few issues.

As if he read her mind, he grinned. "Don't worry. My plans involve pleasure, not business."

Brain cell overload. It was the only excuse she could think of for standing there like a ninny with her mouth open.

Either that or she'd shelved one too many copies of *Cosmo* in the library stacks. The ones with headlines like Hunk Fantasies Can Come True or If He Asks Will You Say Yes?

"Excuse me?" she managed to stammer.

"Come along. We'll get what we need there."

He was heading out the door, with her scrambling to keep up with his long-legged stride, before she could ask the simple questions. Like what did they need? And where were they going?

He never slowed until they'd traversed at least a mile of hallways, three sets of stairs and four posts with armed bodyguards. Ones that saluted religiously as McConneghy came in sight.

A neat trick if you could do it.

"Where?" she tried to ask, but lost the train of her thoughts as she plowed into his broad back.

Rubbing her nose she peered around her. They were in a new area of the villa. Which wasn't unusual, given she'd been limited in her movements thus far to the gym, dining area and her bedroom. But this section was at the very rear of the building, at a level below the main structure, which she could see over her shoulder. If she wanted to look in that direction.

Which she didn't, given what was in front of her.

"A pool?" she muttered.

"Of course it's a pool." If his tone hadn't been light she would have had to slug him and deal with the consequences. "I thought a few laps would be nice."

Heavenly was more like it. A librarian's salary didn't run to luxuries such as regular pool access, but every once in a while, in the dead of a South Dakota winter, she'd splurge and spend several hours at the local YWCA in their overly chlorinated, nothing-like-this pool.

The pool before her was shaped like a kidney bean, with glazed tiles on the bottom, an overhead glass canopy and lush tropical foliage discreetly set around the perimeter. Definitely heavenly.

There was one little detail, though.

Glancing down at her silk outfit she cast the man beside her a look she knew only a woman possessed. The one that said—Get a clue.

"I don't know about you but I'm not used to swimming in my dress clothes."

He had the audacity to grin, and nod toward a lattice-enclosed area.

"There's a changing room inside. And several swimsuits sized for Elena."

"But—"

"All new, of course," he added. The man was a bloody mind reader.

"She keeps unused swimsuits on hand just in case?"

"It's a prerogative of the rich and indulged."

Go figure. Still, the librarian in her hesitated. There was something too decadent, too frivolous about spending the middle of an afternoon, or even the later part of one, splashing around a pool. It wasn't work. It was pure play, and responsible, practical adults did not play in the middle of the day. At least this one hadn't been raised that way.

"I thought you'd enjoy this," he said at her side, those laser eyes of his boring through to all the secrets in her soul.

"Yes, but—"

"But?"

"It's hard to explain."

"Try, anyway."

The man was relentless. No news there.

She looked longingly at the pool before sighing. "You, of all people should understand."

He gave her one of those arched-eyebrow looks that made her want to cringe before he asked. "Come again?"

"You know. Duty, honor, country."

"You've lost me."

Yeah, like that would really happen. She tried again. "Tell me, in all honesty, that you'd be able to stop in the middle of one of your days to splash around in a pool? You know, responsibility before pleasure. That kind of thing."

He looked at her, really, really looked at her a few moments before lowering his head and shaking it. At first, with the small muscle spasms impacting him, she thought he might be choking, until she realized he was laughing. At her. The beast.

"What's so all-fired funny?" she demanded, finding it hard to hold her temper before his mirth. She didn't think Lucius McConneghy laughed aloud a lot.

"You are." He wiped one eye. "You're telling me you'll feel guilty for taking a swim?"

The man nailed it in a nutshell. Another nifty trick.

"And if I do?" she countered.

"Get over it. Take your swim. Enjoy it. You've earned it."

She was sure there was some thread of logic she could unravel to refute what she knew deep down she wanted to do. But the water was calling. Loudly.

"Fine." She'd simply have to ignore the last twinge of decadent irresponsibility. "Maybe just this once."

The suit she found in the changing room was like everything else of Elena's. Too revealing. No one-piece maillot in basic black for the future queen.

But there was something about the quick intake of Lucius's breath when she appeared in it that was well worth her initial discomfort. Especially when it took him a moment or two to clear his throat and respond when she asked if he was joining her in the pool.

"No."

The answer stopped her descent into the shallow end.

"What do you mean no?"

"I mean I'll sit over here and read a magazine while you enjoy yourself."

Great. She got to play while he still had to work. That made it real easy to relax.

"What now?" he asked when she remained standing in the shallow end.

"Do you ever get to stop being in control?"

By the look on his face, one quickly banked, she thought she'd hit a hot button. But his voice betrayed nothing. "I'm on duty as long as you're in Vendari."

Not the answer she wanted to hear. Though why it should bother her was new. She'd known all along theirs was nothing but a temporary, if very intense, relationship based on an unusual circumstance. Of course there'd be no relaxing in a pool. Together. Or anything else—together. Except staying alive.

His voice broke through her musings. "You've gone quiet on me when you should be swimming and enjoying yourself."

"Of course."

The look she gave him tugged at him in ways he'd never known were possible. Disappointment. Vulnerability. A brave smile plastered over what? Did it really matter that much if he didn't swim with her?

Lucius didn't even realize he'd been holding his breath until she slid farther into the pool and submerged her head.

It had seemed like a great idea, a little while ago. Letting her take a few laps in the private pool, one only himself, the king and the king's brother ever used. Elena would never appear here as there wasn't enough of an audience around for her. But, by the light in Jane's eye, she could appreciate what a sanctuary this small enclave meant. A respite from public scrutiny. A way to stretch out knotted muscles and be off stage, if even for a few moments.

At least that's what Lucius had wanted for Jane.

He watched as she began to swim sure and methodical laps through the water. Her form strong and sure. Her figure holding his attention more than it should, even all-but-invisible though the churning water.

The lady was getting to him. Big-time. And that was a danger he'd have to guard against. Admiration was one thing. Anything else could compromise the mission and jeopardize her chances of survival.

"The water really is very nice." She'd stopped swimming and was treading water in the deep end. "Are you sure you have to stay over there?"

No siren's call ever sounded so sweet. Would it hurt to join her? His own guards stood on the other side of the far door. Lord knew he had his own share of clenched muscles and tension to release.

Yeah, like that's why he wanted to slide into that water beside her.

"Lucius?" she said while he dithered. The first time she'd ever called him by his first name.

He was a goner.

"I'll grab a suit." He rose from his seat, ruefully shaking his head. Ten minutes. He'd give himself ten minutes to swim a few brisk laps, and be done.

Easy.

Until he heard her laugh. He'd crossed to the far side of the pool, closest to the men's changing room when her laughter stopped him.

She'd silently glided to the edge of the pool across from him and was waiting there. For him. A big grin across her expressive face. Her eyes glowing, even from this distance.

"I'll race you to the other side if you ever get in here," she teased. She was flirting with him. Actually flirting.

"You think you can win against me?" he asked, more to hear her response than anything else.

"You betcha, big guy."

"Wanna bet on that?"

Her grin deepened and his heart flip-flopped.

"I will if you will."

He was beyond being a goner if a simple smile could make him feel as though a sledgehammer had just broadsided him.

"It's a bet." He turned to take another step when the room erupted before him.

Then all went black.

"Ekaterina, if you say he's going to be fine one more time, I'm going to scream."

"Yes, mademoiselle," came the soft reply, one that made Jane feel as if she was plucking wings off a butterfly.

It wasn't the maid's fault that Jane was trapped in this bedroom that had felt more like a cage for the past three hours. That news was impossible to get. Or that, except for knowing Lucius was alive, though hurt, there'd been a wall of silence ever since the king's brother, Eustace, had pulled her screaming off Lucius's still body. The one she'd dragged bleeding from the pool.

"I'm sorry, Ekaterina." Jane crossed to the far window. "I'm not doing real well with hearing nothing."

"What is it you need to hear?"

She whirled to see Lucius standing at the open doorway between the two rooms, the king's brother at his side.

"You're—"

"I'm not dead. No."

He sounded so cold. So remote. And he looked like hell. A raw gash across his forehead. Bruises darkening his jaw. A sling cradling his left arm.

But he was alive. And there. Less than ten feet away. A few steps and she could touch him, make sure with her own hands that he still breathed. But not with Eustace Tarkioff looking on. And Ekaterina.

"No one would tell me anything." She kept her tone as composed and calm as his. "I didn't know how bad…"

"A few cracked ribs. Sprained wrist." He raised his left arm slightly and couldn't hide the wince. Or else she was beginning to see below the stoic exterior too well. "Nothing that won't heal within a few days."

"You could have been killed."

"Only a slight possibility." It was the king's brother who answered. "The explosive devise was a small one. A direct hit might have done serious damage, but, as you can see, the major is fine."

"Fine? You call almost getting killed fine?"

"Enough." Lucius's voice cut her to the quick. It wasn't a request but an order. "His highness is correct. If the bomb was intended to kill someone, it would have."

And that was supposed to make her feel better?

"But I thought you said Elena—" Too late, Jane caught herself and glanced at Ekaterina before correcting her words. "I thought you said very few used the pool. If someone had wanted to harm…me, why plant a bomb there?"

Lucius's expression tightened. The king's brother's paled as he answered. "Perhaps someone who did not know your habits. Sloppy work by sloppy people."

There was something more going on here. Jane wasn't an idiot, as much as these two were treating her like one, but there was something else happening here besides a near-miss experience for Lucius. And herself too, for that matter.

But obviously she was going to be kept in the dark.

Fine. Lucius had told her to trust no one the first day they'd arrived in Vendari. She'd been forgetting that little point. Lucius was alive. Hurt, yes, but everything about his manner told her she was way out of line for being so concerned.

They were back to square one with Jane as a pawn. Whatever she thought might be happening between her and Lucius was obviously not going to happen. They were not friends. They were nothing but strangers caught up in a deadly game.

Now all she had to do was keep reminding herself of that fact and she just might get out of this crazy place alive. Not unscathed. It was already too late for that. Or it wouldn't hurt so much that not once since he'd entered the room had Lucius looked at her. Really looked at her. No quick smile or nod of assurance. Nothing.

She'd been a fool to think things were changing between them. But that was over. Even librarians knew to be wary once burned.

Jane found the next several days passed swiftly. Though there was a new group to meet and greet every time she turned around, there was also a certain pattern to the hours, and to her time spent with Lucius McConneghy.

They'd moved to the palace the day after the incident, as it was being called. Living in the palace was actually very much like living in the villa, only on a larger scale. More soldiers at every corner, bigger rooms, longer hallways. Early mornings she'd meet Lucius to share a short and constrained breakfast. He'd brief her on the upcoming functions, his tone as dry and impersonal as if he were her lifelong social secretary. Then the limo would arrive to whisk them somewhere where the inevitable speeches took place, with her offering a few words and the pressing of flesh.

She was actually becoming quite good at it. Though McConneghy gave her no more words of encouragement. In fact he barely talked to her at all except to brief her on who'd they'd be meeting, what she was expected to do and the need for her to eat more. As if she could with her stomach churning constantly.

The evenings also fell into a general pattern. Her schedule was still being kept light, so they'd return to the palace by late afternoon or early evening. She'd change into another of Elena's form-hugging dresses and join McConneghy in the formal dining room.

Thus far, the king had only made cursory appearances, for which she was thankful. It was hard enough keeping her composure under McConneghy's cool, gray-eyed stare; no telling what she'd do with the frowning inspection of Tarkioff.

Conversation over the evening meals was as sparse as that between them the rest of the day. No more periodic smiles or small talk to put her at ease. If anything, McConneghy pulled further behind his enigmatic mask of control and composure, leaving her feeling both alone and lonely.

The old Jane, as she was beginning to think of her librarian self, would have accepted the silence; after all most meals through her childhood consisted of a similar routine. But now she wanted something more.

But, and against her better judgment, she found she wanted to know more about the major, about where he came from, what he did outside of this particular mission, how he felt about any number of things. But if she thought No Trespassing signs were erected before, the electric fence around any questions was even worse now.

She wanted to point out she wasn't a master spy or someone who was going to use any golden gleams of information to harm him. But it was obvious the man had spent most of his adult life being reticent.

That shouldn't be her concern, she reminded herself after a particularly grueling day. Another silent and strained dinner awaited her and, if she missed that short time period when the major seemed to grow closer to her, maybe it was better to be safe than it was to be sorry.

Stuffing away regrets that would only mean pain in the long run, she paused outside the dining-room doorway, pulled up the front of her dress a bit, brushed back her hair and took a deep breath. She stepped forward and stopped in her tracks.

"Your Majesty." She glanced around for McConneghy.

"Major McConneghy is detained this evening." Viktor Tarkioff's smile slashed against the darkness of his skin, his eyes looking small and squinty in the light of the candle glow. "I thought it was appropriate that I keep you company in his place."

He moved toward her, extending his arm for her to lay her hand across. It was silly that she hesitated. After all what could this man possibly do to her?

"Thank you." She let him lead her to a seat near his at the far end of the table. "I know how busy you are."

"Not too busy for a beautiful woman."

She told herself this might be the best time in the world to find out if she could convince the king to let her return home. He leaned forward to help her scoot her chair forward and she took a deep breath.

"I have not seen much of you and the major these last days." He spoke before she had a chance. Once in his own seat he reached for a glass of amber-colored wine. "I fear he has dominated all of your time in my country. People will begin to talk soon, of the interest my political advisor has taken in my fiancée."

Jane felt goose bumps along her arms. Surely the man was joking. Or did he expect her to step into this charade with no one to help her, no one to protect her? That was the only thing McConneghy was doing. His job and nothing more.

"I'm sure you're mistaken, Your Highness. Major McConneghy has been nothing but the soul of discretion."

"Indeed." The king's tone said one thing, his expression another. "But I do not wish to spend my meal discussing the major. Tell me how you've found Vendari?"

With a whisper of relief, Jane launched herself into a

glowing report, most of it sincere. Vendari was a beautiful country, with breathtaking scenery and hardworking, charming people. But she also was unable to ignore the grinding poverty, lack of sanitation facilities, the primitive conditions she saw even as the limo drove through parts of the capital city. She held no doubts there was much more she was not allowed to see.

But the king did not appear to be the type of man who wanted to hear about those impressions.

"I'm glad you're finding your stay enjoyable," he said, as the main meal was set before them. "I have worked hard to make my country the power that it should be, but it has not been easy."

Vendari a powerful country? Jane choked on the bite of rice pilaf she had just swallowed. It was a little like calling a kitten a lion in disguise. Obviously the country possessed some type of strategic value or McConneghy would not be going to such lengths to ensure its continued peaceful existence. But a powerful country?

"I understand that Vendari is very important to my country." At the risk of antagonizing her host she decided to probe. "But I'm not sure exactly what it is Major McConneghy offers your country in return."

"So the good major has chosen not to boast. I will explain then. The major is a conduit between his country and mine."

"A conduit?" She'd thought he was a political advisor. "A conduit for what?"

"Your country is a big country. So very big. But it is not always the big countries that are the most important."

"Like Vendari?" It was a stab in the dark.

"My dear, the world is a very complex place." He was obviously ignoring her question. "Your American way is sometimes so simple. You see something you want, you go in and take it."

"That sounds like colonialism."

"It is one of the prerogatives of power."

It sounded as though he approved. But what did this have to do with Vendari and the United States? Or with the major?

The king continued, swirling the wine in his glass. "There are times when big countries find it more expedient to avail themselves of the strategic importance of smaller countries."

"Like Vendari?" she repeated.

"Vendari is very strategic in this region. We are small, but small does not always mean powerless. Though only a fool gives away the horse *and* the grain."

Okay, now he'd lost her completely. Fortunately he seemed in love with his own voice and continued.

"Vendari has needs. Your country has needs. Your major is the conduit between the two."

"So in order to get what the United States needs in this area, the major helps you get what you need?"

"Exactly."

"And what does Vendari need?"

"Many things. We have a very long history. Unfortunately it contains a lot of instability. Not all see the wisdom of a strong ruling house. And when some are unhappy, it is all too easy for those with souls of vipers to align themselves with like-minded individuals in a country."

"Like Pavlov Rostov?"

"So the major has briefed you on certain aspects of the situation."

"Mission," she said automatically, then wanted to groan aloud.

"There are those who wish to sit where I sit. I must ever be vigilant of those who seek to usurp my power. The major's job is to keep me pleased. If I am pleased, I might be able to help his country more when they need our strategic location. It is really very simple you see.''

"Yes, I see." She didn't, not really. But maybe that was because she didn't really care about Tarkioff and his power base, not when her thoughts dwelled on Lucius Mc-Conneghy. How could someone choose a life so much in the shadows? How could he walk the fine line between his country's needs and another's? It was a position fraught with land mines. One wrong step, and there would be no winners, only casualties.

"I am surprised your Major McConneghy did not explain his position more clearly."

He'd have to talk to her to do that, she thought peevishly, but there was more to it than that and she knew it. McConneghy didn't trust her. Ever since the explosion in the pool room he'd made it perfectly clear that they both might be involved in the same strategic mission, but he was on one side of the fence, and she on the other. And it hurt. More than it should.

"The major is a man of few words." Maybe she was getting the hang of this say-nothing-when-you-talk, political way of communicating.

"One must always be wary around a man with his own agenda."

"Wary sounds a bit extreme. I would think that one must trust to a certain extent their—" What did he call Lucius? "their advisor." She noted the king's frown and quickly added, "Though I realize a man like yourself needs to be an astute judge of character and trust would not come easily."

He preened under her words.

"And as such a judge you would know whom to trust and whom not to," she added.

"True. Very true." The words slurred slightly. The king was getting downright foxed.

"And I would also think you would not allow a man you were wary about to become too close to you—or those you care for."

He eyed her silently before remarking, "Are you saying that since I use the major to keep certain areas of my life under control, that thus I should trust him?"

She wondered if the real Elena knew she was described as "certain areas." "You don't trust him?"

"My dear Miss Richards." The king obviously forgot how dangerous it was to speak her real name where anyone could overhear, or he was too tipsy to care. "A man in my position trusts no one. No one at all. Is that clear?"

"Yes. Perfectly clear."

"In fact," he leaned closer until the scent of his wine breath wafted over her. "I have grave concerns about your major."

This surprised her. "What kind of concerns?"

"You know you are very much alone in my country."

The shift of conversation had her blinking. That and the look in the king's eye. Not that he shouldn't be looking at her, after all she was the spitting image of his wife-to-be, but still, it was unnerving.

"We were talking about the major."

"Ah, yes." He glanced at his empty wineglass and shrugged. "You, too, should be worried about the major."

"Why?"

"You are a pawn. One in a very vulnerable position."

"I know that someone has attempted to take your fiancée's life before and tried again the other day."

He waved his hand as if to dismiss such a casual concern. "There is more than that."

It was her turn to lean forward, aware of how empty the room was, of how, except for the king's rather labored breathing, it was cloaked in silence.

"What is it you feel I should know?" She hoped she was ready for the answer.

"You walk two very different tightropes."

"Two?"

"Ah, yes." He waved his hand as if encompassing more in the empty room. "The major says he wants to protect you, no?"

"He has mentioned it." There was something here, beneath the words spoken, a tension creeping into the room, into her very bones.

"Did he also mention that you are being used to lure in those who attempted to harm my Elena?"

The words took several seconds to register and when they did Jane felt cold, icy cold. "You mean I'm being used as bait to attract the individuals who have already tried once to kill Elena."

"Of course, my dear Miss Richards."

"I had not thought about that." It made sense of course. Perfect sense. Too bad that didn't help the large lump in her throat.

"You see, Miss Richards. A very vulnerable position. It is why the major watches you so closely."

Of course he did, she realized. She was his cheese. A very compliant, gullible, willing hunk of cheese and she had believed him when he told her he would protect her.

"You mentioned two tightropes. What is the other one?"

"Ah, think Miss Richards." His hand layered over hers. "Do you not realize that if the major thinks he controls your destiny—you also control his."

"I don't understand."

"To the world at large you and I are to be married, are we not?"

Jane tried to sort out the nuances beneath the words she was hearing. "Yes, I guess you might say so."

"And yet the major, he is with you every day."

"Yes, he's with me."

Protecting her, or at least that's what she thought he had been doing. Now she knew better.

The king leaned back. "So it is obvious."

As mud. "I'm sorry, but I'm still confused. I don't understand what the major escorting me, or your fiancée, has to do with my controlling his destiny."

"It is still two weeks until my marriage, and here you are, a beautiful woman, alone and vulnerable in my country."

"Yes?"

"And it would be only natural that you might seek the protection of the man whom you think could help you should you need help."

"The major?"

The king leaned forward. "It would be an incorrect assumption, Miss Richards. For I am the most powerful man in Vendari."

Well, the man certainly didn't lack for ego.

"The major operates from a rather traditional perspective. He tends to think as a warrior, one from the old school."

"Meaning?"

"It would be in your best interests to choose the man who could truly help you should you need it."

"And that means you?"

"A man in my position can dispense favors to those who please him. For those who displease him—" He waved his hand again, a diamond ring winking in the candlelight. "I reward those who deserve rewards. For the rest, they are as nothing."

The room grew cooler. "Meaning?"

"If you do not do your duty, then the major has failed in his. He will not have kept me happy and relations between our countries cordial. He thus would become a liability." The earlier uneasiness in Jane's stomach congealed into a lump of cold, hard fear. ''Vendari can become a very dangerous place for those who displease me.''

As if it wasn't already, she wanted to point out, but instead decided to make sure she understood, perfectly, what the king was implying. ''Are you saying that by continuing in this…mission, that I will be protecting the major's role in Vendari?''

''Yes.''

''But if I don't, what then? He will be fired? Asked to leave Vendari?''

The king picked his teeth with his pinky before replying. ''Or he could meet with an accident. All too common, I'm afraid.''

''And my country would not protest the life of one of their conduits?''

''They would protest. I would send my regrets. We would start our political dance again. It is life.''

''And why should I worry about the life of a man who is using me?'' She knew the question sounded legitimate, especially to a man like Tarkioff, who appeared to have no scruples whatsoever.

''A very good point.'' He lifted her hand to his lips, keeping his gaze on hers as if watching for a reaction. She refused to give him one, no matter how hard it was to sit there, calmly and coolly, while a snake touched her. ''But I have seen women taken in by him before.''

''By Major McConneghy?''

''Yes. His charm is a tool he uses and uses well.''

First McConneghy had lied to her, telling her he'd protect her when all along he'd been using her as bait. And now, now to discover that those looks, those heated, soul-scorching looks he'd given her were only more lies. He'd played her like a master. How easily she'd responded to him, believed he cared, even when he'd warned her not to trust him most of all.

"So you are warning me not to be deceived by the major? To follow his directions, but not to trust him."

"You are very perceptive."

If only he knew. But the night's revelations were already too heavy to bear without admitting how naive, how truly gullible she'd been. And here she'd thought she was changing, growing as a woman, learning to assert herself, and it had all been a lie. She was still the small-town librarian with the experience of a gnat in the relationship department after all.

"So you see, Miss Richards, it is important you realize the dangerous game you've been involved in. And who can truly help you."

"I thank you for your advice, Your Highness."

Too little, too late, she wanted to add, but was interrupted by another voice.

"It sounds as if I have missed a very illuminating conversation."

The words came from the doorway, hard and razor-sharp. Jane wanted to pull her hand from the king's grasp, to turn toward where she knew McConneghy stood, looking no doubt lethal and in control at the same time.

But she felt too raw, too wounded to expose her expression to him. A man she'd come to trust too quickly, to depend upon too easily.

What a fool she'd been.

But not any more.

Lucius relaxed his shoulders, muscle by muscle. A trait he'd found useful on long stakeouts and in tight situations, but it did nothing for the churning in his gut. Jealousy, green-tinged and soul deep. He wanted to tear Tarkioff limb from limb and the longer he held Jane Richards's hand the greater the need grew.

Not that she minded it in the least. She hadn't even turned

to glance at him since he'd interrupted their little tête-à-tête. And here he had rushed through the debriefing of his team to get back to her, worried that she might be at a loss, might be bothered by being alone too long.

He was thinking like a fool. A damn fool.

"I'm not interrupting anything?" He knew his words sounded hoarse and jagged and still she didn't turn to look at him. But she didn't have to, not in this room, with its walls of mirrors, each one of them searing her image on his soul, as if it wasn't already there.

She looked pale, too pale, but then she'd looked that way often over the last days, as if the strain was catching up with her. But now there was a bleakness about her eyes, the ones she kept downcast, hidden from him. Even as Tarkioff hovered over her like a hawk scenting prey. The man had a smug expression on his face, a calculating look that told Lucius he should have arrived earlier.

"You are finished with your meeting, Major." It sounded casual enough, but Lucius hadn't been born yesterday. "You've completed all the important things advisors must complete."

"It appears that this meeting was more important." He crossed into the room, noting Jane's imperceptible flinch. One that rocked him deeper than he'd ever thought possible.

The king relinquished Jane's hand, which she quickly slid to her lap. A sure sign of agitation. "We were just discussing you. You and the dangerous games a man in your position plays."

Games within games, he thought as he stepped closer to where Jane sat, keeping her gaze averted, as if she were memorizing the thread count in the tablecloth.

"By all means feel free to continue your conversation." He spoke to both of them but kept his gaze locked on only one. "It sounded very educational."

She looked at him then, not directly but through the mirror across from them, the one that threw two images back; him like a dark shadow over her shoulder and her—like a child deceived. The realization dazed him: him of the nerves of steel, the cold control necessary to do his job, no matter what the cost. And yet with one indirect look she shook him, made him hesitate, unsure of just what had put that look there.

"Elena," he said the name automatically and saw her recoil from it, from him. Without thought he extended his hand, meaning to reassure with a touch when he didn't seem able to with words, but she rose to her feet, so fast she knocked the chair over with the movement.

"I...I...good night."

She sounded desperate, frantic to leave. What in the heck had happened while he'd been away?

"I'll escort you to your room."

"No." She looked at him then, her expression warding him off as much as the near panic in her tone. "I can find my own way. I don't need your help."

I don't need you.

"I think it'd be best if I—"

"Good night." She was gone before he could stop her.

He waited until he heard the sound of her shoes clicking across the marble floors die away before he rounded on Tarkioff.

"I don't know what you said here tonight, but I warned you once that she will not be hurt."

"My dear Major—"

"I won't warn you again." He turned on his heel, knowing he'd learn nothing from Tarkioff, not trusting himself to be in the same room with the man much longer.

He caught up with Jane before she'd reached the far wing of the palace.

"Wait up."

Either she didn't hear him or chose to ignore him.

"Damn it, I said wait." This was not the place to talk, not when there were servants nearby who could hear them.

He laid a hand upon her arm to slow her down, pleased he managed restraint, angered when she shrugged it off.

"I know the way." Her words sounded as brittle as his.

He held the oath threatening to escape. Aware it was another measure of how this woman had burrowed beneath his defenses. His control had been razor-thin ever since the event at the pool, when, distracted by her, he'd allowed himself to be caught off guard. A mistake he wouldn't let happen again. But one look at her tonight and he knew his tenuous grasp on his emotions was slipping. Again.

When they reached her room he'd find out exactly what was going on.

But she had her own agenda once they arrived at her closed door. One that had him wondering how he could want to shake a woman at the same time as admire her.

"Good night, Major." She used her prissy librarian tone. A defense mechanism as good as any he'd ever witnessed.

"We're going to talk."

"No." Her look had him wanting to wrap her in his arms and tell her it'd be okay. As soon as he figured out why it was there. He had no doubt who had put it there—Tarkioff. But knowing the king, it could be for a dozen different reasons. Trying to detect the right one was like looking for a bomb in the dark.

"Listen, I know it's been a long day. Having dinner alone with Tarkioff probably didn't make it any easier." Her expression remained a mixture of condemnation and hurt. But damn if he knew how to take away either. "If it's any consolation I'll make sure eating with Tarkioff alone won't happen again."

"It's not."

"What's that mean?"

"As you said, it was a very illuminating dinner." He

thought he saw the glimmer of tears in her eyes. She was killing him by the minute. "Now it's late and I'm tired. Good night."

She turned from him and it took all his years of training to let her close the door in his face.

He'd promised to protect her and so he would. Tomorrow they would talk. Tonight he'd find out just what Tarkioff had said to her. Tonight he'd walk away.

But not tomorrow.

Chapter 7

It took every ounce of willpower Jane possessed to dress herself in Elena's clothes the next day. Where before they gave her a sense of strength and power, now they mocked her. How could she ever have thought of herself as strong enough to deal with men like McConneghy and Tarkioff? She was so far out of her league it was pathetic.

And that hurt. Humiliation upon humiliation, a little like dousing an open wound in vinegar. How could she have blindly trusted a man, believed he was helping and protecting her when all the signs said just the opposite?

Well maybe not *all* the signs, she had to admit, brushing her hair with absentminded strokes. He had been truthful with her in telling her she was at risk from the first. But he'd neglected to tell her the whole truth and from whom she was at risk. And when he'd warned her against trusting him, he'd neglected to mention that he'd be doing everything within his power to make her trust him.

And that's what really hurt. That she had fallen for the

small gestures of kindness; the way he would offer his arm for support before she had to face strangers, the way he made sure she could meet the little people instead of remain isolated, even the way he would nag at her to eat more, as if he cared that she kept up her strength. When all along he was using her, playing her for a fool and setting her up to be a target. Could she be any more naive?

Walking down to the breakfast room like a condemned prisoner taking her last trip, she debated options, discarding one after another. There was no way she could continue to act like the fool she'd been. Nor did it make sense to confront him with what she'd learned. He'd only twist it around, try and soothe when there was no balm for betrayal.

The only thing that made sense was to truly become a stronger, less dependent woman, who, though she might not have a lot of experience in the world in which she now was, still could protect herself. She could be cool. Aloof. Trusting neither McConneghy nor Tarkioff. It made sense, as much as anything had since she'd woken up in that small cramped room.

With a silent prayer for strength she stepped into the dining room, not surprised to see McConneghy already there, not surprised to feel the intensity of his gaze on her. He looked as he always looked: calm, cool and in control.

She cleared her throat and steeled herself. If she could get through the next minutes she could get through anything.

Slipping into a chair, she reached for a cup of fresh-squeezed orange juice, sure it was going to taste like grains of sand sliding down her dry throat.

"Would you like a croissant?" His question sounded calm enough, but she could hear the strain beneath every syllable.

"No, thank you."

"Some eggs and bacon?"

"No."

"Some toast?"

"No."

"You've—"

She speared him with a glance. One she knew could scorch. "I'm not hungry."

"You've got to eat."

"I'm a grown woman. I'll eat when I'm hungry and I'll make that decision. Is that clear?"

He considered her words and her, his gaze steady and penetrating. She told herself not to waver or shatter beneath its force, no matter how hard it was to hold out against it.

"All right," he said at last, though she doubted they were through the worst of it. Yet. His next words proved her right. "Then if you won't eat we'll talk."

Instead of responding directly she stood, folding her cloth napkin and laying it upon the table with cool restraint. "If I recall correctly today's schedule is fairly full. I think it's better if we get on our way."

She watched his brows arch, the lines around his mouth deepen. His voice, though, was calm. Almost too calm. "We'll leave *after* we talk."

"Why the sudden urge to chat, Major?" If she didn't know better she'd say she was getting into the swing of being sharp and snippy. "You've been downright sullen for days and now you want to talk?"

"Sullen?"

"Sullen. And rude."

She was beginning to feel like a child trading barbs over the back fence. Until he changed tactics on her.

"What did he say to you last night?"

She could have sworn she heard frustration, or maybe regret, then dismissed it. Any compassion on her part was pure foolishness. Hadn't she learned that this man would only use it against her? "Are you talking about the king?"

"You know darn good and well I am." Emotion under-coated each word.

She glanced at her watch, sure her legs would buckle at any minute. Confrontation was not in her vocabulary and here she was, sparring with a man who made life-and-death decisions all the time. A man with years of experience of heading straight into confrontations, eyes open. He probably even liked doing it.

She held her ground. "Let's say my conversation last night was on a need-to-know basis."

If the man's gaze became any more glacial she'd be suffering from frostbite.

"Need-to-know basis?"

"Yes, need to know. You understand that concept." She splayed her fingers on the table for support more than drama, surprised he couldn't see clear through her bluff. "You've called the shots thus far, Major, and I tagged along. I had little choice. But things have changed."

Lucius slowly and deliberately placed his own napkin on the table, pleased he had not shredded it before he rose to his feet. He watched Jane's eyes widen, but remain steady on his. Whatever had gone on last night, it had had at least one effect; the woman he'd thought of as vulnerable, needy and unaware of her own power was metamorphosing before his eyes. He wasn't sure if he wanted to shout hallelujah or lower the boom.

"You think things have changed." He kept each word evenly spaced as he leaned forward to meet her belligerent stance. A move that placed him in a position to smell the warmth of her skin, count the scattered freckles across her nose, and notice the intensity of arousal in her eyes. Damn, if that image wouldn't keep him awake through another long night.

"They have changed. You're not the only one who can dictate orders around here."

"Care to make a bet on that?"

Indecision flickered in her gaze, as if she'd backed herself into a corner without a clue how to get out.

"I don't have to make a bet." That prissy tone again. He must be masochistic to be aroused by it. "I can and will take care of myself. No more meekly following your orders while you set me up as a pigeon."

Now they were getting to the real issue.

"You knew what you were getting into before you ever landed on Vendari." Or at least as much as she needed to know, he amended silently.

"Not quite. I think you left a few details out."

"What are you talking about?"

"Never mind." She backed away, standing stiff and straight, her hands fiddling with the folds of her dress, her eyes wary once again. "I believe it's time to leave."

"Not until you get one thing straight here."

"And what would that be?"

Damn if he didn't want to haul her up against him and kiss that upper-crust, straitlaced superiority off her lips. Instead he lowered his voice, surprised she didn't flinch from it.

"While in Vendari, you're my responsibility. Mine alone. And if you want to get out of this place in one piece you *will* follow *my* orders to the letter."

"Oh?" He thought she meant it to be belligerent, but it came out too breathless for that.

"You're not in Kansas anymore, Jane."

"I never was." She gave him a look that could slay dragons. "And if you remember correctly, I'm from South Dakota, *not* Kansas."

He remembered, he thought, as she walked away in a cloud of Chanel No. 5 and swishing silk. He remembered only too well.

The woman was going to be the death of him yet.

* * *

Jane watched the soft greens of Vendari slip past the limo's windows, surprised the chill from inside the car wasn't withering everything in sight. McConneghy sat across from her, his long legs stretched in front of him, dominating the space, his expression as friendly as a shark waiting for dinner.

Was it only a few days ago she'd thought they'd progressed to having a friendly relationship? It was amazing what a few days could do.

She caught her fingers folding and unfolding the cream-colored silk of her skirt and stopped, but not before she noted McConneghy's attention on her hands. That and the flash of a smugly superior smile.

Her parents used to employ a similar tactic when she'd misbehaved or displeased them. Disapproving silence once made her disappear into her room, caused her stomach to roil, and left her stammering when asked a direct question.

Once, when she'd broken a Sèvres china cup belonging to a great-great-grandmother, she'd spent nearly a week walking around on tiptoes. Aware there was nothing she could do to make the eggshell pieces whole again, waiting for the slashing, biting words that would tell her in no uncertain terms what a failure she was. But they never came. Just the tight-lipped silence, glances that looked through her and a tenseness that was a thousand times worse than any outburst.

With a small humorless smile, she wanted to let Lucius McConneghy know she wasn't going to be cowed by his displeasure. Not when she'd been taught by pros and knew, no matter how long, nor how heavy the silence could be, she could outlast it. Maybe.

"We're here." His voice sliced through the silence like steel through air.

She involuntarily flinched, knowing McConneghy was

watching her every move. Nothing to be ashamed of, she told herself, ignoring his outstretched hand as she slid out of the limo. Just because she possessed nerves and he didn't, there was no need to be ashamed of them. So why did she feel she'd given something away? Exposed a chink in her armor, a suit she knew had gaping holes. And why did it matter? Who cared if McConneghy knew she was a mass of raw nerve endings and insecurities? His opinion was nothing to her. Nothing.

If only she could remember that.

"Mademoiselle Rostov," a plump-faced man with sweat along his upper lip greeted her. "We are most honored by your visit."

"It is my pleasure. I thank you for inviting me." Was it only days ago she would have stumbled and stuttered over the polite phrases that slipped so quickly from her tongue now? Her smile no longer felt frozen, nor her legs like jelly, and, for chunks of time, she forgot she wasn't Elena Rostov.

But today McConneghy's scrutiny made her remember. Did he expect her to expose them all? She glanced at him and realized that's exactly what he was waiting for. It was there, in the tenseness of his stance, the way his own gaze remained riveted on hers, the deepening of the creases bracketing his eyes.

And what if she did? What if she turned to the smiling gentleman even now guiding them to a raised wooden stage in the middle of a parking lot jammed with onlookers and casually remarked that it was all a ruse, she was not Elena Rostov and would he be so kind as to find her a flight back to Sioux Falls.

"It won't work." McConneghy whispered at her side, his thoughts matching hers line by line.

"I don't know what you mean." Though lying to a man who missed nothing was pointless.

"This way, Miss Rostov," someone remarked to her right.

She turned, feeling McConneghy's arm brush hers, his body acting as a warning. There was no escaping it. Of escaping him. It was then she heard the sounds.

Firecrackers? It sounded like the Christmas Eve party her parents held, one she had watched from between the rails of the second-floor landing. Her father had exploded a bottle, its cork sailing across the room as people laughed and cheered. But this sound was like multiple bottles popping.

The next minutes slowed as time and sound froze.

Open-mouthed dignitaries revolved around her, yet no voices came. A muted roar rose and fell, but far, far away, like an ocean's pulse in the distance.

Hands reached toward her.

Nothing seemed real.

Until a hard body slammed her to the ground. Gravel bit into her palms, her cheek, her knees.

Reality rushed home with a crash.

"What—"

"Stay down." McConneghy's voice shouted in her ear, his body grinding her into the asphalt parking lot. "Do exactly as I say."

She would, when she caught her breath, which she could do if he'd just budge a little.

"Quit squirming."

He held her head tightly down.

"I said hold still."

"Can't breathe." The pressure eased. A little. When it did, she was aware of several things at once. Screams intensified. It was no longer a wall of sound but individual bursts, high-pitched and hysterical. The other awareness? McConneghy's body covering hers, enveloping it; a lover's intimacy. Though there was nothing romantic about being sandwiched between a man who paid no more attention to her than to the hard ground still grinding into her skin.

He had raised himself on one arm, his gun drawn and poised, his whole attention focused on scanning the milling, pushing crowd. The only clue that he wasn't his calm, cool self was the beating of his heart, the pulse she could feel racing with her own, measure-by-measure, as he lay pressed against her.

"Stay still." She wondered if he was dictating to her or to the feet running this way and that just beyond where she lay.

As far as she could tell the popping noises had stopped. Either that or the shouting drowned them out.

"When I say three we're going to get up, keeping your head tucked as low as possible, and head for that stack of chairs there."

She couldn't see anything except pavement and running shoes.

"What chairs?"

"Follow my lead."

As if she had any choice. But he was already counting.

"One."

Wait, she didn't know which direction they were running.

"Two."

Was he crazy? What if her legs didn't work?

"Three. Go."

His gun-free arm pulled her into a low crouch, holding her and covering her at the same time. She felt like a humped camel with a shield. A shield propelling her forward.

"Run."

The man was going to be the end of her. How could she run bent over like a question mark, unable to see in front of her and with his legs so intertwined with hers they could have passed as a four-legged creature instead of two?

"Stop being difficult." His words brushed against her.

Of all the…thoughts fled her as they reached the rectangular pile of chairs sandwiched one on top of another. He squeezed her between their metal solidity and his own. Now she knew how a piece of lunchmeat felt. She squelched the thought while trying to kneel on scraped knees and keep from having a chair leg's permanent indent on her cheek.

"For cripes sake, hold still."

"Quit squashing me and I will." She knew he was trying to do what he saw as his job, but did it mean he had to turn her into a mass of black and blue bruises in the process?

He shifted, not by much, and barked orders into a small black disc attached to his sport jacket. Had she noticed that there before? Or, like so many other things about this man she wasn't willing to see or deal with, had she turned a blind eye to it?

Like the final drop of water that fills a bucket to overflowing she found herself wanting to shut down. The conversation with the king, a long, sleepless night, the confrontation over breakfast and now this, unfolding before them, all merged and jumbled. It was like a shouting match with too many voices joining in all at once. The result—a need to cringe from the onslaught, back away, and regroup.

"Jane. Jane? Got it?"

She shook her head, aware that McConneghy must have been talking, or more like dictating something to her. But she'd blocked it all out.

There was something different about his voice though, that got through to her. His voice and his words. It took her a moment to realize what it was. Her name. He'd called her by her real name. Not Elena Rostov or Miss Richards. He'd called her by her real name.

Lucius told himself to keep his voice level, his manner calm, no matter how much adrenaline surged through his blood. He ignored the fear he wasn't ready to deal with, a fear out of all proportion to what he should be feeling, and all centered on this woman. The one whose eyes gazed up at him, too large in the paleness of her face, whose whole expression said she was one step away from shock or hysteria.

Not that he blamed her.

"It's going to be all right. The team's contained the problem." When she didn't respond, he added, "Just a man celebrating the birth of his child next block over."

"I don't understand." She remained crouched where she was until he put his hands beneath her arms and slowly pulled her to her feet, feeling as if he was dealing with fine crystal, ready to splinter at any moment.

"The gunshots came from a man firing a pistol into the air. Celebrating the birth of his first-born."

"Gunshots?"

He didn't know if he wanted to shake her, bring back some of that fire he'd heard in her voice only moments ago, or pull her into his arms and make her promises he knew he couldn't keep.

"Sit down over here." He practically had to drag her to the nearest chair, feeling her tremors as he eased her into it. He snagged the arm of a woman who looked as though she could get things done and demanded, "Get…" for a second he almost said Jane, but caught himself. An indication of how unstable he was. "Get Miss Rostov a glass of juice or a cold soda. Something with plenty of sugar in it. If you can't find it anywhere else check for some in the limo. And bring her a blanket."

The woman looked at him as if he was crazy. The morning sun was already high and hot in the sky; asking for a blanket was like asking for more sand in a desert. But once the woman's gaze shifted to Jane sitting in the chair, she nodded and left.

Lucius crouched down beside Jane, taking her hands between his. Ice would have felt warmer.

"There's nothing to worry about. It's all over now." This time.

She looked at him as if he were a lifeline, reaching inside him to tug at emotions he thought locked away. "Those were gunshots?"

For a moment he wondered if she'd already snapped until he remembered who she really was and where she'd come from. In that other world, the one he tried so hard to protect, he'd almost forgotten people could live their whole lives without being exposed to the type of violence he lived with day after day. Guns, bombs, exploding land mines, it was as alien to her life as porch swings, slow summer evenings and babies were to his. Something he'd do well to remember.

"A street over, a man shot several rounds from his pistol into the air to celebrate the birth of his first-born." He spoke with calm, deliberate words, willing the dazed expression to leave her face, the mute appeal in her eyes to disappear.

"Was it a boy or a girl?"

He shouldn't have been surprised. He was beginning to understand that to her, the unknown man would be an individual with a name, a face, an importance simply because he was alive. To him, the man was nothing until his actions impacted the mission. Another difference to keep in mind.

"I don't know if it was a boy or a girl. I'll find out."

She gave a smile as an answer, a small tremulous smile that tore through him like a torch through ice cream. He decided he'd make sure he discovered from the proud but foolish papa not only the sex of his child but its name, birth weight and whatever else, anything to coax another smile from her.

"Major?" A voice spoke near his elbow. "The drink you asked for. And the blanket."

He stood and accepted both, aware Jane was still not true to form when she said nothing as he pressed a cold can into her hands and unfurled the blanket loosely around her shoulders.

"Drink this. Slowly but steadily." He crouched beside her again, aware he'd have to leave any second yet loath to do so. Especially as her gaze followed his every move, as if drawing what strength she still possessed from him.

He watched her grimace as she tasted the sugar-laced liquid, then square her shoulders and swallow again. Finally she was following orders.

The mike at his shoulder squawked and he knew he'd run out of time. "Stay here. I'll be back as soon as I can."

"Where—"

"Three of my team will be stationed around you. You need anything, ask one of them."

She continued to look at him, her gaze less shocky than moments ago, replaced by a remoteness he didn't care for. Without being aware of it he took her hands between his, willing some warmth into them, not caring who noticed his actions.

"Everything will be all right. There's just a few details to clear up."

He wondered who he was reassuring as he rose to his feet, releasing her hands in the same motion. He nodded to Sanchez, who stationed himself behind her, glanced at Elderman to her left and Williams flanking her right. She was as covered as she could be in case the incident had been only a ruse. A ploy to relax their guard long enough to take advantage of the confusion, to make their move.

"I'll be back."

He meant it as a promise and left.

Jane didn't know how long she rubbed her fingers back and forth along the icy sides of the soft drink she gripped like a buoy, feeling the water bead beneath her touch. Sounds spilled over her, the rush of voices no longer screaming but still holding fear beneath their clamor. If she raised her head she would see the profiles of two of McConneghy's team.

A bubble of hysteria threatened to escape but she wouldn't let it. She knew if she did, she'd never be able to get beyond the fear. Better to focus on the incongruity of her, plain Jane from Sioux Falls, huddled beneath a scratchy blanket in a parking lot in a country she'd only vaguely heard about less than a month ago, being guarded by armed men. She'd had nightmares that made more sense.

"Mademoiselle Rostov?" A woman's voice called to her, softly. Three men immediately turned, startling Jane with the speed and precision of their movement. From statue-still to red alert, she thought, aware her hand had crumpled the thin aluminum can before she could stop herself.

"Mademoiselle Rostov." The voice came again as Jane shifted her gaze from firearms held ready to an older woman standing nervously a few feet away. The woman was not dressed in the pressed suits of a delegation member, but the full skirt and work-worn blouse Jane had noticed many of the general population wore. "I have brought you something, mademoiselle."

Was she a threat? A terrorist in disguise? Is this how Lucius viewed all strangers?

The woman swallowed deeply and advanced forward a step, her hands clutched around a small, brightly colored bag extended before her.

Afraid one of her silent, efficient guards would shoot first, ask questions later, Jane stood, letting the blanket slip from her shoulders.

"Wait." She didn't know if it was Elderman or Sanchez she spoke to and right then didn't really care. She addressed her next words to the woman. "You must not come closer. Please."

"It is for good luck." The woman extended the bag she carried, letting it dangle between callused fingers. "The herbs will bring long life and felicity."

Long life or another bomb?

The woman moved closer and Jane reacted. It wasn't fear for herself but fear for the men around her. Would they die protecting her? Or have to live with the decision to take one life instead of risking another?

She couldn't let them do it. If the woman meant to kill her, so be it. But only her. She could live with that more than with the thought of others suffering because of her.

Brushing past her nearest guard before he could react, Jane stepped toward the woman, but before she could reach her, a hand jerked her to a rough stop.

"Are you crazy?" It was Lucius. "Williams, check the bag. I'll deal with you and Elderman later."

"It's not their fault." The words slipped out even as McConneghy was hustling her away from where the woman still stood, her expression as dazed as Jane felt.

She wondered if her words registered with McConneghy as he pushed her into the front seat of a compact car.

"Of all the pea-brained, idiotic—"

He stormed to the driver's side, slid behind the wheel and began muttering through a clenched jaw. And he was talking about her.

"I beg your pardon."

"Don't get prissy on me. Not now, lady."

She'd never been prissy in her entire life. "I am not prissy."

"You're prissy with a capital *P*." He shifted gears and the car lunged forward, taking the city streets with hair-trigger precision. "Are you trying to get yourself killed?"

"I didn't do anything—"

"You were walking up to a total stranger. She could have had anything in that bag."

"I know that."

He gave her a hard-eyed glance before his gaze shot back to the road.

"But I wasn't about to let anyone else get hurt because of me."

"You can't possibly be that stupid."

Jane told herself she wouldn't cry. Not in a million years. Just because it had been a rough day, a very rough day so far, and now she had to endure insult added to injury, did not mean she would cry. Sniffing a little was okay. But definitely no tears.

"Do you think that you, who have the self-preservation sense of a gnat, are better equipped to deal with a killer than my trained team members?"

Okay, maybe one or two tears. But she wiped them away quickly.

"I told you to stay put. That didn't mean expose yourself to the first stranger that approached."

He made her sound like a stripper. Or an idiot. Or a combination of the two.

"I bet you gave Williams one of those big-eyed looks of yours. Twisted him around your pinkie before he knew what hit him."

Who was he talking about? She'd barely dated and here he was making her sound like Mata Hari in disguise.

"Or did you use that voice on him? The one that makes you feel like a heel for not jumping high enough, fast enough."

That was it. She'd had all the guff she could take in one day. She only wished her throat wasn't choking up on her with a lump the size of the Grand Canyon. "Stop it. Just stop it. I didn't do anything wrong and I'm not any of those things you're calling me. So just stop it."

He shot a glance at her, no less hard than the one before, but warier this time. As if he'd heard something in her voice she'd hoped she'd kept hidden.

They drove in silence for a space, the city giving way to small patches of farms with chickens scrounging in the yards and sparse, rocky earth plowed in crooked furrows. Jane kept her face turned toward the scenery, her hands cupped into a useless ball in her lap. When McConneghy spoke at last, several miles had slipped past and his voice sounded less harsh and more husky. "I can't protect you if you don't help."

"You wouldn't have to protect me if I wasn't here in the first place." The words welled up and erupted before she could control them. But they felt better than the dazed helplessness of earlier.

"The point is you *are* here." She thought she heard him sigh before he shifted the car down to take a series of tight corners. "I'm dealing with reality. The reality here is you put yourself and my men in jeopardy by not staying where I told you to stay."

He must have taken guilt lessons from a Grand Master. Either that or he understood her well enough to know she would argue with him until the day after forever if it impacted her alone. But the fact she might have harmed others, even unintentionally, she couldn't accept.

"I didn't do it to hurt anyone. I was trying to protect people. You of all people should understand that." When he said nothing she added, "But you said everything was okay. That it wasn't anything to do with Elena."

"I said what you needed to hear. It could have been a feint to divide and confuse my team."

"Oh."

This then was his world. One where he couldn't accept a peasant woman's gift at face value, couldn't trust anything, or anyone. Where he must always be on guard.

"It was a girl."

"Excuse me?"

"I said it was a girl." He glanced at her, his expression unreadable. "The man who had a child. It was a little girl, eight pounds, five ounces. He's naming it Elena in your honor. I suggested Jane as a middle name."

Now the tears refused to be held back. She turned her head, hoping he wouldn't see, or if he did he would blame the wind rushing through the open windows. How dare he rant and rave one minute and then be kind, take the time and trouble to find out about the man and his new child for her sake?

"What now? I thought you would be pleased."

Didn't anything escape the man's attention?

"I am pleased." She swallowed the rest of her pesky emotions and gave what she hoped was a final sniff. It was then that the scenery around her registered. "Just exactly where are we going?"

He cast her another of his enigmatic looks. One he must have perfected in the cradle, before shrugging. "You'll see in a few minutes."

Did the man ever give a straight answer? She glanced around the interior of the sports car. "Why aren't we in the limo?"

"It attracts too much attention."

And a fire-engine red, low-slung sports car whizzing through the countryside didn't? But before she could point out the error in his thinking the vehicle crested the hill and the brilliant blue of a tiny, moon-shaped lake lay spread before her.

"Oh." It was so inadequate a word, but anything else would have been, too. The lush green of the hill sloped steeply down to a ribbon of sand, white against its darkness. Soft, lapping waves washed against its flat line, a brilliant landscape of contrasting blues, sky and water.

It took only minutes before McConneghy steered the car down a zigzag road and pulled it alongside a flat verge of vinelike bushes leading toward the lake.

He cut the engine, the sound of birds filling in the void.

"What are we doing?"

"I thought you'd like a break."

He was out of the car and reaching into the back seat before she could ask another question.

"Come on." He opened her car door, extending one hand, the other clenched around a woven basket.

"I don't understand." Understatement. Yet she took his hand, feeling its solidity beneath her own. "Where are we going?"

"We're here." He actually smiled, his teeth looking white against the tan of his face, his eyes appearing more blue than gray with the lake as a backdrop. "I thought you needed to get away."

He was going too fast for her, as usual. Not letting her catch her breath before he shifted her world end to end. How could she keep any sense of equilibrium when he kept muddling everything?

Sand slipped through her open-toed shoes, feeling warm and soft as he guided her across the empty beach, his hand tucked securely around hers as if she'd escape if he released it. They might have been the only two people in the universe for all she could see when they finally stopped. On the other hand this could be like the pool. Another beautiful spot hiding danger around every corner.

She watched as he unfurled a large square of cloth from the basket before pulling her down onto its surface. She tucked her knees beneath her, ignoring the sting of her scratches.

"I don't understand any of this."

"It's a picnic." He gave her what might have been a teasing look. Except he didn't tease. He dictated, ordered, arranged, but he never teased. Or at least not with her. "It's nothing fancy, but it'll keep you from starving."

"But when? Why? How?"

He stopped unpacking long enough to look at her, his eyes as unfathomable as the distant water. "You needed to get away for a bit. This was the quickest way to give you a break. One of my men grabbed food while I arranged for the car."

Of course, she thought, hurt already overshadowing her earlier pleasure. He wasn't doing this for her. He was doing this as the quickest, easiest solution to a glitch in his mission. This was not an intimate getaway to what had to be one of the most beautiful spots she'd ever seen in her entire life. This was the most expedient way to soothe the bait's frazzled nerves. When would she stop thinking like a naive ninny and grow up?

His gaze remained steady on hers for a few more seconds before he finished his unpacking and settled beside her.

"You went quiet on me."

She had no answer to that. Not when it was the truth. Not when he sat so close his arm brushed against hers every time he leaned across the cloth.

"You all right?" He actually sounded concerned, she thought, finding the lump back in her throat.

"Yes. Of course I am."

It was a lie, but he didn't have to know everything.

"You sure?"

"Of course I'm sure."

He must have heard what he needed to hear, because he smiled then. Right before he leaned forward and covered her lips with his.

Chapter 8

She told herself it was because he took her by surprise, because it had been a wild day, because it was senseless to fight. Whatever the reason, after a second or two she did not pull back but leaned in, ignored common sense telling her to be wary and gave herself up to the sensations bombarding her.

He tasted as she'd known he would. Dark, dangerous, exotic. His lips were firm beneath hers, coaxing, but only a little, as she needed no slow seduction. Instead her hands slipped up the smooth cotton of his shirt and tangled into the thickness of his hair before she knew she'd moved.

His tongue touched her lips and she parted them. Wanting to taste more, needing to taste more. His left hand cupped her head, fingers splayed through her hair, tilting the angle of her head to devour more. It was as if he possessed and begged at the same time.

She wanted to feel him touch her, feel the strength of his fingers across her skin, know the surety of his holding her close—embracing, protecting, giving as well as demanding.

She'd been kissed before but never like this. Oh, no, never like this. It was an awakening: hard, fast and desperate. There was no gentleness, though she could have sworn that's what she wanted. There was no tenderness though she knew he was capable of it. This was raw, barely leashed need and she couldn't get enough.

Her. Plain, ordinary, everyday Jane was being claimed, branded and devoured, and he was doing nothing more than kissing her. But maybe she could change that.

She heard a deep moan, his, she thought, and leaned deeper into the kiss. It was heady. Exhilarating. Frightening. And she wanted it to continue forever.

Lucius knew he'd crossed the line in that split second of time between thought and desire. But never in his wildest dreams had he expected what he found. When had sin tasted so sweet? He felt her tremble, savored the stroke of her hands along his scalp, the play of her tongue meeting and matching the quest of his. And he was lost.

He couldn't get enough of her, didn't want to stop the spontaneous combustion shredding his control second by second. His fingers danced in the silk of her hair and he knew the movement was branded onto his soul. She uttered a small, exquisite sigh as he deepened the kiss and he felt emotions churning within him he'd never known he possessed.

This was a woman who could make him forget. A dangerous woman. This was madness. It was career suicide. It was nirvana.

The strident cry of a wild hawk broke through to him, its predator's call like a jagged edge of lightning against his senses. He pulled back, aware of the flushed face of the woman before him, the kiss-swollen lips tempting, the dazed expression in her eyes, fluttering open, telling him loud and clear there'd be no resistance to finishing what they'd started. And that alone kept him from taking what his system demanded.

She was vulnerable, today more than ever, and there was no way he'd betray that. No matter what the cost to him.

"What?" She posed it as a question though he knew she was as stunned by what just happened as he was.

He pulled back, physically placing some distance between then as if that was going to help douse the fire still roaring through his veins.

"It's time to eat something." He was pleased his voice sounded calm, nothing like the tempest keeping his pulse high, his heartbeat matching it. "You skipped breakfast so you'd better get something in your stomach."

He turned away from the stunned hurt in her gaze, knowing he should apologize even while he battled with the urge to repeat the last moments all over again, and take them further. How in the hell did he get himself into this mess? What had happened to his legendary control? His priorities?

He felt the seconds ticking past, long, slow, agonizing whacks of time, the only thing he could give her right then to gather herself together. It wasn't much, but then he hadn't given her anything else except fear, confusion and terror thus far.

"Is this another part of your plan to soothe the bait?" He heard the bitter-edged anger in her voice. Better that than unrealistic expectations, he told himself. Much better.

"Eat." He tore off a chunk of bread, handing it to her without looking.

"So you're not going to answer?"

"If you want me to tell you I'm sorry, I will." He bit his own bread, wondering if he'd choke on it.

"You've been relatively honest so far. No need to start lying now."

She nailed that one, he thought, not pleased with the realization.

"Tarkioff mentioned you were not above using seduction as a tool, but I thought he was exaggerating."

He glanced at her then, glad to see color in her cheeks that was not arousal. It meant she was fighting back. She had to fight back to survive the next two weeks, but it didn't mean he liked being the target.

"I wouldn't trust everything Tarkioff says."

"You don't care for him, do you?"

He wondered if she meant it as a statement or a question. "Most people hear the word *royal* and assume the pomp, the pageantry, means greater than real-life people."

"And you don't."

"I know being born to a title doesn't mean you deserve that title."

She flinched at the hardness of his tone. A hardness he hadn't realized escaped until it was too late.

"You don't like Tarkioff?"

"No." The least he could give her was honesty. "He's the man I must work with in this country, nothing more. After the wedding my duties to Tarkioff will end. Which is none too soon for me."

"Why?"

"There's a phrase about absolute power corrupting absolutely. It's founded in truth."

"Does that apply to the king's brother too? And Elena?"

Loaded questions. If only she knew how loaded. He hedged his answer. "I have found it a challenge to find simple men in places of power."

"Do you enjoy living in a world where you trust no one?"

No one had ever asked him that particular question before. No one would have dared. One more sign that he'd allowed this woman to get too close.

"I didn't make this world." He swallowed some bloodred

wine. "But I can't afford to hide my head in the sand and get the job done."

"Ah, the all-famous mission."

When had she gotten so quick with her tongue? What had happened to the woman on the plane, intelligent but reserved? Another few comments and she'd be drawing blood. Not that he didn't deserve it.

"I do what I have to do." He paused, then continued. "I won't pretend not to have enjoyed what we just did, but it was a mistake. It won't happen again."

When she didn't reply, he glanced at her, at the crumbs of bread shredded in her lap, uneaten, at the curl of her lips, ones he could still taste, but holding no passion now. He expected scorn, and told himself he could live with it, but what he saw instead startled him. There was no bitterness in her gaze, no look of a woman used and turned aside. Instead there was empathy. A compassion so deep he thought he'd drown in it, so compelling it shook him to the core of his being.

He was a soldier, used to meeting steel with steel, but in Jane Richards's eyes he found what he'd been searching for his whole life without knowing it existed. Not for him. Never for him. Here was a haven, a respite from the battles he fought year after year, here was acceptance that what he did and what he might be were two separate things, at least some of the time. And if someone had placed a pistol to his head with the trigger cocked, he couldn't have been more terrified.

"It's time to go." The words came out abrupt and husky and the smile playing about her lips told him he'd just given himself away.

But she didn't taunt him. Instead she brushed the crumbs from her lap, rose slowly and stood, gazing toward the lake. The image of her there, the breeze tousling the hair he knew smelled of citrus and honey, caressing the fine line of her profile, would remain with him forever. A reminder of what might have been if he were another man and she another woman, in another place and time. But it could never be now, because he wouldn't allow it. He couldn't allow it. Not while her life remained in the balance. Her life and the mission.

Jane accepted the silence as they drove back to the palace. She would never have considered herself an experienced woman of the world and yet she knew something had changed between her and McConneghy at the lake. And it wasn't because of that kiss, the one she could still taste if she ever so gently ran her tongue along her lips.

No, something else had happened between them and she relished the timeless quality of the drive to figure out just when and how things had shifted between her and the man sitting tight-lipped and silent beside her, his competent hands caressing the wheel with the same strength and control that he'd caressed her.

Maybe that was it. McConneghy hadn't been controlled when he kissed her. His hands hadn't remained passive and sure, but had roamed across her face, her skin, her hair, like a crazed man memorizing something he'd never possess. And later, when he pulled away from her, erected that shield between them that felt layers thick and impenetrable, she thought she'd glimpsed something in his gray-eyed gaze. A hunger replaced by a bleakness that broke her heart.

She never thought to see such loneliness in another's eyes. An emotion that touched her own core. Touched and tore. She expected to be alone, having been raised with elderly parents, no siblings to share her life, no connection to anyone except her co-workers, tenuous relationships at best.

But why did McConneghy look like he'd breached an invisible barrier only to withdraw behind his shell of control and aloofness? Surely a man who advised rulers of small, strategic countries could not be lonely. A man who looked like he did, who moved like he did, who possessed grace and leashed power, tenderness and strength, intelligence and responsibility, surely a man like him could not be so alone that he'd need, or want, even for a short space of time, a woman like her?

Could he?

The walls of the palace rose before them. Too soon, she thought, way too soon. But there was no denying the armed sentries saluting their vehicle as it roared beneath the arched gates and over the cobbled courtyard.

"I'll have Dr. Illiyich come up to your room to look at your scrapes."

Jane glanced at her knees, where dried blood adhered shredded nylons to her skin.

"There's no need." Was that her voice that sounded so calm and serene? After the day she'd had? "I'll just wash up with soap and water."

"I'll have the doctor come, anyway."

So they were back to dictator and peon. She sighed as she opened her car door, not waiting for either McConneghy or one of the security men to come running.

"Fine." She smoothed the front of her skirt, knowing it was a hopeless cause. She felt stiff and sore, souvenirs from being scraped across the pavement, her hair must be a mess from the wind and someone's hands, and her swollen, well-kissed lips told their own tale. No doubt the real Elena was going to have to live down this arrival for the next few months.

Suddenly McConneghy was at her side, his hand beneath her elbow, guiding or maneuvering, she didn't know. Her legs felt rubbery and it seemed like a long way across the courtyard and up that waterfall of steps.

"I'll send up a tray of food for you."

"I'm not hungry."

"You need to eat. It's not going to do anyone any good if you collapse from starvation."

"But I'm not—"

"Do what I tell you."

The man was getting on her nerves. One minute kissing her senseless, the next acting as if nothing had happened; dictating with one breath and being overly solicitous and concerned with the next. Did they teach confusion as a psychological weapon? If they did this guy was good. He was better than that, he was the best.

"I'll try." There, that should keep him happy and off her case. At least for a little while.

"Don't try—do." They'd drawn even with the double-wide palace doors. "I won't be joining you for dinner."

Of course it wasn't disappointment she was feeling. It was relief. Wasn't it?

"Will the king visit me?"

He must have heard something behind her words because he waited until they'd crossed the front foyer then pulled her to a stop, out of the reach of eager ears.

"You'll be dining alone."

She held back her sigh.

"When do I see you again?" She wished it sounded a little less breathless, but it was too late to steal back the words now.

"Tomorrow morning. I'll be in a meeting till late this evening."

There was nothing more to say. And yet they stood there, his gaze seeming to ask something of her, his hand still anchoring her arm, his body shielding her from any curious onlookers who might cross the far hallway.

When he broke the silence, she didn't think he said the words he meant to say.

"You'll be all right?"

"Yes. Fine. I'm fine." At least she would be if she could

escape to the haven of her room, away from the intensity of his gaze.

"Till tomorrow then." He released her arm and turned away. Only then did she remember the words spoken by the king the night before.

"McConneghy," she uttered his name and watched him pause as if preparing for a blow. Yet when he turned toward her his expression betrayed nothing.

"Yes?"

She stepped closer, meaning her next words for his ears alone.

"There was something else Tarkioff said last night that I think you should be aware of." She knew they were both thinking of earlier, of the lake and her accusations.

"What was it?"

"He said if you no longer pleased him, then accidents could happen."

"Accidents?"

"I think he meant that you could get hurt."

"That is not news. It's part of my job description."

Was the man being dense on purpose?

"Lucius, the king said that if he chose, Vendari could become a dangerous place for you."

She didn't know what to expect, but it wasn't his slow smile. One that looked almost sad. "Then I'll have to share with the king that Vendari is already a dangerous place for me. A very dangerous place."

With that he walked away.

She stood as if rooted to the floor, wondering why she expected sanity in a day that had started rocky and gone downhill from there. Obviously she was dealing with a madman. It was the only plausible answer.

She turned to limp to her room. It was there she found the small bag lying in the center of her bed. A brightly woven bag she'd last seen in the hands of the woman hours earlier. A bag smelling of crushed herbs and promising felicity and long life.

The man had done it again.

Hours later, her sense of disorientation hadn't dwindled. The doctor had told her she'd be sporting a few colorful bruises and scrapes, as if she hadn't figured that out for herself. Dinner had gone off without a hitch, though it was lonely in her bedroom with only her own thoughts: convoluted, jarring, discordant thoughts. Thoughts that refused to disappear no matter how she wrestled them.

How could they disappear when all it took was a look at the connecting door between her room and McConneghy's to trigger images better left buried? Images that built upon one shared kiss. She never would have thought of herself as possessing a wild imagination, but she was painting some pretty graphic and erotic images of what might have happened if Mister Control hadn't pulled back.

Darn the man, anyway. If only she could lump all the churning emotions within her and blame them on raging hormones or lust. Not that either had ever been a problem before, but maybe she was susceptible to cool mountain breezes and hard-eyed men with wounded gazes. But it was more than that, a lot more. It was enough to keep her tossing and turning once she'd gone to bed, the thought of sleep impossible.

For a while she'd grabbed on to the Stockholm Syndrome as a possible solution to her internal turmoil. True, she technically wasn't a hostage becoming emotionally attached to her captor, but for all intents she was vulnerable to McConneghy as her ticket to survival. And it was a documented, scientific fact that the position created unusual responses often confused with attraction, co-dependence and even infatuation.

But darn it, she wasn't feeling infatuation. She had absolutely no trouble seeing McConneghy's less than sterling qualities: his tendency to assume command and expect to be obeyed. And his ability to communicate left a lot to be desired, especially when you were on the receiving end of one of his terse, need-to-know non-answers. And what about his way of getting high-handed, blaming her for getting out of line when it was all his fault? No, it was definitely not infatuation she felt for Lucius McConneghy.

But then what was it? She didn't think it was love, it couldn't be. Love was soft and warm and gentle and McConneghy made her feel none of those things. True, she didn't have a lot of experience in the love department. She'd learned early on that her parents might have wanted a child at one time, but they had never wanted her. Not a realization that created an atmosphere of giving and receiving love.

But she knew love came slowly, built over time, contained trust and caring, at least that's how she'd always pictured it. It didn't happen over days, with a man who hoarded secrets like a miser's gold, who was willing to use her even while he told her he was protecting her, and who no doubt would laugh himself silly, if he ever did laugh, if he knew the train of her thoughts.

She wouldn't blame him, either. She could hardly believe she was even thinking such things. Wasn't she in enough of a mess, far, far from anyone who knew her or might be able to help her, set up to be a decoy for a woman she'd never met, on behalf of a country that wasn't her own, without being betrayed by her own emotions?

With a sigh that floated across the dark room she sat up in bed, threw off the linen sheets and reached for her robe. It wasn't much of a robe, not like her sturdy flannel job back home but, she doubted Elena Rostov wore anything that didn't shout seduction.

The French doors along one wall of her room, and the stillness of the night beyond them beckoned. Anything to chase away her thoughts, even a moonlit balcony that could have been straight from a Romeo and Juliet scene.

As she opened the door and stepped out onto the balcony shared by her room and the one next door, the night air felt cool against her fevered skin. A storm must be in the offing because it felt humid, thick with anticipation, charged with the same electricity that kept her from sleeping.

It cocooned around her as she stepped into its inky darkness, the balcony floor rough against her bare feet, the sound of the wind sighing through cypress trees beyond the palace gates, a random breeze lifting her hair from where it lay heavy against her back.

She leaned forward, pressing her palms flat against the waist-high railing, feeling the solidness of its iron beneath her curled fingers. The bark of a dog wafted on the breeze. Such a familiar sound. One she'd expect to hear in Sioux Falls, but not here in late August while she stood in a gossamer-thin gown in the silence of the night. Overhead, a thousand stars glowed and she felt alone. So very alone.

"Couldn't sleep?"

The familiar voice startled her with its closeness. She turned to glance toward its sound, surprised in some ways to see the dark outline of Lucius silhouetted against his own open balcony door, not surprised at all in others. Maybe her earlier thoughts had conjured him. But if they had, he wouldn't be standing half in, half out of his doorway, and she wouldn't be all the way across on her side of the balcony, feeling very tongue-tied and awkward.

As if he translated her very wish, or maybe it was fear, he stepped from his room, not moving next to her, though anything within a football field was too close.

Her fingers curled over the iron railing, sure to leave imprints where it bit into her skin. She felt her whole body tense, a fight-or-flight survival mechanism she recognized but couldn't suppress. He'd made her feel that way from the first moment she'd seen him and it had only increased over the time she'd known him.

"You were quiet on the drive from the lake."

"I think I was tired."

"And yet you can't sleep."

She shrugged, looking away from him, sure he could see too much that she wasn't ready for him to see. "It's so peaceful out here. You can forget…" The words trailed off. She thought he knew what she wanted to forget.

Silence slid between them, a silence deep enough that she could hear the pattern of his breathing behind her. Its slow, even pace acted like a rasp along her nerve endings, a painful torture scraping her too-tight emotions.

"I used to study the night sky when I was growing up. My grandfather taught me the names of most of the constellations."

It was the first time he'd volunteered any of his past with her. She didn't want to read too much into the casual comment, even as it was strange to think of him as a little boy, not as intense, as focused, as sure of everything.

"Where did you grow up?"

"Houston, for the most part."

That surprised her. "But you don't have a Texan accent."

"We traveled a lot when I was young. Never stayed in one place long enough to acquire an accent."

She glanced at him again, noting the way he stood casually, but still aware, like a large cat that could be still and yet poised to leap at any moment. His gaze was focused on the sky, but she didn't doubt for a moment he knew exactly what was happening around him—including her staring at him.

"Were your parents transferred a lot?"

"Military. My father was an air force fighter pilot."

That made sense. She could see him growing up in a military family.

"And why Houston?"

"He was killed in a training mission when I was about ten. My mother's family was from Houston so we ended up there." There was no anger in his tone, no bitterness or regret, but she couldn't help feeling all those things for him. "It's a McConneghy tradition."

He'd lost her there.

"What's a tradition?"

"The military. Since the first McConneghy arrived in the States they've served their country."

"How long has this been going on?"

"Since the Civil War. Shamus McConneghy paid for his family's passage from Ireland with the money he was given to fight in another man's place."

"Fight and die?"

"I don't think he planned it that way."

Duty and obligation to country must have been passed to him through the gene pool.

"Tell me some of them managed to fight and come home."

There was enough of a pause for her to know she didn't want to hear the answer.

"My great-great-grandfather was only wounded in the Spanish American War. It took him two years to die of the injuries."

"And the others?"

"They did their duty."

She couldn't help but wonder if the wives and children of his ancestors had had any say in the cost of that duty. Or were these women stronger and braver than she could ever imagine herself?

"Is your mother still in Houston?"

"No. She died of cancer when I was in college."

"I'm sorry. That must have painful for you both."

"She kept it pretty much to herself. Until the end."

She thought of her own parents. They'd both passed away within months of each other shortly before she graduated from college, but then it had been expected. They'd been in their late forties when they'd had her so she'd always accepted that she would be alone as an adult, and possibly sooner. But to have your parents taken from you without being prepared for it was hard for her to imagine.

"Do you have any brothers or sisters?"

He glanced in her direction, his face showing no expression. "One brother, one sister. Both younger."

Of course, the feeling of responsibility. At ten he'd have become the male head of the family. No wonder he shouldered obligation and responsibility so naturally. Everything in his life would have trained him for that role.

"Are you close to them?" She found she really wanted to know, to hear about his childhood, his family. It made him less a stranger, more a real person.

"When I'm stateside, between assignments, we try to get together. My brother lives in D.C., so we see each other as often as we can. Trish lives in Ohio, but we do holidays whenever we can."

"Are you an uncle?"

"Yeah, Alex has two boys."

She couldn't help the smile. The thought of him giving pony-back rides and getting mussed was too strong an image to ignore.

"Both terrors, but my sister isn't married yet."

"And are you?" She was surprised she'd never thought to ask the question before. Or maybe she was afraid of the answer.

"Am I what?"

"Are you married?"

He shook his head, his expression unreadable. "No."

"Ever?"

"Almost. Once." He shook his head again. This time the

gesture nearly breaking her heart. "This isn't any kind of career that's easy on a relationship."

She thought of his ancestors. The ones who had died in the line of duty and knew they weren't the only ones who paid the price.

"So it became a choice between your job and a wife."

He hesitated for a moment, than shoved his hands in the pockets of his chinos. "Something like that."

"And the job always comes first."

There was no hesitation this time. "Yes."

"And your family. Do they know what you do for a living?"

He looked momentarily sheepish. "They know I work for the government."

"And are away from home a lot."

"Yeah."

"But they don't know any more than that?"

"They're better off not knowing." His words sounded as though he'd wrestled with this issue already and had come to a decision. Not an easy one. "I didn't want them to worry. To wonder every time I went away if I'd be back. It's not an easy burden to ask of anybody."

And he obviously didn't expect anybody to be willing to assume it for him, she realized. Not the woman he thought he'd marry, not the siblings he'd helped raise. No one. No wonder the man seemed so alone. He was.

She wanted to reach out to him, to offer comfort in some way. It was a little like the country mouse wanting to console the city cat, a very large, very powerful, predatory city cat.

She turned her head to stare at the darkness spread before her and heard him move, shift ever so quietly until she knew he stood right behind her. So close that if she stepped back she would press against him, feel the heat and solidity of him engulf her, know the same sense of security she always felt around him. A funny emotion to feel about a man she knew was using her.

"You've gone quiet on me again." The huskiness of his tone washed against her. A very dangerous feeling.

"I was wondering why you told me about your family." It was the truth, too. "You have large Do Not Pry signs any time a conversation gets too personal."

She heard the low rumble of his laugh, felt it curling like a slow fire in her belly.

"Force of habit." His fingers had reached up to lift a lock of her hair. Lift and let fall. A simple gesture that had her breath hitching. "In my profession it's not wise to get too close to anyone."

"Are you warning me off?"

"And if I was, would you be smart enough to heed the warning?"

"Not likely."

She could feel his smile in the darkness.

"How did I know that was going to be your answer?"

"I always thought of you as a very perceptive man, Major."

"Perceptive but foolhardy."

That surprised her. The words and the self-deprecating tone. She made to turn, to see his face, but his hands on her shoulders stopped her. His hands and his words.

"Don't turn. I only have so much will power."

Now what did he mean by that? Then she glanced down, forgetting she was wearing a gown and robe that defined gossamer. But she was still only Jane Richards beneath the silken folds and she was surprised he couldn't see that.

Lucius knew it had been a mistake, stepping onto the balcony instead of back into his room once he realized he wasn't alone. His third mistake of the day. The first had been pulling her into his arms at the lake and tasting her, feeling her immediate response to him, replacing fantasy with a reality that was much more difficult to forget.

His second had been in letting those few moments simmer and stew within him all day, a slow boil of arousal that had been painful for its duration and intensity. Never before had he been unable to compartmentalize emotions from his work. Time and time again while he'd debriefed his team, and then the king and his brother, his thoughts had been elsewhere. And not just anywhere, but focused on one person, one woman who was playing havoc with his life while he doubted she had a clue.

And now, standing here, where he could feel the silken resiliency of her hair beneath his touch, inhale her essence with every breath he took, was torture more excruciating than anything he'd been trained for.

"Now you've gone quiet on me." He heard the husky, breathless quality of her voice and told himself he didn't dare respond to it. Not if either of them wanted to remain unscorched.

"I spoke with Tarkioff earlier." He watched her flinch, knowing his words caused the reaction.

"I don't want to talk about the king."

She sounded like a sulky child.

"Talking about him would be safer."

"Than what?" Now there was a taunt in her voice. A woman's dare, willing to risk all rather than walk away from what might be only emotional pain.

He raised his hands to cup her shoulders, sure that there at least they'd be safe. As long as he didn't pull her back into his embrace, didn't let them trail from shoulders to the line of her throat, her breast bone, lower; didn't let them forget they were there for his protection as well as hers.

"You know this is an impossible situation."

He heard her laugh, a soft whisper of sound that was almost his undoing.

"I figured that out for myself."

"Then you can figure out what would happen if there was the slightest hint that the king's intended was involved, in any way, with his political advisor. His foreign political advisor."

"The king called you a conduit."

"It's as good a term as any other."

"And what if—" She paused as if unsure of her next words, or his reaction. "And what if this same political advisor was involved with a librarian from Sioux Falls, South Dakota?"

"There is no such person. Not in Vendari."

"Oh."

He couldn't help his smile. Not at the disappointed, frustrated sound in her single word reply.

"But what if—"

He tightened his grip, just slightly, but enough to stop her voice in mid-sentence.

"There can be no what ifs. You are who you're pretending to be and I am the mission. It can't be any other way."

"Because you say so?" Now she sounded defiant.

"Because it's the way things are. I told you I'd protect you and I can't do that if—"

"If what?"

That was it. He still was a man, no matter what his mission or priorities dictated. And as a man he responded to the question, spoken and unspoken, he heard in her voice.

With one move, surprising them both by its suddenness he twirled her until she faced him, no darkness of night hiding her wide-eyed expression from him, no double-edged words hiding his hunger from her.

"If I do this."

His mouth descended on hers, devouring what he knew he couldn't have, desperate for one last taste, one last touch before he put the impossible behind the both of them. And it might have ended there, one last torrid kiss to haunt him the rest of his life if she hadn't met his passion with her own.

She molded the length of herself against him, soft, full breasts pressed against his chest, her hands twined around his neck, her thighs entangled with his. What began as lips to lips became body against body and her thin wisp of a gown created no barrier.

Not that armor plating would have kept him from touching right then. Touching because he wanted to take, and somewhere, in the recesses of his rational mind he knew he could not go that far. But there was nothing rational about what he was feeling right then.

His hand slid between them, cupping the exquisite fullness of her breast, knowing it would feel right beneath his touch, feathering his thumb across the tightly beaded nipple, exalting in the moan of pleasure his movement elicited.

"Lucius." It sounded a cross between petulant demand and aching request. She shivered against him, but he doubted the night breeze caused the reaction. Nor his response of drawing her closer, as if by sheer force of want alone they could become one, end the torment they seemed destined to inflict on one another.

"Lucius, I want—"

"Shhh." Their time was brief. All too brief and more poignant because of it. He couldn't give her what she wanted, what his own body ached to take, so they had to be content with what they could do.

He deepened his kiss, ignoring the throbbing of his lower body, the sweet, sweet friction caused by her pressing against him. He'd never thought himself a saint, only a man with responsibilities to fulfill, obligations to meet, but if he walked away tonight he'd deserve every medal for courage above and beyond the call of duty.

Because that's what it took to step back, drop his hand from the satin of her skin, pull his lips from hers, feel the cool night air wash between them—the kind of courage he hoped never to experience again.

It took a few pleasure-drugged seconds for Jane to realize he was doing it again; arousing her body to a frenzy of need and want and then pulling away. Slowly opening her eyes, as if awakening from a very deep sleep, she focused on him, aware of the tautness of the skin across his face, the stillness of his body.

His expression told her he expected her anger. He darn well deserved it for leaving her aching and needy. But she wasn't going to let him get away with it.

Anger he'd only deflect. He'd pull his mantle of duty and obligation tight about him, accept the responsibility of his actions, and hers, and curse himself. She knew it as she knew the beat of her own heart. She could read it in his face, in the deepness of the lines carved there, in the tenseness of his stance. He was a warrior, prepared for battle and ready to accept the cost. And the pain.

But she couldn't let him do that. Wouldn't let him do that. She was a woman grown, responsible for her own wants, her own actions. He hadn't seduced her, given her fancy words and softly spoken lines. Not unless barked commands counted.

No, he'd been honest, at least in this between them. Other things, well, that was another matter. And one that had to be dealt with. But not now.

Now she stepped forward, noticing the almost imperceptible tightening of his features as if he expected, and felt he deserved, the worst she had to offer. But instead of slapping his face, she raised one hand, a tentative hand she could feel shaking and laid it alongside his cheek.

His eyes betrayed his surprise. And his wariness.

She found that she wanted to soothe. Tell him it was

okay, that she understood his sense of right, wrong and responsibility, even if it meant her body felt unfulfilled.

"I won't believe you if you tell me this was a mistake." She offered a smile, one that felt as unsure as her hand that she now slowly slipped to her side. "I wanted this as much as you did. The only difference is I'm honest enough to know it's not going to go away just because it doesn't fit into your definition of a mission. It's not nice and tidy, but it's real. And you'd better learn to deal with it."

She stepped to the side then, not sure if she could make it all the way to the French doors and beyond on legs that felt like limp spaghetti. The Jane she used to be wouldn't have been able to, she knew that much. But the new Jane, the one who'd stepped into the shoes of another, who'd faced crowds of strangers and kept on going, that Jane could do it.

Did she have any choice?

Chapter 9

Lucius glanced at his watch. What was keeping her? The one thing he'd come to depend on with Jane was that she was punctual. She might have the rest of his world head over heels, but at least she'd never thrown off his time schedule. Until now.

He glanced up as the door began to open.

"It's about time—" The rest of his sentence disappeared as he tried not to swallow his tongue.

"Do you like it?" she asked, as if she didn't see him standing there thunderstruck and speechless. "Ekaterina helped me choose something special for tonight."

And then she turned and he felt his gut plummet to the floor. Special? That damn dress could cause a riot. It *would* cause a riot if even one man looked at her the way he knew he was looking at her. He felt the slam of jealousy, white-hot and potent, screaming through his veins.

"Don't you like it?" There was the slightest edge of hesitancy, of doubt in her voice, as she glanced at him.

He grabbed on to it like a lifeline.

"I've seen handkerchiefs with more material to them."

He thought he might have hurt her with the abruptness of his words until she straightened her shoulders, making him wonder if that damn dress would slip off with such a move. Realizing that they'd never make it to the function if it did.

"I see you're still cranky." She said it with pouted lips. At least that's where his attention was snagged. Had he kissed those same lips? Where had he found the strength to stop kissing them?

"Let's go." It was more command than request, but darn if he was going to let her know how she'd rattled him. That was the last thing he needed going into an assemblage of most of the movers and shakers in Vendari. He felt like he was leading fresh meat to a pack of piranhas, the biggest fish being Tarkioff himself. One look at Jane in that dress and the man would feel no compunction at taking what he saw as belonging to him anyway.

So much for trying to protect her. What had happened to the straitlaced librarian who had quaked in her boots the first day he'd led her onto a crowded stage? Now he was walking down the hallway with a sweet, seductive siren who smelled of Chanel No. 5 and tasted like forbidden fruit. He knew, he had yet to forget her taste. Forget or stop craving.

"I think you look very nice in your tux. Very, suave and dangerous."

When had a woman's compliment made him want to blush? "Thank you."

"Aren't you going to tell me I look nice in my dress?"

He dared not even look at her dress, not at the way it swirled around her hips when she walked, at the way it molded every curve like a lover's hands.

"It's a nice dress."

"Are you going to be sulky all night?" He thought she

might be goading him. Not a wise thing to do in his present mood.

"I'm not being sulky."

"It's hard to tell."

"Did you ever stop to think what that dress is going to do to Tarkioff?"

He heard her quick intake of breath. "I didn't wear it for Tarkioff."

Lust slammed into him with the power of a locomotive.

"Who'd you wear it for then?"

"Ahh, Mademoiselle Rostov and Major McConneghy. It is a pleasure to see you."

Jane was never so pleased at an interruption in her life. She couldn't remember the name of the funny round man who was even now extending his pudgy hands to them, but she knew she owed him more than she could ever repay. Another few seconds beneath McConneghy's glare, within reach of his slashing tone, and she would have hit him with her beaded bag. Not a very effective weapon, but there wasn't much else at hand.

Maybe her plan wasn't such a good one after all. What did she know about seduction? From Lucius's look, very little. He was supposed to move toward her, not growl and scowl. Maybe she should have read a few more articles in those *Cosmo* magazines before she'd shelved them.

"Please. Please." The man gestured to a gathering throng near double doors leading into what looked like a large hall or ballroom. "His highness sent me to look for you."

Thank heavens, she thought, before she saw the glances shooting her way, then silently sliding away. Maybe the dress was a little too daring? No time to retract now. The best bet would be to stiffen her spine, make sure her smile remained firmly in place and bluff her way through. Something librarian Jane knew how to do with her eyes closed. Something that would be easier to do if Lucius Mc-

Conneghy wasn't impaling her with his gaze. Condemning or devouring, she didn't know.

"Ahhh, my Elena. You look enchanting." The king's voice sounded as slick as an oil spill. But at least he seemed to appreciate the effort she'd made.

The smile she gave him was only a little tentative. She ignored McConneghy at her side and extended her hand, which Tarkioff raised to his lips. She thought she heard McConneghy growl.

"If you will stand by my side, my dear." The king phrased it like a request but she'd been in Vendari long enough to know better. Squeezing in between Tarkioff and his brother, Eustace, was a tight fit. Tighter still when McConneghy clung to her side like a burr to socks.

"What are you doing?" she whispered, keeping her smile pasted in place.

"Protecting you."

"You can't do that if you smother me first." Too late, she thought of a dozen different ways he could press down upon her, each one more graphic and erotic than the last. She could have sworn the temperature in the room jumped ten degrees.

"I'll take that risk."

Were they still talking about being smothered? Jane didn't think so, not with McConneghy's shark smile and the intensity of his gaze. Maybe she'd gone too far with her dress? Hadn't she seen a documentary about little fishes getting eaten by bigger fishes only because they dared to swim in the wrong part of the pond?

Fortunately she didn't have time to dwell on her unpleasant thoughts as the receiving line began to swell, each individual requiring a smile, a handshake and a few words of greeting. And to think she used to envy royalty who had to do this for their living. But at least they didn't have McConneghy breathing over their shoulder. He stood just behind her, out of the direct line, but closer than her shadow. Every time she shifted she could feel the brush of his sleeve against hers, sense the slightest of whispers of his hand across the bare skin of her back.

Right then and there she decided if she was ever to be tortured, she'd be a failure at holding back. Not when every nerve ending, every ounce of awareness she possessed was attuned to his next move, the next accidental touch, the lightest of impersonal caresses.

The man was killing her, second by second and he didn't even know it. Or did he? After a hint of roughened fingertips crossed her lower back, causing her to stiffen in order to fight the sensations they ignited in her, she began to wonder if Lucius McConneghy wasn't playing her for a fool. He'd be a master at this game of cat and mouse, while she knew she'd never get beyond amateur status.

But why? Was he trying to punish her by taunting her in just the way she had meant to tease and taunt him? Or was he trying to show her how far out of her comfort zone she'd traveled? That wouldn't be too hard to do, but darn, she resented his being able to get away with it.

What if she turned the tables on the always-in-control major? What if, instead of flinching every time he brushed against her, she, too, played his game? Hadn't she decided to dare tonight? What was the point of screwing up her courage if she was going to run at the first sign that things weren't going the way she planned?

What would Elena of the silk clothes and diaphanous nightgowns do if the man she wanted was standing within inches, trapped as surely she was trapped in this receiving line? For the first time that night Jane felt a real smile. The old Jane wouldn't have dared—the new Jane could hardly wait for the fireworks.

Lucius cast a cautious glance down the line. At the rate it was progressing, he'd be an old man before it petered out.

Old and broken. Surely the Grand Inquisitors did not need the rack and thumbscrews to bring a man to his knees. All they would have had to do was place him within touching distance of the woman he ached for, close enough that he could inhale the scent of her skin with every breath, hear the pattern of her breathing, feel the texture of her skin now and again when she accidentally brushed against him, and the man would crumble.

Lucius knew he would. He was crumbling now and there wasn't a damn thing he could do about it. Not with every eye of Vendari upon them. What had happened to his legendary control?

Before he could pull together what shreds of it he thought he might have left, Jane stepped back. Far enough back that he had no choice but to stop her movement with the palm of his hand against her lower back. Either that or have both of them tumble against the windows behind them.

It was a big mistake. The second he felt the softness of her skin beneath his touch, the curve of her spine begging him to caress, he knew he'd crossed an invisible line. One spelling doom for his mission, spelling doom for himself.

"Stay still." He all but hissed the order in her ear. Aware how tempting it'd be to nibble on her earlobe even as he was telling himself fools who played with fire got singed.

She slanted him a glance over her shoulder, one filled with teasing laughter. "I beg your pardon. I didn't mean to bother you."

Like hell she didn't.

She ran the tip of her tongue across her lower lip and he thought he'd have to beg.

"If I'm standing too close I can always move away."

Not in this lifetime. Not while his hand still rested on her lower back, a position he knew they were both excruciatingly aware of.

"Just do your job and I'll do mine."

He could have sworn her eyes sparkled right before she turned to greet another man who bent too low over her hand. Didn't these guys have wives or mistresses to get home to? How was he going to survive if she decided to dance with a few of them when he was ready to lunge for their jugulars as it was?

It might have been less than an hour, though it felt like a lifetime, when the last stragglers were greeted and charmed. By that time Lucius felt like chewing glass. If he didn't know better, he could have sworn Jane was purposely brushing against him, rubbing her sleeve against his arm, stepping back so her foot tangled with his. Either that or she'd become terribly clumsy.

Did the woman know how many eyes were watching her every move, his every reaction? Even Tarkioff had given him a warning glance or two, which did not bode well for diplomatic relations. As the receiving line broke up and guests began to mingle freely in the minutes before dinner, Lucius knew he'd have to make his move.

He waited for his opening, when Tarkioff was snared by the Minister of Transportation and Jane had stepped away from his side. It was now or never.

"Miss Rostov." He spoke the words loud enough to turn several heads. Good, the last thing he wanted was the gossips to wag about private assignations. "If you have a few minutes we could discuss that earlier problem you had."

He watched her eyes widen, as if figuring out what game he was up to, yet her voice was poised and cool as she replied, "Problem?"

"Yes, the one we discussed last night."

There were several if he recalled, but it was a better bluff then none at all.

"Oh, that problem." She gave him a high-wattage smile that did not bode well for his equilibrium. "You want to talk. Now?"

If the truth was known—no. What he wanted to do was drag her from the hall, count the seconds before he could get that excuse for a dress off her and bury himself deep inside her. But somehow he didn't think the assembled guests needed to know that much.

"Now would be a good time." He saw the wariness in her gaze increase. Good. He needed her wary.

"Fine, Major McConneghy. You lead and I'll follow."

That would be a first. "Right this way."

He placed his hand beneath her elbow, not trusting himself further, keeping his gaze focused straight ahead and not on the curve of her cheek in profile, and definitely not on the line separating black dress from creamy white skin along her back.

It was the longest ten yards he ever walked.

Jane wondered how long they'd be able to keep up the facade of polite acquaintances. Not long, she guessed by the look in Lucius's silver-smoked eyes and the way her heart skipped from double time to triple time. She'd thought the stories she'd read of lust and temptation had been just that, stories. Now she knew otherwise.

They drew near a set of open French doors, the night air offering a faint breeze, cool against her flushed skin.

"This is far enough," he said.

"What did you want to talk about?" She waited until they were standing side by side but not one second more. Not when her nerves felt as taut as they could.

"Whatever it is you think you're doing, stop it."

"You want me to stop greeting the king's guests?"

"Damn it, that's not what I meant and you know it."

So the always cool and collected major was getting a little testy. Maybe the dress was a good idea after all.

"Maybe you'd better clarify what you mean." She sugar-coated the words but they were far from sweet.

He gave her a look that would have withered an old shoe,

but Jane was finding herself much tougher than leather. "You know exactly what I mean. Stop doing what you're doing."

"Meaning what, exactly?"

"Brushing up against me. Giving me those come-hither looks."

"Come-hither looks?"

"The ones over your shoulder and when you cast your eyelashes down."

Oh, that was good. She didn't even know she was doing that, but now she could use it on purpose.

"You mean like this?" It must have worked because he looked downright thunderous. She'd hoped for tempted more than murderous, but she still had a full evening ahead of her. She could work on it.

"That's exactly what I mean. Stop it before you have Tarkioff and half his country calling for my blood."

"Is that what you're afraid of?"

She wondered why she'd never thought of gray as a hot color.

"It's what *you* should be afraid of. We're not playing games. There's too much at stake, including your life."

"I thought we were discussing your life."

He suddenly looked weary. An unfair tactic—she knew she could fight his anger, but not this.

"I'm more worried about your life." He took a deep breath, one that exposed the gun in the holster he always wore. That brought reality into crystal-clear focus for her. His reality.

She looked toward the crowded room, seeing only a swirl of color, hearing only a wash of conversations.

"I mean it, Jane, tone down the sex thing."

"Sex thing?" Now she sounded like a harlot for hire. She'd been after seduction, not sex. Well, maybe not till later.

"I don't think you want the king knocking on your door tonight."

She wanted that about as much as she wanted to be having this conversation, but she held her tongue. He was ruining everything.

"If you don't stop, that's what you're going to get."

"I thought you said you'd protect me?" She threw it in his face, keeping her voice pitched low so no one would overhear, but loud enough to make her point.

"Don't be an idiot. There are things even I can't protect against. Why do you think I've kept you as far away from him as possible?"

Great, first she was a harlot, an inept one if all she managed was anger for her effort, and now she was a fool. But, perhaps, that's exactly what she'd been: a complete and total idiot. It was as plain as the pattern on the parquet floor that the man she'd been trying to interest was about as interested as a Great Dane was in a beagle.

Words caught in her throat. She would not apologize, at least not for trying to be something she was not. Instead she straightened her shoulders and made sure her smile was firmly in place. "Not because you demand it, but because it's what I choose to do, I will endeavor to behave myself."

He slanted her another of his blazing looks, one tinged with something else. "It's not a joke here."

"Believe me, the last thing I feel like doing right now is joking."

His expression became a little less glowering. "It's for your own good."

How many times had she heard that growing up? It was the litany of her childhood, right along with "don't cause any problems," "behave yourself" and "not now." She wondered if McConneghy was a mind reader to so unerringly zero in on the phrases that poked like hot needles in her memory.

Unclenching fingers wrapped so tightly around her beaded purse she was afraid the beads would crack, she was pleased her voice remained calm. "If you're done with your lecture I think I should get back to the king's side."

Not that that's where she wanted to go. No, she wanted to run as far and fast away from her debacle as seductress as possible. But like so many other things she'd discovered since waking in a strange room less than a month ago, she didn't have much choice in the matter.

"I'll be at your side the whole evening."

She wondered if he meant that to reassure or threaten.

"Right. You have your job to do and I have mine."

He laid his hand across her arm. Not a heavy hand, but the lightest of touches, the type of touch she'd thought about in the long hours of the night.

"For what it's worth." He paused, as if struggling to find the right words. "You look very beautiful tonight."

Crumbs to the starving, she thought, sure if she didn't leave soon her mouth would tremble.

"How kind of you." She moved away.

Lucius felt as if he'd kicked a small and helpless creature, but for the life of him, he couldn't understand why. Minutes ago she was twisting him and every man with blood in his veins around her little finger. Now she looked just as seductive, just as enchanting, but with a fragile air at odds with the way she moved through the crowds, in that in-your-face dress she wore like a second skin.

He continued to watch her through what must have been the longest dinner on record, and he'd sat through enough diplomatic meals to be a good judge. She remained poised, nodding her head here and smiling there as if she had been born to the role of a king's wife. In reality, she was doing a better job than the real Elena Rostov, who would have looked bored or mutinous by now. But Jane had retreated somewhere, behind a facade and damn if he didn't want to break through it.

But wasn't she doing exactly what he'd asked of her? Had asked of her since she'd found herself in an impossible situation with no way out? Never once had she thrown a fit. No hysterics. No recriminations. And what had he given her? Orders, which she tended to ignore, suggestions, which were about as effective, and the possibility that at any moment a total stranger might kill her.

She laughed at something Eustace Tarkioff was telling her and Lucius felt the twist of jealousy in his gut. The king leaned toward her and Lucius set the crystal goblet he was holding down, very, very carefully.

With a grim smile he wondered what his superiors would say if he lurched across the table, hauled the king from his chair and planted a fist smack in the middle of that orthodontically perfect grin? So much for putting the mission first. Right then he didn't care a rat's tail about the mission, *or* about the strategic value of the country's relationship to the U.S.

Nothing mattered except getting Jane away from that crowd of people and into his arms, finding a way to take that lost look from her eyes, replacing it with a real smile reserved for him alone. That's when he knew he'd lost all sense of perspective, all need for the distance a mission required.

He lifted his goblet and sipped, tasting nothing.

Jane knew if Tarkioff looked down the front of her dress one more time, she was not going to be responsible for her actions. Red wine down the front of his snowy-white uniform? The remnants of her uneaten meal in his lap? Maybe a fork in an anatomically vulnerable spot?

The old Jane would never have dared, but then the old Jane never had to ward off unwanted glances. She'd never had to ward off glances at all, come to think of it. And the new Jane didn't want to do it now, not while her emotions still felt ground into the dirt by Lucius McConneghy.

And then the man had the audacity to sit at the table and watch her as if she was the only person in the room. Which was ridiculous when you considered how crowded the place was. But every time she glanced his way, she caught the gleam of those intense eyes impaling her, as if waiting for her to screw up—again. Didn't he know she was only human? So she'd made a mistake with the dress, with the whole seduction scene. That didn't mean he had to treat her like an incompetent.

Didn't he understand her nerves were at the breaking point? Or was that what he was waiting for? She closed her eyes with a silent sigh, reminding herself that if she could sit through the yearly budget committee at the library she could survive this dinner.

And then it was over. Blessedly over, as first the king rose to his feet, extending his hand, which she had no choice but to accept, telling herself it would be very inappropriate to cringe as his moist hand closed around hers. She actually felt a real smile as he led her toward the larger ballroom, with its glittering chandeliers and space, lots and lots of space. Here, she thought she might be able to breathe a little, force a little distance between herself and the man she supposedly would be marrying in less than a week and a half.

But she'd forgotten about the dancing. The first strains of piano and violins reached her just as the king pulled her into his arms, until she thought she would choke on the scent of aftershave and hair unguent. Now she worried about losing what dinner she had eaten all over his pristine uniform. Another faux pas for sure, earning, no doubt, another "behave yourself" lecture from McConneghy.

She almost grinned at that, sure if she didn't find some glimmer of humor in the situation, she'd race screaming from the room in a matter of seconds. Or less.

The room swam around her, not in the way of fairy-tale princesses, but more like a nightmare that wouldn't end. The king's soft, meaty hand sweated against her back, bodies brushed past them, conversations ebbed and flowed. This should have been a magic night, might have been if the right man had held her in his arms. But if there was one thing Jane was coming to expect in this unreal situation, it was that McConneghy would have his own agenda.

Then, as if her thoughts bid him to her side, Lucius was there, murmuring polite noises to Tarkioff, his gaze molten on hers. She felt his arms steel around her before she could brace herself for her reaction. An automatic shift into overdrive, with breath backing up in her lungs, her cheeks flaming and her heart doing the rumba, no matter what beat was being played in the background.

"Don't look like that." McConneghy murmured it against her hair.

"Like what?"

"Like you're ready to bolt. I don't plan to eat you."

A shame, her rebellious thoughts interjected before she could control them. A crying shame.

"I don't run." She said it with her librarian's diction.

He offered his predator's grin in return. "If you did, I'd come after you."

Dangerous ground. Very dangerous ground, but the new Jane replied before she could stop. "And?"

"You like playing with fire, don't you?" His voice sounded like molten lava sliding across her senses.

She felt the lightest of touches as his thumb grazed her back, tiny pinpricks of sensations streaming up her spine, along her nerve endings, across her skin. How could so simple a touch make her want to arch and rub, push closer for more and yet bolt at the same time?

She cast her glance downwards, knowing he'd see too much if he looked closely.

"Now I've frightened you."

Funny, she realized with a start, that was the one thing she'd never felt around him. She'd felt fear, but because of the situation, not the man. Though she'd felt other, rawer, more primitive emotions—wariness, kin to awareness only deeper—when he'd looked at her as he was looking now. As if there was no one else in the universe except the two of them, and time held no meaning.

"I've never been afraid of you."

The words were honest. Though there could be a hundred different definitions of *afraid*, as she knew he knew when he grinned and answered. "You should be. You very well should be."

She wanted to respond, even if the words clogged in her throat, but there was no time. In the space between one dance step and the next everything changed.

There was a sound, a loud boom, like fireworks let off nearby. A woman screamed. A glass was dropped, shattering against the floor. She heard it all in the distance, her whole attention focused on the man before her, watching his face change, his mantle of control descend as sure as a suit of armor. His hands tightened fractionally around her—instinct or training? she wondered—before he was dragging her toward the side of the room.

It was happening again.

"Do exactly as I say. No questions. No arguments."

"But what—"

"No questions." He turned from her, nodding toward someone in the distance, the crowd around them already milling like frightened sheep. Another explosion sounded outside, followed by the sounds of men shouting, booted footsteps running.

"I want you to go straight to my room."

"Your room?"

"Mine. You'll be safer there. Don't stop for anyone. For any reason."

"But—"

"Do as I tell you."

There was no gentleness in this man. He was all warrior now, and she was part of his mission.

"All right."

She thought he might have looked relieved, but the impression came and went so quickly it may have only been her imagination.

"I want you to lock the door behind you and make sure all other doors into the room are locked, too."

"Okay." He was scaring her now with the intensity of his look, the tightness of his grip on either arm.

"I'll send one of my men along with you. He'll be stationed outside the door until I relieve him."

Until, or if? she wanted to ask, but swallowed the thought. That and the queasy things it did to her stomach.

"Do not open the door to anyone. Not to Tarkioff. Not to his brother. Not to anyone except myself."

She nodded her head, aware the hysteria in the room around her was building.

"Do you understand?"

"Yes."

"And you'll do exactly as I said?"

She might have been afraid, but she was not an idiot.

"Of course I will."

He smiled, the briefest of expressions and one she knew she'd carry in her memory forever. Another man materialized at his side, one as controlled, as intense as he.

"Keep her safe." McConneghy spoke to the other before turning back to her, pitching his voice low. If she thought he was going to leave her with some warm and touching sentiment, she was wrong.

"If you need it there's a pistol in the nightstand by the bed. You'll have to click the safety off before you use it."

Since Jane's experience with guns was limited to what she'd watched on TV she only nodded her head. If it came to her having to use one, she was in deep trouble. But now didn't seem to be the time to point out another of her short-comings.

"Fine. I understand." She didn't really. Not about the gun at least, but she did about other things. Like the fact that McConneghy was leaving her to head toward the explosions, not away from them. The man had to be certifiably insane. Also brave, responsible and determined, yes, but definitely certifiably insane.

As he turned to leave, she grabbed his arm, not caring if she left nail marks on his jacket. "You'll be careful?"

His predator's grin turned into a pirate's. The man was actually enjoying himself. Well, maybe not enjoying, but he wasn't quaking in his boots, either.

"I'll be careful."

She didn't want to place any bets on that one. Instead she turned away, letting the nameless, silent team member lead her away, telling herself there was nothing to fear. Not for herself.

But for McConneghy?

Lord, she wished she knew the answer to that one.

Chapter 10

Lucius stole a glance at his watch, not surprised to see the smaller hand sliding past three o'clock, feeling it had been a year since he'd left the ballroom instead of hours. His feet echoed hollowly down the empty hallway, a fitting accompaniment to his dark thoughts.

Something wasn't right. His gut repeated the message; the last few hours verified it. The explosives set off in the courtyard had been noise and smoke and not much more. Either they were dealing with amateurs or bumblers who'd make the Three Stooges look competent by comparison. It was similar to the bomb in the pool room. All smoke, little damage.

But the initial attack on Elena Rostov had been planned by a pro. From the explosive devise used, the timing, the lack of a trail to follow afterwards, it had run like clockwork. So was he dealing with two different threats? And if so, how was he going to keep Jane safe from simultaneous fronts?

He rounded the last corner, pleased to see Santiago on alert, as if he'd been standing there minutes instead of hours. The kid was good, better than good, as he was standing outside of Jane's room instead of down the hall in front of Lucius's door. The biggest threat would have come from within the palace. By posting himself where he was, the young soldier might have given Jane a few extra seconds of warning should there have been an attack. Time, Lucius knew, that could have made the difference between survival or not.

"Any problems, Santiago?"

"No, sir," came the quick response. "The king's brother wanted to leave a few of his men, but I suggested they would be better positioned farther down the hall."

Since Lucius hadn't seen any, Eustace Tarkioff must have either rejected the offer or called them off earlier. Another piece of the puzzle to analyze and interpret.

"And the mademoiselle?"

Lucius watched the young man's face relax. "Meek as a lamb, sir."

Then they must have been talking about two different women, Lucius thought, failing to suppress a smile.

"You're done for the night, Santiago. Report back to Elderman and we'll debrief at zero seven hundred."

"Yes, sir." The young man snapped a salute.

"Oh, and good job, soldier." Lucius watched the pleasure seep into the other's eyes. "Especially the decoy in front of the wrong door. Nice touch."

"Thank you, sir."

"Good night, Santiago."

After saluting the departing soldier, Lucius approached the door with the same rush of adrenaline and wariness that he approached any unknown situation. The night's activities had unsettled him, and he wasn't even thinking about the series of explosions, but about the earlier shock waves. The ones that had begun when a door opened and a woman in black had stood before him, more beautiful than he could have imagined, a smile flirting about her lips, a dare in her gaze.

He'd been lost from that moment forward. And not because of the way a scrap of material looked draped across her, or the instantaneous response of his body. It was more than that.

It was the way she knew the servants' names, not for convenience sake, but because she saw them as individuals. It was the way she greeted strangers in a receiving line, or thought to ask about a newborn child.

Whatever he had expected when he'd entered a dim, cramped room to discover a woman taken against her will, it hadn't been Jane Richards, or what she was doing to his world. The mission had faded beside his need to keep her safe. Somewhere along the line she'd become *his* woman, the woman he longed to claim and would fight to the death to protect. There was no point in denying it or ignoring it, neither tactic was going to change reality.

Jane Richards, with her too-large eyes, sweet, sweet smile and stubborn streak that was getting wider every day, had gotten under his skin and branded him. Just as he wanted to brand her, every inch of her. It was a primordial thought, an urge as instinctive and as old as time, which did not sit well. Especially when he knew she deserved more than a man committed to his country, his job and a lifestyle that wreaked havoc on relationships.

He unlocked the door, turning the handle slowly, not wanting to frighten her if she was still awake on the other side. The room was bathed in shadows, a single nightstand lamp casting an amber glow throughout it.

Another woman might have had the room ablaze to ward off the fear, but leave it to Jane to keep a cool head. The shadows gave her the advantage over anyone coming in from the lighted hallway. It even took him a second or two to locate her, curled up in a club chair dragged across the room until it stood halfway between the French doors and where he stood. The woman would have been a natural strategist, he realized, allowing the smile that accompanied the thought.

He entered quietly, closing the door behind him, the sound of her even breathing taking away some of the fear congealed in his gut. She looked nothing like the Siren nestled in her chair cocoon, her legs drawn up beneath the thin silk of her dress, her hair tousled about her shoulders. She looked relaxed and vulnerable, except for the Glock nine-millimeter lying lax in her right hand.

The image slammed against him with the force of a gale. She should have been sheltered from violence, from the ugliness he dealt with on a regular basis. But she wasn't and he'd been the one who'd dragged her out of her safe, secure world into the middle of this mess. Guilt ate like acid through his system.

"McConneghy?" He heard her soft whisper from where he stood, not daring to slip any closer, accepting that even he had limits on his control. Limits constantly stretched too thin around this woman.

"Yeah, it's me. It's all right. Another false alarm."

He watched her sleepy smile, felt his body's immediate response and bit back a groan.

She stretched. A slow, sensuous arch of arms and back that had him entranced and petrified at the same time. Nothing had changed. She still deserved more than he'd offered her thus far, and giving in to the burning need raging within him was only going to compound the situation. But looking at her there, sleep-rumpled and inviting, smiling that soft smile that crumbled his defenses quicker than an Uzi blast at short range, taxed to the limit his resolve to do the right thing.

Jane shrugged off the last dregs of a haunted sleep she'd never meant to indulge in and wondered what she'd done now. Lucius looked like a thundercloud ready to erupt, eyes narrow, skin stretched taut along his nose, shadows hollowing his cheekbones. He'd said everything was okay, but maybe it really wasn't, and he didn't want to give her the bad news.

Standing up, tugging her dress back into place, she felt the gun she'd been holding slip to the floor.

"Careful." He snapped the words out.

"Sorry." She looked at it where it lay, an inert blob of darkness in the dusky room. "I don't think anything broke."

He groaned as she glanced up, then went still.

"I really don't think I hurt it."

"Forget the gun, Jane. The fact you didn't blow off your foot is a miracle, but I should get used to things like that happening around you."

"Like what?"

"Forget it."

The man really was too tense. There had to be something he was holding back. "Tell me the truth."

"What truth?"

She stepped toward him and saw him tense even more. "The truth about what happened tonight. It was bad, wasn't it?"

"You mean the explosions?"

"Of course I'm talking about the explosions. That's why you're so on edge isn't it?"

"Part of the reason." His voice must have dropped an octave, or the room grew suddenly chilly. Something had to account for the goose bumps trilling across her skin.

"What's the other part?" She stepped closer, wanting to see his face clearly in the weak light. This time he definitely groaned. "Are you hurt?"

She was at his side in a moment, stopped only by his palm, raised as if warding her off.

"Don't come any closer."

He sounded in pain.

"What is it? Where are you hurting?"

"Lady, you're killing me here. I think it'd be better if you stepped back."

What was the man babbling about? Could it be a head injury? She stepped close enough to see the pulse point pounding alongside his temple, heard the raggedness of his breathing, watched his features tighten even more.

She lifted her right hand to his forehead, brushing back a lock of midnight hair, expecting to feel blood beneath her fingertips. "You're in pain."

"Damn right I'm in pain."

She knew it. She'd been right all along. He'd been injured in the line of duty, in protecting her, and now he was being noble about it. "What can I do to help?"

He closed his eyes. If it'd been anybody else she'd have thought he was praying. Or counting to ten.

"Tell me what to do to take away the pain. Do I need to get a doctor?"

"No."

"Do you need to lie down?"

"Not yet."

"But you sound like you're hurting."

His fingers clamped around her wrist, drawing her hand away from stroking his face, but not releasing it.

"I am hurting and you're making it worse. Sweet mercy, I'm not made out of stone."

He could have fooled her, she'd never seen any one so rigid. He looked ready to explode.

"If you tell me where you're hurting maybe I can fix it. I had to get my first aid certificate for the library, and I passed with flying colors. Everything, that is, except the applying pressure part, but I'm sure I could manage it if you needed me to.''

"You're doing just fine with the pressure part.''

She found herself smiling. How nice of him to give her a compliment when it was obvious he was hurting.

"Don't look like that.'' The man practically growled the words, his hand tightening about hers.

"Like what?''

"Like an innocent just ready to be gobbled.''

"Gobbled...'' His look stopped her. It dried her words to dust and singed her down to her toes. Why hadn't she noticed it before? The intensity, the power, the sensual hunger all but floored her. Reality dawned, slowly, but crystal-clear. The room was no longer chilly, but hot, too hot and growing warmer by the second.

"You're not really hurt, are you?'' She whispered the words through too-dry lips, unable to turn away.

"I'm not hurt.'' His words rasped against her. "But I am hurting. Big-time.''

He glanced down and her gaze followed his, stopping at the bulge against his suit pants, a very large bulge.

"Oh.''

"If you don't want to finish what we started at the lake yesterday I suggest you retreat to your room.''

"I didn't start it, you did.''

"So I did.'' His free hand reached up to brush her hair from her shoulder. Why such a gentle gesture should make her want to tremble made no sense. But then nothing else did either. "The point's the same. Leave now or deal with the consequences.''

"And if I don't?''

"I'll give you ten seconds to get to the door, Jane. After that—''

"What?''

She didn't know if he was more surprised, or she was, at

the dare in her voice. The old Jane would have been running for the door. The new Jane held her ground.

"I don't want any regrets. We're talking sex here, that's all. No promises, no commitments."

No lies, she wanted to add, but didn't. Even here, she knew he was being noble, giving her an out, making what was happening between them as black and white as possible.

But he was wrong. Everything was in Technicolor—shades red-hot and vibrant, and for once she was going to forget caution and grab on to life with both fists.

"All right, we're talking sex." She watched wariness seep into his gaze, until she added, "Is that all we're going to do—talk? Because if it is, it'd better be a darn good conversation."

He hesitated, questioning her or himself, she didn't know. All she knew was she forgot to breathe until the hand that had played with her hair slipped around her waist, tugging her close enough that she felt scorched by the heat in his gaze.

"Fine. No more talking."

The words barely registered before his lips captured hers. Devoured, more like it. Holding nothing back, demanding, coaxing, claiming, all before she could think. Not that she wanted to think, not when her system sang with its own response, as outrageous and unrestrained as his.

His hand flattened against her back, its heat outlined against her cool skin, pulling her closer, until she felt the long hard length of him melded against her. And she wanted more.

They moved. A silent two-step, until the bulk of the bed pressed against the back of her knees. He deepened the kiss. She responded. Her hand slid beneath his jacket, tangled with the leather of a holster strap and stilled.

"Damn it." He muttered another pithy oath as he pulled back enough to strip his jacket and harness off with a fluid movement. The jacket slid to the floor, the gun was strategically placed on the bedside table. Even now, he remembered his duty first. Not that she expected less.

She thought he should have looked less lethal without his weapon, but he didn't. Not with that heat in his smoke-silvered eyes, that growl in his voice. "Come back here."

He didn't have to ask twice.

Jane didn't have a lot of experience behind her, but there wasn't time to worry about it. In the space between one heartbeat and the next she was in his arms, straining beneath his kisses, tearing at his shirt like a woman crazed.

Crazed with lust. Her—quiet, unprepossessing, plain Jane was making noises in her throat that sounded feral, her fingers were desperate to touch his skin, her mouth opened beneath kisses that all but consumed her, and still she wanted more.

The room tilted and she thought she'd buckled until she felt the give of the mattress beneath her, the weight of Lucius atop her.

"More." It was her voice pleading.

"My pleasure." She heard the grin behind his words, felt the give of her dress as it slid from her neck to her waist, shivered beneath the wave of air across her sensitive skin, her aching nipples.

"Lucius?" She didn't know what she wanted, but knew where she'd find it.

"Is this what you want?"

His wet tongue abraded her right nipple, rough against rough. She almost shot across the bed.

"Yes. Yes."

"And this?" He suckled his lips around her areola until she wanted to scream.

"Yes. Oh, yes, I—"

He moved to her left breast. She shifted beneath him,

arching to grant him greater access, squirming when he took full advantage of it.

"Lucius…"

"Yes, love." The endearment arrowed to her heart even as she accepted that it meant nothing. Not like what he was doing to her body, tensing it, teasing it, taunting it.

"Damn it, Lucius—"

She felt another grin against her stomach. Right before his tongue swirled against the dip of her belly button, his hands pressed against the mound lower.

Her clothes were in the way. Why didn't he pull them off? Why didn't he end the torment? Why didn't he hurry?

But leave it to Lucius McConneghy to bring her to a quivering mass of aches and needs and leave her poised while he dawdled. The man was going to kill her. Exquisitely, one nerve ending at a time, but sweet death was still death.

His hands stroked. Heel of his palm to fingertips, using the silk of her dress, the nylon of her panty hose as a barrier, or a torture device, she didn't know. All she knew was, it was driving her insane. The slow, deliberate rasp, pressure applied, then receded. Again and again.

Her hands clawed at him. Wanting his shirt gone. Wanting his skin against hers. Just wanting.

"Lucius, please—"

"More?"

"Yes, darn you."

"Such unladylike talk." His laughter floated across her senses. "What would the other librarians say if they heard you now?"

"They'd say you're a dead man unless you hurry up."

He stilled, then raised himself until he dominated her line of sight. She was afraid he was going to pull back, as he'd done at the lake, and then she'd have to kill him for sure.

But instead he smiled, a smile so sinful it should have been illegal.

"You saying I'm going too slow for you?"

She wasn't sure if it was tease or taunt. "Well, not exactly."

"You want fast now?"

Her body wanted blessed relief. Her soul wanted him to continue what he was doing forever. Her response straddled both.

"I want you inside of me." The old Jane would never have dared to make such a demand.

His only response was a grin. That and the sound of her dress tearing. Or maybe it was her pantyhose, but that didn't matter right then. Not when she felt the gentle strength of his hands slide between her thighs, stroking, stroking, again and again.

"Lucius—"

Somehow he'd managed to shuck his pants, though his bloody shirt, minus a few buttons, was still stubbornly in place. She felt the pressure of his knee wedge against hers, the quest of his fingers tangle in her curls, the deepening of his kisses.

She'd died and gone to heaven. She knew it. This was not what she'd experienced before, given that her experience bordered on the lean side. But even in her wildest imaginings, she'd never have thought sex could be wanting and aching and straining and needing. The man was killing her.

"If you don't—"

He shifted, moving away from her for a scant moment, long enough to make her wonder if she'd pushed him away with her neediness, until she heard the crackle of a package being ripped open. Always the protector, she smiled, sure that now was not the time to point it out to him.

"Ready?"

She had meant to answer, but he swallowed her words

with his mouth even as he positioned himself between her thighs. Then paused.

She'd waited long enough. With a guttural cry, part defiance, part triumph, she arched upwards, taking before he could change his mind and do the noble thing. It didn't take him long to follow her lead. Thrust followed thrust: long slow glides of pleasure that had her delirious with sensation. In—deep, deep, deeply in before he'd pull almost all the way out, then begin again.

An explosion was building within her. There, but almost not. She urged him on with her hands, her hips, her lips to his skin, but he held to his own agenda. In and out, pressure applied then released. Then he'd shift, going deeper, rubbing harder. The pleasure built. Or was it pain?

She wanted to sob. Or swear. But before she could do either, the pressure shattered, splintered into a thousand pinpricks of sensation washing through her system. Her cry echoed through the room, muffled by his lips against hers until his own shout of release joined with hers.

"Wow." It might have been seconds, or hours later when she heard her voice speak her thoughts. Warm, fuzzy thoughts dwelling on the sensation of Lucius's body warm against hers, his hands wrapped around her, his breathing gradually slowing.

"Wow?" She felt his smile against her hair, his hands stroking against her torso. "Is that a fancy librarian term?"

"Anything else might be too much for your ego." She knew she sounded prissy, as prissy as a naked, thoroughly loved woman could sound with a smile on her lips.

"*Wow*'s a good word. Better than 'that was nice' or 'not bad.'"

"I don't believe you've ever heard either one of those phrases in your entire life."

She felt his lips press against her temple.

"Let's just say you inspired me."

For all she knew he might have used the same phrase with a hundred women before, but somehow she didn't think he had. He'd always been straight with her, a little reticent with information, but when he finally did tell her anything, he'd never sugarcoated it. A nice trait in a man, she decided. A very nice trait.

"You've gone quiet on me." His voice whispered through the room, his hands continuing their slow glide across her skin.

"I thought men didn't want to talk after sex."

"This man wants to know what's going on in that head of yours."

She heard nerves beneath his words. Or maybe it was only wishful thinking, either way, she thought it'd be best to keep things light, no matter if she was feeling anything but.

"I'm wondering how I'm going to get that shirt off you."

He paused, as if looking for what she wasn't saying, then shrugged. "You'll have to work to get it off."

Oh, she liked that idea, and its possibilities. Raising herself on one elbow she grinned down at him, catching the answering dare in his gaze.

"You're playing difficult here, Major?"

"Yup."

Her fingers slid beneath the first button. The first remaining button, which was halfway down that wonderful chest.

"You know I'll show no mercy." She snapped the button off with a flying ping.

"I'm counting on it."

Another button went sailing.

"I won't have any cry of foul play later."

She pressed her lips to the skin now exposed. A slow, long, wet kiss that had him sucking in his breath.

Her fingers slipped lower. Not low enough to stroke that

body part of his already twitching awake, though it was tempting.

"I will allow you to cry mercy if you need to." She ducked her head to hide her grin at his mortified expression and followed with another kiss to his chest. Then a lick of her tongue. She popped another button and he went still.

Her tongue had moved up to circle the dark bead of his nipple, paying him back for the exquisite sensations he'd inflicted on hers earlier.

"Do they teach torture in librarian school these days?" His chest was rising and falling more quickly, his eyes were slits of heated silver.

"Advanced Torture 101. I aced the course."

She felt the rumble of his laughter beneath her lips. She pressed his shirt aside to taste and touch more.

But leave it up to McConneghy to have his own agenda. Before she could continue her quest of devouring him, inch by leisurely inch he rolled her over, slipped on protection, and slid into her in one quick, hard, deep thrust.

When she caught her breath, and the sweet sigh of pleasure accompanying it, she opened her eyes to glance up.

"I'd say that was a cry of surrender."

"I'll show you a cry of surrender."

His words were a promise, which he proceeded to fulfill. Very ably.

Lucius watched the sun creep over the far horizon outside the French doors, listened to the deep even breathing of the woman snuggled against his chest and wondered if he'd ever felt such contentment. It was an emotion alien to his world, to the choices he'd made. But another choice had been made, and the consequences would have to be dealt with. In spite of his words of warning, and Jane's cheeky response, he knew she wasn't the type of woman who slid easily into a relationship and just as casually walked away from it.

In spite of her enthusiasm and daring foreplay, he sensed the shyness, the innocence still as much a part of her as her kindness to strangers. She might look like a siren in that dress she'd worn earlier, but he had no doubt she was as unsure and vulnerable as he'd always guessed. A man could not make love to a woman the way they had through the night without knowing such things.

The question now was what he was going to do about it. The smart thing was to tell her it'd been nice, break her heart clean and fast, then hope like hell she could get through the next days with him playing good guy/bad guy, a role he had down pat. Or maybe he should string things along, put some physical distance between them, but not bring reality into play until he was sure she was safe on the plane and heading back to South Dakota.

Unfortunately, either scenario ended up with the same result: Jane hurt and him responsible. But then, he knew it'd come down to that point, eventually. It had to.

But there was a third option. One he'd been considering since he'd tasted her sweetness, felt the power of her response to his touch. The third solution held the most risk for the both of them, but also its own rewards. What if he chose to accept what had happened, was happening between them and savor it? Revel in it, if the truth was known. What if he chose to take whatever time was allotted to them and allow it just to be instead of cutting it off?

He found himself smiling, inhaling the scent of her hair with the motion, knowing there really was no choice in the matter. She was his and nothing—not duty, not obligation, not responsibility—was going to make him let her go when he could hold her like this.

There'd be a price to pay. There always was. But for now he had Jane. It'd be enough. It had to.

Chapter 11

Jane awoke the next morning in her own bed, alone, vaguely remembering Lucius's arms around her, carrying her securely from his room to hers, playing the role of protector once again. This time of her reputation.

The thought made her smile. That thought and others, ones based on the sweet lassitude in her limbs, the quiet ache of muscles thoroughly used. How many times had they turned to each other through the night? How many times and how many ways? She felt herself blushing and hoped she could bring it under control before Ekaterina, rustling around in the bathroom, spied her.

"Ah, mademoiselle, you are awake at last. The excitement of last night, it must have worn you out."

"It did." She felt the heat in her cheeks increasing, knowing they were talking about two different kinds of excitement. "How late is it?"

"It is nearly noon."

"Yikes." She bolted upright, remembering at the last

minute to grab the blanket to her. Lucius may have made sure she was found in the right bed but he'd neglected to make sure she was dressed in a decent pair of pajamas. "Am I late for any appointments? Major McConneghy is going to kill me."

"No, mademoiselle. The major was the one who told me to let you rest, that you'd be exhausted."

As he should well know, she thought, feeling the heat seeping through her body this time.

"He said he canceled your meetings this morning."

Jane didn't know if she wanted to thank him for his thoughtfulness or smack him for his assumption that she was a lightweight. Just because she didn't have a lot of experience making love through the night…all right, she had no experience…didn't mean she couldn't have bumbled through the day somehow.

"I have a nice warm bath ready for you." Ekaterina's voice broke through her musings. And the thought of a soothing, leisurely soak did sound divine. She would deal with McConneghy later. She just hoped she wasn't going to have to battle through one of his noble-thing, this-shouldn't-have-happened responses. But leave it up to the man to make what could be easy into something complicated.

The old Jane might have caved into such a pack of nonsense. The new Jane wasn't going to have anything to do with it and the sooner McConneghy understood that the better. She knew they didn't have a future together. How could they, when she wasn't sure there'd be a future at all, not if some terrorists, or disgruntled revolutionaries with an ax to grind got their way? So she'd have to take what she could, now, while she could.

"Do I have anything in red in that closet, Ekaterina?" She reached for her robe, trying not to wince from thigh muscles protesting movement. It was bad enough she was going to have to explain the state of her clothes from last night, no need to compound the speculation.

"In red, mademoiselle? Yes, there is a suit and several dresses."

"Not the suit, but maybe one of the others." A woman should always dress for battle. "Something sexy, but subtle."

"Yes, mademoiselle." The maid left, humming, as Jane made her way toward the scented bath. McConneghy was never going to know what hit him. It was not the time to slide back into the old Jane's way. No, it was time to go on the offensive.

She caught her image in the bathroom mirror and paused. It wasn't the well-kissed lips, or whisker burns along her cheek that surprised her. It was the gleam of battle in her eyes. Lucius McConneghy didn't stand a chance.

Lucius ignored the pressure band tightening around his skull, telling himself that blowing up at Tarkioff wasn't going to solve anything. Except maybe to lower his blood pressure. The man was insisting that last night's fiasco was a major threat to discredit his regime and to personally humiliate him.

Maybe, maybe not, but spending the whole morning barricaded within the royal library with the king and his brother, instead of leaving him free to follow up what few scant leads and even fewer hunches there were, was not helping the situation. Fortunately his team had been at work since Lucius had met with them right after he'd left Jane sleeping in her own bed.

The image that thought brought created its own pressure, but this time it wasn't settling around his head. Like glimpses of a lost dream, he'd found his thoughts wandering time and again since he'd been cloistered with Tarkioff and Eustace.

It was Eustace's voice that was soothing the king now. "All measures have been taken to find the culprits behind this incident."

"It's not enough." The king's meaty fist slammed upon the desk. "I want results, not empty promises."

"But, Your Highness—"

"Enough, Eustace. It was your guards who failed in their duties last night. I want them replaced. I will not tolerate incompetence.'"

"But, sir—"

"Replaced and punished. Do you hear?"

"Yes, sir." The Head of Security kept his face stoic, his demeanor under control, but Lucius had noticed the quick flash of temper in his dark eyes. Not that he blamed the man, but it didn't bode well for the days leading up to the king's wedding.

A quiet knock on the far door interrupted any further conversation. As Lucius was closest to it, he rose to answer it. If Jane Richards had meant the scrap of flame and fire she wore with a teasing smile to make him drool and re-member, she succeeded. He was only thankful his back was to the other men in the room. There were some emotions one could not hide, and raw possessiveness was one of them.

"Am I interrupting anything?" she asked in that honey-over-heat voice that made him want to throw her over his shoulder and continue where they'd left off in the wee hours of the night.

Her look told him she was thinking along the same lines, but before he could suggest she meet him elsewhere, the king's voice boomed across the office.

"Come in. Come in. We have need of beauty since we have no competence."

Lucius watched her flinch at the implied criticism of the

other two men in the room, then step around him. He had to give her credit for being brave. Foolish, but brave.

"Thank you, Your Highness." She bowed her head to the security minister. "Monsieur Tarkioff. I really do not wish to interrupt you, as I'm sure you have much to discuss."

"No, mademoiselle. It is our pleasure." Eustace waved her to a nearby chair while Lucius cleared his throat.

"We were reviewing that shameful business last night." The king's voice reflected the stern expression of his face. "I hope it did not frighten you unduly, my dear?"

"That is thoughtful of you to have worried about me." She offered him one of those smiles Lucius knew to be genuine and powerful. "But I can assure you I was in capable hands with Major McConneghy."

Lucius thought he was going to choke. From the way she avoided his gaze and kept her whole attention on the king he knew she was playing some kind of game. He just hoped she knew the stakes.

"Well." Tarkioff cast him a questioning glance. "I am glad Major McConneghy knows his position."

"Oh, yes sir. I agree."

This time it was Eustace who cleared his throat, and hid what Lucius guessed was a grin as the king's expression darkened.

"But have you found the men who set off the explosions?"

Lucius wanted to give her points for neatly deflecting the royal attention. He couldn't have done it better himself.

"We are working on the issue." Viktor Tarkioff slanted both his brother and Lucius looks that said he expected more than that. "But there is nothing for you to worry about. We have increased your security."

Jane glanced his way then, wariness replacing her earlier bravado and for that alone Lucius could wring Tar-kioff's neck.

"Then you feel there will be more incidents?"

Before Lucius could respond, Tarkioff replied. "It is the price one pays. A necessary evil in today's world. A burden borne by those who serve."

"You'll be safe." Lucius could not stomach one more banality. "We've only increased security as a precaution, not because we believe the risk to you has increased."

"I see." He watched her swallow, her fingers smooth at her skirt before she rose to her feet. Her voice remained steady though, as she addressed a glowering king. "I will not keep you from your work then. Thank you."

Lucius was at her side before she reached the door, his hand slipping around her elbow in an automatic gesture. He noted that her gaze did not meet his, and that beneath his touch her skin was cold.

"I will escort the mademoiselle to her room." He said it for the benefit of Tarkioff and his brother, but for the look Jane shot him, he might have just announced he was es-corting her to prison.

"Good day, mademoiselle." It was Eustace's voice fol-lowing them from the room.

Lucius waited until they reached a relatively secluded section of the hallway before he tugged her into an empty room, closing the door behind them.

"Are you trying to cause an international incident or just being stupid?" All the emotion he'd been holding back, the frustration with Tarkioff, the need she roused in him simply by being in the same room, the awareness of the tightrope she walked with her two-edged words, all roared through him, coating his words with an anger based on fear. Fear that what he'd only begun to accept might be possible be-tween them would be cut short if he did not protect her. If he could not keep her safe.

He wrapped his hands around her arms, reassuring himself physically that she was there, ignoring the hurt he saw in her gaze. "This is not a game we're playing. The stakes are too high, the risks too great. If Tarkioff or Eustace even suspected there was something going on behind their backs—"

"Something?" The hurt look deepened in her gaze.

"You know what I mean."

"Are we going back to the beginning? To master and peon?"

"We don't have time for this."

"Oh?"

Now he knew he'd taken the wrong track.

"I have an irate king breathing down my neck, an unexplained incident, worried heads back in the States—"

"And me."

He allowed the sigh building in him to escape.

"I didn't mean it that way."

"Don't worry, Major." She tugged her arm but he only tightened his grip. "I may be slow but I'm not stupid. I know what it means to be a liability. I know very well, so you don't have to explain the nuances to me."

He tried to gentle his voice. Not easy when a woman was glaring at you with pain and humiliation in her eyes.

"Jane, I didn't mean it like that. I just don't have time to explain everything right now."

"There's nothing to explain." It sounded so final it scared him. This was not the same woman who had walked into a room moments ago with fire in her gaze. He'd been truthful though, he didn't have a lot of time to clarify everything with her. No time at all. So he communicated in the only way he was sure would get through.

Before she could protest or evade, he pulled her to him. His lips claimed hers as she opened them in a gasp of surprise, and then he devoured. Slowly, surely he reassured her that what they'd started last night was still there, was still alive and vital and as important to him as it was to her.

When he finally came up for air he noted the passion building in her gaze and the raggedness of her breathing. He knew he felt the same himself, and later, he hoped not much later, he'd do something about it.

"Trust me on this, Jane." The anger was gone from his tone, but not his sense of fear. Fear for her, fear for what she was doing to him without even being aware of it. "We'll talk later, but right now the safest place for you is in your room. I'll send up something to read, some videos for the DVD player. Just stay there, where I know you'll be safe."

He watched her close her eyes as if coming to an internal decision before she raised her gaze to his, clear and determined.

"I'll go, but that doesn't mean I'm going to like it."

"I didn't expect miracles."

She smiled then. A tentative one, but it gave him hope. He took her arm again and made to open the door.

"Lucius?"

He paused. "Yeah?"

"Take care of yourself in the meantime."

"Will do." He would, too, now that he had a reason to.

Jane counted to thirty-two, the number of steps between the main door to her room and the set of open French doors. She knew because it wasn't the first time she'd counted them. It was obvious she and the major would have to discuss the meaning of the word *later*. Another fifteen minutes or so and she'd disregard the silent sentinel posted outside her door all day and a good part of the night and go find McConneghy in person. The man was a sadist to leave her cooped up like this all day, alone, fretting, aching from his kisses. Especially that last one.

She turned at the French doors and began counting backwards, the sweep of silk pants washing against her legs. She was beginning to like silk against her skin. That and the scent of Chanel No. 5. Had it been that long ago that this had all seemed so strange and frightening? Less than a month since Lucius McConneghy had crashed into her life and changed everything?

Her footsteps stilled across the floor, her bare toes glad for its coolness beneath them, its solidness. Something had to be solid when everything else was thrown into confusion. A month ago she'd known exactly who she was, what she was doing, and, if it was a little bland and boring, the texture of her days.

And now? Now everything was up in the air. It was bad enough there were threats against her life, well really Elena's life, but since everybody seemed to have accepted that Jane was Elena that didn't make a lot of difference. No, what was really bothering her could be pinpointed to one man. One impossible, responsibility-driven, too-difficult-for-words man. A man she was falling in love with.

She sat down on the bed, as stunned by her realization as anything that had happened to her thus far.

How could she possibly love a man she barely knew? He was the one responsible for getting her into this outlandish situation in the first place, and he made no bones about not wanting anything more than a physical relationship with her. Of all the men in the whole world, she couldn't have picked one less likely to be her type.

But even that thought didn't help matters. The old Jane might have been willing to ache from afar, well aware that a man like Lucius McConneghy could never love her back and accept that she'd spend her life wanting something that was not to be. It was a sappy reaction, but then she was sappy, or had been. She'd been a doormat when it came to asserting herself, her needs, her agenda. And now? Was she much different now?

With a heavy sigh, she wondered if, once she changed back into her sensible cottons and polyesters, resumed her job at the library and stopped using perfume she could never afford on her salary, she'd also revert to the old Jane's ways. Was being a sap in her blood? Responsibility was bred into Lucius. Heck, the guy went into the military knowing most of the males of his line had died as a direct result of that life. No wonder responsibility was such a strong element of his character.

But did any of it make any difference? She loved him and knew he might care for her. A man who made love the way he had all the previous night had to have some sort of feelings behind such passion, but that didn't mean he loved her. She might be inexperienced, but she wasn't a total fool. He'd said as much before they'd taken that first heady step.

Would she go back and change it? No way. Not one exhilarating, exciting, breathtaking second. But what now? Could she enjoy what they had, stop thinking about the future long enough to experience the present, accept that she might not have a forever, but she could have a here and now?

Before she could make a decision, as if she really thought there was any but one decision to be made, she heard the quiet rattle of the door handle and a voice that made her heart accelerate.

"It's me. Open the door."

She rose from the bed, surprised her legs were as steady as they were, and crossed to open the door. She felt breathless and shaky inside and hoped he didn't notice.

The look in his eyes kept her from speaking. A hot, dark, dangerous look that had her blood heating, her pulse racing even before the door behind him clicked shut.

"I want you." He spoke the three words as a desperate man, his arms pulling her into his, his lips claiming hers.

There was no more conversation as she tasted his need.

This was not the man of last night, the aroused lover still in control, still holding back a part of himself. No, this was a man who was giving as he took, his hands fast and sure across her back, tangling in her hair as he deepened his kisses.

Her mouth opened beneath his, but it wasn't enough. She felt the two of them move until a wall stopped their progress, but not his passion. His fingers slid beneath the hem of her loose shirt, a guttural groan breaking from him as he discovered no bra to hinder their movement.

He touched, stroked, kneaded, even as she felt his hunger grow, hers expanding with it. His hands shifted direction, slipping beneath the band of her pants, letting them slide to the floor, cupping the bare skin of her buttocks.

He pulled her closer to him, lifting and stretching her legs until she felt impaled between him and the hard surface of the wall.

"I can't wait." His movements echoed his words as she felt the thrust of his sheathed shaft against her entrance, its bluntness demanding acceptance. "Tell me yes, Jane. Tell me yes."

She smiled against his hair, feeling more sure of herself in those seconds than in her whole life. He might not love her, but right then and there he needed her. More than that, she wanted him. All of him.

"Yes."

The single word was all he needed as he surged forward, stretching her until she felt the fullness of him deep, deep within her. Then he began to move. Strong thrusts, each one demanding more than the last. It was if all the emotion she'd glimpsed in him from time to time, the feelings tightly leashed and controlled, were slashing at him, pushing at him to dissolve the difference between him and her until it was only them.

His moan of release echoed against her hair, harsh and

wracked, and yet he held her high, her legs wrapped around his waist, her hands digging into his shoulders. She could feel the pulse of his heart quiet against her, hear the raggedness of his breathing begin to slow while they stayed where they were, as if caught in a heartbeat of time. She knew then, without words, that he was already regretting his actions. What she wasn't sure of was the reason why.

"Are you going to tell me this was a mistake?" She surprised herself by the ferocity of her tone.

He pulled back then, enough for her to see the tiredness bracketing his eyes, the exhaustion lining his face. "No. No mistake. I needed you too much for that."

His words warmed her even as he slowly slid her legs to the floor, his hands not releasing her until sure her own legs would hold her.

"I didn't hurt you, did I?"

"No." She responded both to the question and the hesitation in his gaze. "In fact, it was much better than a bland 'how are you?'"

She caught his wry grin, pleased she'd lightened some of the load pressing down on him. No doubt he'd been cloistered with Tarkioff and his brother all day, something that would try the patience of the strongest of men.

He lifted a hand to her face, the gentleness of the act bringing tears to her eyes. She felt his fingers glide across her brow, stroke a strand of hair from her face, memorize the line of her cheekbone and jaw.

"I never want to hurt you." She knew he was talking about more than the last few minutes, but she was at a loss how to take away the regret shadowing his gaze.

"They don't grow wimps in South Dakota." Keep it light, she told herself. Keep it light. "You'll just have to try harder next time."

He rubbed his cheek against the top of her head, another tender gesture so at odds with the strained lines of his expression that she wanted to ask what had happened, but before she could he'd slipped his arms beneath her legs and swung her into his arms.

"Let's try it slow this time." He gave her a smile that could topple mountains and walked to the bed, settling her atop the covers as if she was rare and precious.

If she hadn't already lost her heart, she knew it would have taken flight right then and there.

He slipped his jacket from his shoulders, tossing it on a nearby chair and removed his shoulder harness, his gaze never leaving hers. Yet, when his fingers began to unfasten the buttons of his shirt, for some reason she felt unaccountably shy. A silly feeling given their lovemaking of only moments ago.

Hardly being aware of it, she let her gaze slip, finding respite in smoothing the folds of her blouse while she tried to still the erratic beating of her heart, the sudden dryness in her mouth. Even then she was aware of his movements just beyond the line of her sight, of his steady breathing, of his gaze studying her.

"I haven't frightened you." He leaned forward until his fingers curled beneath her chin, raising it until her gaze locked with his. She could read the concern in his eyes. Those eyes she'd once had thought were hard and cold, without feeling, devoid of passion. Boy, when she was wrong, she was really wrong.

Since no words would come she mutely shook her head instead.

He knelt beside her, his splendidly naked body heavily aroused and yet his voice soothing, his gaze steady on hers.

"There have been times I would have given a fortune to have you keep quiet." She knew he was trying to make her smile with his teasing tone, so why did she feel like crying? Especially when he added, "This isn't one of them."

She swallowed, but still couldn't force words past the lump in her throat.

He removed his fingers from her chin and slipped them lower, to the top button of her shirt.

"I'll stop any time you want me to."

She knew he would, though that was the last thing in the world she wanted right then. Her head shook in negation and his finger slid a button from its hole.

"You deserve courtship, with red roses and candlelight dinners. I don't have any of that to offer you. Not here and now."

She wondered if there were more to his words but lost the thought as the last button gave and she felt his fingers slip between the open folds of silk.

Her breath caught and held as callused fingertips slid ever so gently across her skin. There was no pattern to the movement, no heat to the touch. Nothing but an exquisite gentleness at odds with the driven, determined man she thought she understood. Through eyes growing heavy with pleasure she could see the cost of his control.

She wanted to give him something, anything, in return for the sensations racing through her.

"We don't have to go slow."

"She speaks at last." His lips ever so tenderly brushed her forehead. "But you're wrong. We do need to go slow. This time."

"Why?"

"Because I want you to know, to feel what you've put me through all day. Away from you, thinking about the taste of your lips."

He kissed her deeply.

"About the feel of your skin when I do this."

He squeezed one nipple ever so gently.

"About the sounds you make deep in your throat when I touch you here."

One finger slid between her thighs, rubbing softly, then more urgently. She arched beneath him.

"I've wanted you until I couldn't see straight."

The pressure increased, building to an ache.

"Until I could think of nothing but getting back to you."

He slid two fingers into her, teasing her until she wanted to scream. Or beg.

"Of burying myself so deep within you I'd never find my way out."

And he did. In one sure, strong stroke he entered her, finishing with his body what he had started with his hands. They slipped over the edge together and she knew there'd be no going back. Not for either of them.

Chapter 12

Later, when the shadows of the night had lengthened and she lay across the bed, Lucius's head pillowed between her naked breasts, his breathing deep and even, she asked a question that had been bothering her ever since her unpleasant dinner with Tarkioff days ago.

"Lucius?"

"Ummm." She knew he wasn't asleep, just relaxed. Rare enough for him that she should have felt guilt for wanting to know something perhaps better left alone.

"How well do you know Elena? The real Elena I mean."

"Elena Rostov?"

He was hedging and she knew it. "No, I'm talking about Elena Dela Santos, the opera singer." She tugged a lock of his hair.

"Ow."

"You deserve worse than that. Of course I'm talking about Elena Rostov."

He rubbed his forehead, but she heard the wariness in his voice. "What do you want to know about her?"

"I want to know how well you know her."

"That's an open-ended question."

She'd gone this far, no time to back down now.

"I was wondering if…" This was harder than she'd thought. "If…you know."

"If we were lovers?"

The way he said it made her feel petty and nosy instead of just a new lover seeking some reassurance.

"Yeah, something like that."

"We weren't."

The words dropped like splattered grease in the quiet of the room.

"Because you didn't want to or because she didn't want to?"

She wondered where she got the guts even to think of asking such personal questions, and then, when one silver-tinted eye slitted open, wondered why she could not have left well enough alone.

With a smooth move startling her in its suddenness, she felt Lucius's hand snake up to cup her head and pull her lips to his. Only after he thoroughly kissed her did he answer.

"Elena, like you, is a very beautiful woman. But that's where the similarities end."

"Meaning?"

He stretched. A great delaying tactic, she realized as she watched the play of muscles in his chest and arms.

"Meaning Elena assumes the world is made to notice her."

"Meaning men."

"Yes, men in particular."

"And you didn't?"

"I'm here as Tarkioff's advisor, not Elena's plaything."

She knew he'd never be any woman's plaything, but the image made her smile. At least, she told herself it was the image and not the fact that he was doing with her exactly what he wasn't willing to do with Elena.

"I see."

"I don't think you do." He rose to one elbow, all relaxation gone from his expression. "There never was, never would be, nor ever will be anything between Elena Rostov and myself."

"But we look exactly alike." Why would Lucius be attracted to her and not Elena?

"Anybody who was with either one of you for longer than ten minutes would know you're nothing alike."

"But I thought I was doing a good job impersonating her?"

He didn't have to grin at her tone.

"You are. Almost too good."

"What do you mean by that?"

"Jane, you're the most real person I've ever met," he said, really throwing her for a loop.

"You're losing me here."

Instead of answering right away he gave her a kiss. A soft, gentle kiss she felt all the way to her toes.

If he was trying to distract her he was doing a fine job of it. A darn fine job.

"You're real and Elena is all smoke and mirrors."

"Meaning?"

"You see people, with their hopes and dreams and lives and treat them as if they're important."

"Of course they're important."

"Not everybody sees life that way."

"Like Elena."

"Like Elena."

He glanced away, as if gathering his thoughts before he spoke. "You're the kind of woman that a man wants to protect and defend and ravish all at the same time."

Her?

''You tie up a man's thoughts until they're in knots.'' He sounded frustrated. ''And at the same time make everything perfectly clear.''

As mud, she thought, wondering what he was really trying to say? Did he care about her? More than he wanted? Less than he thought he should?

He pulled her back into his arms, confusing her even more. ''I know I got you into this mess and I sure as hell am going to get you out, but only if you help. You could try the patience of a saint.''

Her? *He* was the one not making any sense.

''I want you to keep your eyes open. Be aware of every situation. If it doesn't feel right, back away. Trust no one.''

He'd said that to her before if she recalled. Very emphatically, but she figured now was not the time to point it out. Nor his just as emphatic follow-up sentence—the one that told her to trust him least of all.

Over the next several days Jane replayed Lucius's words over and over again, trying to capture their urgency, their shadow of fear, but it was hard, really hard, when everything else in her was smiling. No, make that grinning.

She thought he had said something very important, even if he couldn't say the words out loud. He loved her. Or cared for her very much. She could wait for the L-word. For a while. And in the meantime every day gave her another twenty-four hours to spend with him, by his side, sometimes in his arms, many times near enough that she could simply look at him. Look and absorb as if she could capture rays of sunlight to warm her future when they'd go their separate ways. If they did.

But she wouldn't think such gloomy thoughts. The old Jane might have dwelled on them, allowed them to taint the present with the reality that nothing this wonderful could possibly last. But the new Jane intended to savor.

Late at night, when Lucius would come to her after long, frustrating meetings with Tarkioff, when his need for her was urgent and desperate, she'd want to pull him into her arms and tell him it'd be all right. But those times would slip past, lost in the intensity of his loving, swept aside by passion so strong she felt like kindling before its fire.

But it was hard to ignore the worry she'd catch in his eyes, the way he'd look at her as if trying to figure out a particularly difficult puzzle. So she did what she could to help. She kept things light between them. At any moment he could be snatched from her, their impossible paradise in the middle of tension destroyed, her own life snuffed out, but it didn't touch that inner part of her that felt sure, somehow, that things were going to be all right.

Maybe not peachy-keen kind of all right. How could they be when she would be heading back to midsummer in Sioux Falls in a matter of days and he—who knew where his next mission would send him, or with whom?

But she refused to think of such things. Instead she found delight in touching him, in sneaking her hand into his right before their limo would pull up to another function, of catching the surprised, then wary look he'd shoot her. He made her laugh. He made her ache. He made her want a tomorrow, while aware that every moment together was also bringing the time they'd be apart that much closer. No one had warned her that love could feel so poignant and so painful.

Lucius glanced at the memo clenched in his fist, then at his watch. They were running out of time. Now he understood who was behind what was going on, but not why. Tarkioff's wedding was less than three days away and they were no closer to finding out the why behind the threats on Jane's life—Elena's life—than they were before. And without the why they were never going to fix the problem.

Funny that he didn't give a tinker's damn right then what it meant to relations between his country and Vendari. Or what it meant to his career or the careers of his team.

None of it mattered. Not when it was Jane caught in the vortex. Something was going to break open, and soon, Lucius's gut told him as much and his experience reinforced the warnings. But he was in the dark as to the why, what, how and when. In other words, if he'd been blindfolded in a dark cave, he couldn't have felt any more out of touch.

And then there was Jane. Sweet, wonderful, trying-her-hardest-to-keep-a-smile-on-her-face Jane, and she was breaking his heart. He, who should have been protecting her, was being protected by her. Every time she took him into her arms, accepted him into her body, soothed when he felt the most frustrated, she showed him in a hundred ways the depth of her emotions, the strength of her commitment to him. He didn't deserve it, any of it, yet she kept giving, kept her smiles bright for him and right on the mark.

He was tempted to stick her on the next plane back to the States and take the fallout. He would, too, if he was sure that would be safest for her. But his concern was that once she was out of his sight, out of his direct sphere of influence, she'd be vulnerable in ways he didn't want to imagine.

She'd been kidnapped once already because of her likeness to Elena Rostov, why not again? And there lay the crux of the problem. If she stayed in Vendari, continued her charade until the day of the wedding, she was in danger, and if she left, she was also in danger.

Since he couldn't fight on two fronts at once, while every instinct screamed at him to get her away—as far away from him and Vendari as he could—he knew she'd be safest where he could see her, touch her, protect her.

He was betting her life, and the best part of his, that he was making the right choice.

He glanced back at his watch when he heard the door

behind him open. Relief surged through him the moment he recognized Jane's hand on the door, just one more sign of the strain he'd been feeling the last week.

"Am I interrupting?" she asked, stepping into the room in the cautious way she'd moved the last couple of days. As if by walking warily, not stirring the space about her much, she might become invisible. He wondered if it was a trait from her childhood, a childhood he doubted had given her much sense of security and assurance. He'd at least had that much. Too much responsibility at too young an age, but he had known that his mother had needed and wanted him.

"Come in." He waved her into the library, thankful it was empty for a few moments. "The king and his brother might intrude at any minute."

"If the Head of Security is with the king is it important?"

"A formality."

She had enough to deal with without his concerns on top of them.

She offered him a tentative smile, as if gauging his mood before trusting her own reaction. "I was hoping to find you alone."

He opened his arms and she stepped into them. It was that easy. In spite of everything he'd done to her—brought her to this isolated country, embroiled her in a potential revolution that didn't amount to a lot in the scope of world affairs, taken advantage of her vulnerability to become her lover—in spite of it all, she came into his arms without hesitation. It staggered him.

"I'm alone." He brushed a kiss across her hair, wanting more, knowing at any second they could be interrupted. "I thought you were going to spend the day in your room."

"I've memorized every square inch of those walls." He heard the frustration in her voice and bit back a smile. His kitten was a lioness at heart, though he doubted she thought of herself that way.

"There's a dinner this evening."

"The dinners are hardest of all." He felt her frown as she rubbed her cheek against his chest, setting off an explosion of need throughout his system. "I feel like you're so far away from me, even though you're in the same room."

"It'll be over with soon."

He felt her tense immediately and wanted to bite his tongue. They'd both sidestepped the issue neatly. Never acknowledging that one day she'd be on her way, he on his, but they'd both known it was inevitable.

"I don't mean to complain." She pulled out of his arms and stepped back, a tremulous smile that tore at his being touching her lips. "I just thought, maybe for a short while, sometime today we could get away. Find an excuse to take a drive or have a picnic somewhere."

He watched the way she wrapped her arms about her as if holding herself together, and decided, though it'd take a lot of rearranging and adjusting, it'd be worth it to take the shadows from her eyes.

"I have to do this meeting with Tarkioff and his brother for a few moments." Her expression looked crestfallen. "But I'm sure I can work something out. It might not be for long."

"Even an hour or two away would help."

"I'll make it happen."

A genuine smile touched her lips, darkened the intensity of her eyes. He felt as if he'd just handed her the world on a golden platter, a feeling that only increased when she reached her palm out to lay it upon his cheek.

"Even a few minutes alone with you in the middle of the day would be wonderful." He thought he saw moisture in her eyes until her gaze dropped, along with her palm. "I'll go get ready."

"Is one of my men with you?"

"Yes, sir." She gave him a snappy salute in response to his tone. "It's Elderman. The young one with the thick eyelashes."

"Good." Though he'd never had one of his crack team described quite that way before, he told himself not to groan. Later he'd have to razz the young man about it. It was too good to pass up. "I don't want you going anywhere without him or one of the others. Is that clear?"

With an indulgent grin she patted his cheek. "If I had a nickel for every time you've told me that I'd be rich."

"It's for—"

"I know, I know." Her rich, deep chuckle sent its own message to his libido, though he could ill afford to act on it. "It's for my own good. I've heard that a few times, too."

"And I'll keep saying it until it gets through."

"You're so cute when you're being all stiff and official."

He did groan this time. "Damn it, I'm not trying to be cute, I'm trying to keep you alive."

"I know you are, and you will." She'd reversed roles on him again, being the one to reassure rather than the one who needed reassurance. "I trust you implicitly."

Maybe that was part of the problem, he thought. She trusted him too much. She thought he was better than he was, but he was only a man. A man who would do anything to keep her safe.

"Jane, I..." He wanted to tell her, at least once, what she meant to him. But before he could, he heard the rattle of the door handle.

He watched Jane turn toward the door, his attention focused solely on her until he saw her expression change, her eyes grow wide, her smile disappear. Only then did he follow the direction of her gaze. He expected to see Tarkioff or his brother. He expected anything except the person who walked through the door.

Jane wondered for a split second whether she was awake or dreaming. The sense of unreality was strong enough to have her doubting that what she saw, or who she saw, could be real. It was like looking into a mirror, only one that walked and talked and smiled, a cold, calculating smile that sent goose bumps crawling up her arm.

"How quaint." The voice was even and well-modulated, carrying the lightest of accents over the sheen of concession. "I didn't expect to find you both here, though this will make everything so much easier."

Jane turned to glance at Lucius, surprised at the rigidity of his stance. This was not the same man who only moments ago was holding her, teasing her. The man before her was all business. Cold, controlled business.

"What are you doing here?" Ice coated his words.

"Now, darling, that's not the welcome I was expecting. Especially from you."

Jane told herself the words meant nothing.

"I don't understand." It was her own voice, sounding more unsure and frightened than she wished, though it was nothing to what she felt like inside.

"Well, aren't you going to introduce us?" The other woman asked, her gaze still locked with Lucius's, her blood-red lips turned up in a mockery of a smile. "Though I'd say any introduction would be unnecessary."

"Jane, I'd like you to meet Elena Rostov." Jane could tell by the other woman's flinch that she didn't appreciate the order of the introduction, nor the contempt in Lucius's tone. "The real Elena."

The real Elena, indeed, Jane thought, wondering how anybody could have believed she, Jane, was the woman before her. Except for height, size, features and coloring, it was like comparing apples to oranges. This was obviously a woman of the world, smooth, effortlessly in control, sure of herself, her words purred, her movements were sultry, even her expression was more assured. Jane had never felt more like the country mouse, or the third wheel.

"Nice to meet you." She knew the woman didn't hear her words. Elena's attention was too focused on Lucius.

"You don't seem pleased to see me, darling."

"I'm not."

It was Jane who flinched this time.

"You must learn to be more diplomatic, Major." The woman moved into the room, her smile as tight as her tone. "That is your role, is it not? To facilitate relations between our two countries."

"Why are you here, Elena?" Jane could see that Lucius had not moved, yet his voice sliced through the room. "How did you get in here?"

The woman's laugh did nothing to ease the tension. "That was so simple. Your man assumed I was your impostor."

Jane felt like day-old dog meat.

"He asked how I'd left this room but I simply waved him off."

Lucius's expression did not bode well for the young man. "It still doesn't explain why you're here."

"No, it doesn't." The woman ran her hand along the back of an overstuffed chair, an exaggerated gesture befitting a B-grade movie. Her expression appeared amused. "But I believe you'll have to wait until the king and Eustace join us."

The words sounded innocent enough, but Jane could feel Lucius tense at her side. Whatever was going on, he didn't like it.

"You know you've placed both your life and Jane's in danger by being here."

"Oh, don't be so stuffy, darling." The real Elena fluttered her lashes. If she hadn't seen it herself, Jane would have thought the gesture impossible. But somehow on the other woman it worked. "You've always been too serious. All work and no play makes for a dull boy."

Obviously Elena did not know Lucius very well, Jane realized, if she thought him dull and serious. The knowledge reassured her. She could see Lucius being taken in by the woman's sultry beauty, but never by her layered seduction.

Before she could feel too sorry for Elena, though, the door opened again and the voice of Eustace Tarkioff boomed into the room.

"It makes perfect sense. You must trust me on this, Viktor."

Whatever the other man's answer might have been was cut off as both men spied the woman poised dramatically against the plush chair. It was a good pose, Jane had to give her credit for that, even as she watched gazes swing back and forth between Elena and herself.

She didn't blame them for being speechless, though she wished somebody would say something soon to break the strained silence in the room.

It was Elena who spoke at last. "Come in, gentlemen, and close the door behind you."

The Head of Security did as she said, though his mouth remained open, his gaze wary.

"You all look as if you're seeing a ghost, though you know full well I have been alive and well." Her laugh sounded a little strained to Jane's ears.

"Of course, my dear." It was Tarkioff who stepped forward and placed a kiss on the cheek she turned to him. "It was just that we were not expecting you like this."

His glance swung to Lucius and back to his brother.

Jane felt like an invisible reflection until Eustace looked her way, then spoke up. "This was not the plan."

"Plans can change, as you should well know, dear."

There were currents beneath currents here. Jane couldn't quite put her finger on what was happening. Or why. Whatever it was, Lucius must have noticed, too, as he stepped slightly forward and closer to her side, almost shutting her out of the conversation and the triangle of people standing across from them.

The king regarded his brother with a quizzical expression.

"Dear?" he asked at last, pinpointing for Jane one of the lines of tension radiating like a spoke from the woman before her.

Before Eustace Tarkioff could answer, Elena laughed again and spoke to the king this time.

"Don't be any bigger a fool than you already are, darling."

Ouch, Jane thought, watching the king's features tighten, but it was Lucius who jumped into the fray.

"I think it's time for your explanations, Elena. Yours and Eustace's."

Now nothing made sense. Why was he lumping the beautiful woman with the reserved, quiet Head of Security?

"I knew you'd catch on. Eventually." This time Elena's laugh sounded genuine, her gaze lingering overlong on Lucius. "It's too bad for your plans it didn't happen sooner."

"What plans? What didn't happen sooner?" Jane was as surprised as the rest of the room when it was her voice demanding answers.

"Stay out of this, Jane." Lucius's voice brooked no objections. A sharp slap across the face would have stung less.

"Be kind, darling, tell the poor girl what she wants to know."

Jane didn't care much for being "the poor girl," but she was glad somebody was suggesting she be let in on the secret. If not a secret, whatever it was the rest of the room seemed to know about. All right, maybe not the king, who also looked genuinely baffled.

"It's simple enough." Lucius spoke as if even an idiot

could figure it out. "Let me ask, though, how long have you and Eustace been acting together?"

Elena and the king's brother acting together for what? Jane wanted to know, but Lucius had stepped forward again, all but shoving her out of the way.

"That's idiotic." It was the king's voice echoing through the room. "Tell him, Eustace. That is absolutely preposterous."

"I'm afraid he is right, Viktor." Eustace turned toward Lucius, his face no longer amiable and conciliatory, but hard and measured. "We have been acting in unison since the beginning. It was I, after all, who suggested the union between our dear Elena and the king."

"Of course." Lucius's voice sounded different, as if he was encouraging a slow student.

"So the first assassination attempt was a ploy?"

"No, darling, it was real enough." Elena answered, and Jane thought her shudder was real. "Though not planned, it did serve a purpose."

"And the explosions at the pool and on the night of the dinner here at the palace?" Lucius might have been asking for a bus schedule for all the emotion behind his words.

"Crude, but effective don't you think?" The younger Tarkioff's voice cut in. "Elena knew you would get suspicious if there were no more attempts on her life."

"And if I was too suspicious I'd have looked closer into the first attempt."

"There was always that possibility, Major."

Elena glanced at the Head of Security as if saying, "See, I told you he was a bright boy," but Jane thought she was the only one who caught the gloating glance.

The king, who, up until this time had remained mute, asserted himself. "Explain, Eustace. Why have you gone behind my back to perpetuate this threat upon my fiancée? It makes no sense."

"But it does." Eustace's voice held none of the diffidence it normally did when addressing his older brother. "Because Elena is not your fiancée."

"Of course she is—"

"Be quiet, you fool." Elena's voice cut through the room, sharply honed and lethal. "The whole engagement has been a sham. I would no more marry you than rut with a pig."

The woman's words reverberated around the room in the sudden silence. Even Lucius seemed taken aback as he reached one hand out to pull Jane closer to his side and slightly behind him. She wondered who was going to sling the next mud.

As if ignoring his fiancée's, or pretend fiancée's words, the king turned to his brother. "Eustace, I order you to explain yourself."

"Gladly, Your Highness." The man's words sounded straightforward but not his tone. Not one bit. "I have been working with the Rostov family for years."

"You've *what?*"

For the first time, Jane felt sorry for the king. This was more convoluted than some of the soap operas she sometimes caught before work.

The younger Tarkioff ignored his brother's outrage as he continued. "There never was any intention of Elena marrying you."

So did that mean Jane was pretending to be a pretend fiancée, she wondered, feeling a little of the hysteria she'd experienced weeks ago when this whole mess had first started. It was a measure of how far she'd come that she could very definitely recognize the symptoms.

Tarkioff stepped forward, his face the color of ripe tomatoes. "This is outrageous. I don't believe you for a moment."

"Believe him." Lucius's words slashed through the

room. "I'm sure your brother is very serious about what he's saying."

"That's a wise move." Eustace Tarkioff smiled, but it didn't reach his eyes. Funny she hadn't noticed before how cold they were. Cold and determined.

"But why have Elena become engaged to me? Why plan for a wedding if there was to be none? It makes no sense."

Jane thought the king was sounding a little hysterical himself until Lucius's next words seeped into his awareness. "Why? Because by your engagement to Miss Rostov you legitimized her right to co-rule Vendari."

"The right to what?"

"That's right, Elena, isn't it?" Lucius stepped closer to the other woman, leaving Jane to feel abandoned and still in the dark. "The people of Vendari have accepted you as their king's new wife, have taken you into their hearts, have even rallied around your bravery despite the threats to your life."

"That was a nice touch, wasn't it?" Elena's brows arched, her gaze remaining firm on Lucius. "And you helped with it, protecting your little pretender here with such solicitous care. It was touching, very touching, but absolutely pointless."

"So while you were safe until whoever made the first attempt on your life was found, Jane continued your charade to ingratiate the brave Elena into the hearts and minds of the people of Vendari."

"Something like that." Elena did not sound quite as assured as she had seconds ago. Jane wondered if it was Lucius's proximity, or his tone that disturbed her.

"And Eustace kept up the pretense closer to home when it wasn't your life that was in danger at all."

"Explain yourself." The king uttered the words Jane wanted to, but couldn't get around the lump in her throat.

"Simple, Your Highness." Lucius paused, closer to

where the other three stood now than he was to Jane. She couldn't see his expression but could guess at his harshness. He'd been used, royally used by the sound of things, and she held no doubt it did not sit well. "We have been working under the assumption that the ultimate threat all along was to Elena's life. That if she died before your wedding, the country could become destabilized enough to result in an attempt to overthrow Vendari by Rostov's people."

"Yes, but—"

"But the real threat has been to you, not your fiancée."

"But how?"

"If you were assassinated right before the wedding, or perhaps on the day of it," Lucius glanced at Elena as if for confirmation, which she gave with the slightest of nods before he continued, "then it would be natural for the woman who has won the hearts of so many these past weeks to step in and rule in your stead."

"A woman? It wouldn't happen. They'd never accept a woman as ruler."

"Perhaps. But there was a contingency plan. Your brother."

"Eustace?"

"If Elena needed a puppet husband, what better man than your brother, your Head of Security? The people would rally behind the two of them. It's very simple and straightforward."

And might have worked, too, Jane realized glancing from one face to another in the room. It very easily might have worked.

It was Tarkioff who asked the question hovering on the edge of her awareness.

"What happens now?"

As if invisible strings had been pulled, Jane felt the tension in the room escalate. No one moved. No one spoke. But the fear became palpable.

She wanted to hide. To scream at Lucius to hide. To do something, anything to break the tautness of vibrating nerves. Then she saw the gun. A long-nosed, blunt, ugly weapon gripped in Elena Rostov's hand.

And it was pointed straight at her.

Chapter 13

Like the day the gunshots had rung out in the town square, Jane felt that stretching of time, the slowing of everything in the room as if movement happened one frame at a time. Even the voices became painfully drawn out. The gasp of breath she heard sucked in—hers, she thought. The harsh bite of Lucius's tone, angry almost, but only one syllable released. A very clear, unrelenting, "No."

"Too late, darling."

The gun wavered but never shifted. It was Lucius who moved, sidestepped until he was right beside her.

The man was using himself as a shield to protect her, and all Jane could do was remain rooted to the floor. As if her brain impulses were not connecting to her muscles, she could hear herself screaming inside to push him out of the way. To save himself. But nothing happened. She couldn't make anything happen.

"A gallant but wasted gesture, Major." Elena's words slid into the stretched silence.

"This was not what we planned," Eustace said.

"Plans have changed, darling. But only slightly."

"But why kill her?" It was the king, sounding more perplexed than concerned, as if it didn't matter that her life hung in the balance as long as he made sense of why she was about to be shot in cold blood.

"She is unimportant." Elena gave a shrug, as if they were discussing exterminating a bug rather than a person. "You've known that all along."

Jane wished they would stop talking around her as if she couldn't hear their words. Such cold, callous words.

"If we change the plans now, there could be problems." Eustace said, though no one turned to look his way. Not when the gun remained steady.

"Listen to him, Elena." Now it was Lucius speaking. It sounded so reassuring, so matter of fact, Jane wondered if he'd forgotten that he, too, stood in the line of fire. How could he be so calm when she couldn't even breathe? "Eustace knows what he's talking about."

Did Lucius know about the plan? Was he working in cahoots with Elena and the king's brother? Why else was he talking this way?

"It's not too late to go back."

Elena glanced at Eustace, then dismissed Lucius's words. "It is too late. It's time for a new plan and she's a liability."

Hadn't that always been her role in life? Jane felt surprise at the anger the realization brought. Anger that gave her enough clarity of thought to move, not away from the gun but toward it. She doubted she could outrun a bullet, but she'd discovered there was something she could do. She could make sure Lucius wasn't hurt in the process.

His hand snagged her arm, grasping so tightly it hurt. His expression told her he knew exactly what she was doing, and he wasn't going to have any part of it.

But this time she wasn't going to let him have his way. Not this time.

"Don't worry, Miss Richards." It was Elena's voice that stopped the struggle of wills between her and Lucius. "We still have need of the major. He will not be hurt."

She might have liked the other woman better if she knew she'd spoken out of compassion, but from her expression it was clear that wasn't the motivating factor. Not when her whole attention was riveted on Lucius like a cat on a bowl of fresh cream.

Now the power struggle was between them, with Jane on the outside, watching heated gazes clash.

"This is ridiculous." The king sounded petulant and put-upon. "Eustace, you and I will discuss this matter. Now."

No one moved.

The king spoke again. "I tell you this has gone on long enough. I demand a resolution."

He received one.

Jane, her gaze glued on the face of the woman before her, waiting for that last second when the gun would jerk, was the first to see the change.

It was as if Elena Rostov's eyes glazed over, her features tightened as her gun hand moved, ever so quickly, ever so silently. Seconds only, but it felt like forever. The dark barrel of the weapon arced and settled. This time pointing dead center on the king.

"Elena. Don't."

It was Eustace's voice that cried out. But too late. The gun snapped. Once. Twice. Again. Ugly, rasping sounds exploding through the room. Four times in all. Short, abrupt, lethal pops.

The king's face registered surprise. A questioning expression that begged for understanding even as a wide circle of red spread across his chest.

Lucius's hand, still banded about Jane's upper arm,

swung her behind him, as if he could hide her from the figure of the king toppling forward, one hand reaching toward his brother. A brother as frozen in place as the rest of the group.

"Eustace?" It came on a gurgle of breath, swallowed by the heavy thud of shoulders slamming against the carpet.

It was that quick. From a living, breathing man, befuddled by the pace of events unfolding, to a crumpled mass, lying still and silent.

Jane felt separated from reality. From where she stood, behind Lucius, all she could see was Viktor Tarkioff's outstretched hand, red-stained and motionless against the patterned carpet.

She closed her eyes, afraid she was going to be sick, knowing if she didn't pull herself together, she was going to run screaming out of the room. Though she doubted Elena would let her get far.

"You didn't have to—" Eustace Tarkioff's voice sounded as bewildered as his brother's.

"I did and it's done." No regrets from this woman, Jane thought. Not one teeny, tiny ounce. "It was only a matter of time. I just moved up when it happened."

Jane could hear the breathing in the room. Eustace Tarkioff's hard and ragged. Elena's short and shallow, as if she'd run a hard race. Lucius's calm and controlled, as if dead bodies fell at his feet on a regular basis. Which maybe they did. Could that be why he seemed to be the only one in the room unaffected by what just happened?

Eustace's expression changed. Grief was there, regret maybe, but then came a dawning realization that Vendari now had a new ruler—himself.

Elena looked bored. As if she'd had a dirty chore to take care of and now it was time to focus on other things. Jane didn't want to think yet of what those things might be, or of how she fit into them.

But Lucius remained exactly where he'd been seconds ago, his hand steady on her, his expression focused on the woman with the gun still in her hand. His expression gave nothing away. The man had to be made of granite.

"What now?"

Eustace spoke the words, but it wasn't Elena who answered. It was Lucius.

He moved first, releasing Jane's arm to kneel by the body, checking for a pulse along the king's throat. As if anybody could live after having four bullets pumped into their body from only a few feet away.

"He's dead."

The words echoed around the room.

"Of course he is, darling." Elena smiled with her words. Jane decided if Lucius was made of stone, this lady was made of steel, shiny bright and hard, razor-hard. "I am nothing if not thorough."

It was then Jane wondered why no one had come running into the room. Surely somebody should have heard the shots. Or had they been loud only to her? But what about Lucius's man stationed just outside? Was he to open the door any second and meet his own death?

Lucius's next words answered her unspoken questions. "Your silencer is useless now."

That's why the bullets had sounded like loud pops. Elena had used a silencer. Maybe that was why the gun looked different, too. Different from the one Lucius had told her to keep close not too many nights ago. That night they'd first made love.

It was that thought that had her shaking. Where was the man who'd held her in his arms, made her laugh, made her body sing? Was this the real Lucius McConneghy before her—cold, lethal, discussing weapons with a murderer who'd just pulled a trigger?

He glanced at her then. One quick, silent look as if he'd

heard her thoughts aloud before he turned back to Elena Rostov who was staring at the gun in her hand.

"Then I shall have to find some other way to eliminate your American friend."

American friend? Eliminate? They were talking about her again and she didn't care for the words being used. The shaking grew stronger.

Lucius rose to his feet, the move smooth and controlled. Almost too controlled, she thought, reading the tenseness of his shoulders, the way he held his body as if ready to spring. But his words were at odds with what she saw.

"Is it necessary?"

What was he saying? Is it necessary? She couldn't believe what she was hearing. What happened to "No way," or "Over my dead body"? Hadn't he said all along he'd protect her? Was this his definition of protection?

"Of course it's necessary, darling."

Jane was getting really tired of Elena's slow, casual way of talking, as if discussing murder exhausted her. She absolutely refused to think of the words spoken. The "of course" words.

It was Lucius who answered, but not in the way Jane expected. Not at all.

"Then I'll handle it."

What?

She turned, shock making her movements jerky, her body refusing to accept what he was saying. She wanted to demand an explanation. Force him to tell her he was joking. But no words would come. All she could do was stare, willing him to look her way, to meet her gaze and repeat his words.

But he kept his gaze averted.

"Don't play me for a fool, Major." Elena's voice held contempt. "I know how it would offend your sensibilities to eliminate a pawn. Especially if that pawn was a woman."

Pawn? Was that how Lucius had seen her all along? It couldn't be. It just couldn't be.

"I have a mission to complete." The words were delivered calmly, rationally. How many times had she heard him say them before? The mission came first—always the mission. So why hadn't she believed him?

He spoke again, his gaze still locked with Elena's until it shifted momentarily to the dead man on the floor. "Aspects of the mission have changed, but fundamentally it remains the same. My country wants to see a strong presence ruling Vendari. They never indicated who that strong presence must be, only that it remain friendly to our interests."

Was he crazy? How could he be talking about political policy at a time like this? Maybe he had a plan? This was Lucius—of course he'd have a plan.

"So you will have me believe you will help take care of our liability here?" Elena cast a brief impersonal glance Jane's way before continuing, "Our only witness to what really happened in this room who does not have a vested interest in keeping it quiet?"

"I would have preferred not to have to kill her." Lucius shrugged and Jane's heart plummeted. "But I will do whatever is necessary to complete my mission."

No. No, this couldn't be happening. Lucius wasn't really saying such things. He couldn't be. This was the man who only moments ago was talking about a picnic with her. Who had told her, again and again, he'd protect her. Maybe he was buying time for his men to rush in and save them? That had to be it. Lucius would never kill her. Never.

She didn't even know she'd made a sound, but it escaped anyway. A soft, choking sound that drew all eyes to her. She could feel them, though she looked at only one face, one set of clear, gray eyes.

Without thinking she found herself shaking her head, denying what she'd heard, wanting Lucius to tell her in some way that everything he'd just said was a lie. A ploy. Something.

But he didn't deny it. Not with his words. Not with his look. Not even with his eyes, so glacially cold she could feel the goose bumps crawl up her arms.

"You will kill Miss Richards?" Eustace asked the question in his blunt manner. Not hiding it behind double talk.

Silence wavered like a tangible beast in the room until Lucius spoke. "I will take care of it."

Jane stepped back, an instinctive, age-old reaction to a threat. A threat coming from a man she loved. Or had that, too, been a lie? Had she given her heart, soul and body to a man who lied with his? Who used her, knowing it could come down to a moment like this, to a cramped room with one dead body and two ruthless people playing with others' lives as if they had no meaning. Playing with her life. Only it wasn't a game and it was Lucius who was going to pull the trigger.

"You said you'd protect me." She whispered the words aloud as she took another step in retreat.

"I told you to trust no one."

Hysteria bubbled within her. He was right, he had told her not to trust anyone, especially him. But had she listened? No. Like a fool she'd walked into his arms and believed what she wanted to about this man. And in spite of everything, she still believed it. She still loved him and that's what was hurting most of all.

"Jane." He spoke it softly, as if it was only the two of them in the room. "It will be quick. I will not hurt you."

The man had said he was going to kill her, but he wouldn't hurt her? Ha!

Even Elena seemed to have a problem with that statement. "I want it done now. Where I can see it."

"Perhaps it would be for the best—"

"No." Elena interrupted Eustace's statement, looking at

only Lucius as she continued. "It must be done here and now. As a sign of good faith between our country and the 71major's."

Oh, that was choice. Not only was she going to be coldly executed, it was going to be on the altar of diplomatic relations. A sacrificial goat so that one country would be pleased with another.

"It will be done. But in my own way. It does not need to be painful."

She wondered who Lucius was trying to reassure—them or her? If it was her, it wasn't working.

"You can't do this." She'd always heard of people begging for their lives and realized it was more than that. She knew, in her heart of hearts that if Lucius killed her, something in him would be lost forever, too. She could read it in his eyes. In the coldness of his words. She wasn't just fighting for her own life here, she was fighting for his, too. "You can't do this, Lucius. There's got to be another way."

He shook his head, denying her statement or denying what he was about to do, she didn't know. She had to try harder.

He stepped forward.

She stepped back.

"I'm no threat to anyone here. Who's going to believe a librarian from Sioux Falls? If I say anything I'll be locked away in a mental hospital for years."

He stepped again.

The couch stopped her retreat.

"Lucius, think this through."

"I have."

She swallowed. "You can't kill me. I love you."

She saw the flicker of shock, or denial, in his eyes, the briefest darkening of their color, the tightening of his jaw before he stepped closer.

"I warned you to trust no one."

"Didn't you hear me?" She wanted to shout it. To hit him over the head with it. Anything to break through to him. "I love you. Don't do this. Don't do this to me. To yourself."

Instead of responding he reached into his pocket and pulled out a palm-sized radio. They all heard his tense words. "Elderman, bring Gomez and the package. Now."

Jane gulped air into her lungs. It must be a code word. Any second now the long-lashed young man assigned to guard her and another would break into the room and stop the insanity. Then Lucius would take her into his arms, tell her it had all been a lie and make everything better.

She spared a quick glance toward Elena, the concern on her face indicating she was obviously thinking along the same lines.

"Eustace?" Elena combined a question and command in one word, but it was unnecessary. Before the dead king's brother could move, the door swung open and two men stood poised in the threshold.

"Thank heavens," the words escaped Jane before she knew it. Relief made her tremble, clutching the back of the couch for support now that the nightmare was over.

But Lucius didn't look relieved. If anything he looked tenser, as if preparing himself for battle instead of celebrating a win.

"Close the door behind you." He barked the orders, reaching his hand toward the black nylon bag Elderman cradled in his. "Give it to me."

What did he need with a bag? Why didn't he tell his men to disarm Elena, the other Elena? To bring further reinforcements in case Eustace decided to make a move?

She glanced from the two young soldiers to Lucius who was unzipping the bag.

"What are you doing?" It was Elena who spoke first.

"I told you I'd take care of the problem." Lucius extracted a small vial and then what looked like a plastic tube. No, not a tube, a syringe.

"No." The guttural cry tore from Jane's throat. "No. Lucius, you can't."

"I must." The statement sounded so calm next to her own outburst that it stopped her from reacting for a split second. Long enough for Lucius's two men to flank her, one on either side.

She never looked at them. Not when they stepped closer. Not when they banded her arms with their hands. Not when they held her immobile. Her whole attention was focused on Lucius. On the precise, controlled movements of his hands as he assembled the syringe, slid the gleaming needle into the vial, pumped liquid through it until it beaded and bled from its tip.

"No, Lucius." The words came as a whimper as he turned toward her, his gaze as bleak as she'd ever seen.

"It has to be this way, Jane. It's the only way."

He walked forward until he stood directly in front of her, his size blocking her view of the other two in the room, his attention as focused on hers as hers was on him.

She looked deep into his eyes and saw his resolve. He believed he was doing the right thing. She read it there. Read his regret, his grief, but foremost his intent to see his mission through.

As if something broke within her she screamed. Not a wounded sound this time but a cry of rage. Of an anger so deep and so bitter it slashed through her.

She pulled her arms from her captors, surprising them with her move, surprising herself. But there was nowhere to run, nowhere to hide. It was the same scenario all over again. The one she'd woken to only weeks ago. She was the hunted and Lucius the hunter. But she was not about to be a victim.

She'd changed between then and now. She would no

longer go along meekly with another's plans for her. Not even Lucius's plans. Lucius, who she trusted with her life, with her heart.

And he'd betrayed them both.

"Jane." He made it sound so soothing, so cajoling, as if pleading with her to understand. But she wasn't going to make it easy for him. He could reject her. Reject the love that she'd offered to him with no strings attached. But she wasn't going to make it easy for him.

She swung around. One foot connecting with a shin, another snagging a leg from behind. She used her elbows, her knees and found space before her. She lunged forward. An arm encircled her waist, lifting her from the floor in the same move, slamming her against a rock-hard chest.

Lucius's chest. She knew from his scent. From the words uttered against her hair.

"Don't fight this, Jane. You'll only make it worse."

Worse? The man was going to kill her and she was supposed to go along meekly?

She didn't think so.

She bucked against him, slamming her head back and forth, clipping his chin, using her feet against his legs, her fingers against anything she could reach.

"Enough." He grunted the word, squeezing her tighter, one arm securely about her waist, pinning both arms, the other across her upper chest, his leg scissoring hers between them.

But she wasn't about to give up. Not yet.

She fought.

He held her tighter.

He uttered words to her, breathless words that meant nothing. She was tiring and they both could sense it.

Tears wet her skin. She could feel them, feel the pain welling up with them. He'd lied to her. He'd lied to her.

The refrain echoed in her head, drowning out his voice, feeding the struggles she refused to cease.

"Elderman. Now."

He held her tighter until the room started to darken. She couldn't breathe. There was nothing left to fight with. He'd lied to her.

"Hold still. It will be over in a minute."

It was over before it started, she thought, feeling the prick of the needle against her skin, aware of Lucius's arms wrapped around her.

"You lied." The words were spoken aloud this time. It no longer matter who heard them. Who knew what a fool she'd been. "I loved you and you lied."

Elderman stepped back, but Lucius's grip did not lessen. If anything it intensified until she could feel the numbing sensation begin—in her hands and feet first, then up her legs and arms.

"You lied." The words mingled with her tears, but it no longer mattered. "How could you lie?"

His hold released, or maybe she no longer could feel it as the coldness seeped through her. She could feel herself slipping, realized it was Lucius moving, kneeling down, her weight still cradled in his arms.

The image of the dead king flashed before her. Soon she'd be laid out beside him, as cold, as still.

She struggled, but it was useless.

"Shhh." It was Lucius's voice, as it had been once before, saying nonsense words as she faded. She thought he'd been kind then. How she could have been such a fool?

"Why wasn't I enough?" Her words sounded slurred, her sight dimming. But she could still make out Lucius's face bending over her, his eyes agonized. Hadn't she thought they were cold before? There was nothing cold in them now. Now she could see emotions so deep and anguished she wanted to weep for him.

But he'd made his choice. And it hadn't been her.

"Don't fight it, Jane. Damn it, don't fight it."

He almost sounded as if he was trying to reassure her. His hands brushed her hair from her face, dried the tears still fresh there. She wanted to smile at that. Tell him it didn't matter any more if he killed her, not after he'd broken her heart. But the words wouldn't come. Not those at least.

"I loved you. You lied and I loved..." the last word faded away, the cold almost complete, the room almost dark. She could no longer see his face, nor feel his arms around her, but she could still hear.

It was Elena's voice demanding, "Is it over?"

"It's all over."

They were the last words she heard before the darkness came.

Chapter 14

Five weeks, ten days and fourteen hours. Jane glanced up at the institutional clock in the library's basement break room. Fifteen hours. It was a good sign that she'd stopped counting the minutes. It was, wasn't it?

Five weeks, ten days and fifteen hours and no word. Nothing. Not an e-mail, or a letter, or an archaic telegram. Nothing. The sooner she accepted that he had never really cared, the better. The other alternative? He was dead. And as painful as the first realization was, she knew it was nothing to accepting the second.

Her throat closed and the piece of whole wheat bread in her hands crumbled. She glanced at the clock again. Fifteen hours and four minutes.

The TV made a small hum in the background of the break room. Jane hadn't even realized it was on until Sue Dobson, the children's librarian, spoke.

"There, Jane. That's you."

Jane glanced at the small screen and froze.

Elena Rostov. Or was it Elena Tarkioff now?

Sue's voice droned on. "That's the woman I was telling you about that looks just like you."

Several gazes turned toward Jane. Marion White from circulation. Ted Peters from the bookmobile.

Marion's voice chimed in, "You're right, Sue. Isn't that the woman who's been on the news these last weeks?"

"Almost every night. She's some princess in some east European country. It all sounded so romantic at first."

More like a nightmare.

Sue continued her litany. "Seems like she was going to marry the king. Only he was assassinated."

Murdered.

"Then his brother stepped up and was willing to both become king and marry her."

More than willing.

"Only they found out the brother was behind the king's death."

"What?" That snagged Jane's attention.

"Honey, haven't you been listening to the news lately? Or reading the papers?"

"Go easy, Sue." Marion interjected with a shake of her head. "Can't you see Jane's still mourning her aunt? It was your aunt who passed away wasn't it?"

"Yes. My aunt." The words rasped against her throat.

"Hard to lose someone you love and pay attention to the everyday things at the same time. It's no wonder you don't know what's happening halfway around the world."

"What is happening?" Jane asked. Not wanting to know anything, unable to let it go. A moth to the flame.

Sue spoke up. "They feared there was going to be a revolution."

"But?"

"But when all the dirty details came out, both the brother

to the king and the woman who looks like Jane were exposed as murderers.''

''They were? But what happened?''

Was he alive?

''It's been quite the soap opera.'' It was Ted Peters nodding. ''It seems the U.S. was involved with the king. The murdered one. Some then wondered if we were behind the king's death.''

No. Not the king's.

''But now there's some second cousin on the throne and things finally look like they're going to even out.''

''Without bloodshed?'' Jane asked, aware she held her breath.

Sue looked at Marion who looked at Ted.

''I didn't hear of any deaths,'' Ted said. ''Though there usually are a few causalities in this type of thing. Innocents who get in the way.''

Didn't she know it?

''So that's it?'' Her voice shook but she steadied it. ''What about the U.S. involvement? Aren't there advisors and such?''

Gray eyes. Wary, lonely, deceiving gray eyes.

''Doesn't anybody know what happened to them?''

Ted stood, carefully folding and refolding his paper napkin. ''Probably were. Probably still are. Us small fish are the last to know what's happening with the big fish.''

So true.

Marion rose, too. Just as the intercom buzzed and Doreen Bellows's voice crackled over it. ''Jane? Jane Richards? There's a patron in research who insists on speaking to you.''

Jane looked at her barely eaten meal but it was Marion who answered. ''Doreen, can't someone else handle it? Jane just started her break.''

''He's very insistent.''

Marion's brows arched as she glanced at Jane. "He?"

"Probably Mr. Witherspoon." Jane stuffed her sandwich back into her paper sack. "He's researching Sumerian tablets and—"

"He has a bouquet of yellow roses." Doreen's voice cackled again.

"No researcher ever brought me roses." Marion grinned and winked.

"Me neither," chimed in Sue.

"Don't look at me." Ted grabbed his archeological magazine. "But if I had someone waiting for me with roses I wouldn't be lagging."

She wasn't lagging. Catching one's breath wasn't lagging. Surely there was a mistake. There were any number of reasons a man with roses was asking for her. Any number.

She was still reassuring herself when she walked around the corner and froze.

Any number of reasons except this one.

"Are you all right?" Lucius stood less then three feet away, his face looking drawn and wary, a bouquet of vibrant sunny roses clenched in his hands.

This was not happening to her.

"You're alive?"

"Of course I am." He sounded surprised that she'd even asked.

"Why are you here?" She was barely aware she asked the question. There were so many questions crowding through her thoughts.

She watched him flinch before he stepped forward. "I needed to see you. To make sure you were all right."

He made it sound so simple. This man who had upended her life. This man who made her want and ache, cry and beg. Who had woken her heart only to break it clean in half. She could kill him for it.

"Well? Are you?" he asked, his voice rough.

"Oh, I'm just peachy keen. Now you can leave."

She knew they were alone. At least for the moment. But any second a patron could walk past the small desk and filing area. She was not about to have a public scene at her place of work. And no doubt he knew that.

Her words were bitter, her actions automatic, the numbness she'd come to live with over the last months intensified. The old Jane would have been flustered, pleased that he'd sought her out. The new Jane could only remember how fragile the last weeks had been. And why.

She heard his sharp intake of breath.

"Jane—"

"I mean it, Major. You know where the exit is. Same door as you came in." She didn't dare raise her hand to point the way. She was afraid it'd shake too much.

"We've got to talk."

"We're no longer in Vendari, Major. You're no longer calling the shots. I'd like you to leave."

Where were the words coming from? The hurt? The pain? The betrayal?

She'd loved him and he hadn't trusted her. Not once.

Well, she'd been a fool before, but that Jane had disappeared. She might not be wearing designer clothes and silks any longer, but neither was she plain Jane now. Crushed Jane—yes. But only if she let herself be swayed by this man.

"You're upset," he said.

"You noticed."

He ran a hand through his hair. A move not in sync with the calm, controlled man she knew.

"Look, I know there's a lot to explain and this isn't the best place to do it." He spoke as if she wasn't standing there glaring at him.

Do not relent. Do not believe his tone. He broke your heart. Remember that. He broke your heart.

"No explanations are necessary." If only her emotions

could feel as cold as her words. But they didn't. They felt shaky and unsure. He'd hurt her—unbearably, but now he was back. And he wanted to talk. As if she'd believe that.

Why did she care?

"We will talk, Jane." He made it sound like a promise, and a threat. But before she could protest he moved, with that lethal, quiet grace of his. Closed the space between them. His arm was about her, pulling her close, his lips claiming hers. Hard. Possessive. Demanding.

She wanted to fight, to protest. Something. Anything. Except what she did. She stepped toward him instead of away. Met his heat with her own. It was a kiss she knew neither would be able to forget.

All her resolve to remain aloof crashed with the taste of him.

Damn the man.

When he raised his head, his gaze impaling hers, he smiled, a knowing, warrior's smile.

"My part in this whole mess was inexcusable."

Understatement.

"And I made some mistakes."

Big-time.

"But I'm not the only one."

What?

As if he'd read her unspoken thought, he replied. "You said you loved me, Jane. Love means trust. You should have trusted that I'd never have done anything to hurt you."

He knew he'd caught her off guard. It was intentional. He'd take any advantage he could get to win her back. He had, too. She was his life. Her kiss gave him hope and he clung to it as he'd clung to his sanity the last weeks. The ones without her. The ones where he didn't know how she was, if she'd forgiven him. Communication had been impossible until Elena and Eustace were both safely behind bars and the new king installed.

But now he was here and she was in his arms. At last.

"Jane?"

"The news said Elena and Eustace were arrested."

"I didn't come to talk about Vendari." The words sounded blunt, harsh, almost desperate.

"Well." He could see her trying to emotionally distance herself. Pull away from him. "That doesn't leave much for us to discuss."

He knew it wasn't going to be easy. Never had he expected it to be this hard. Where was the Jane who put herself out to be kind to total strangers, the one who faced an impossible situation head-on, the one who'd told him she loved him? The woman before him looked like her, but held herself still and distant.

She was killing him by the second and didn't seem to care. Not that he deserved more. Not after what he'd done to her.

"If it will make a difference I'll apologize to you." The words felt like sandpaper rasping along his throat.

"For?" Her arched brow reminded him of the other Elena, then he remembered there was only one Elena. And one Jane.

"Do you want me to start at the top of the list or just hit the highlights?" His own voice sounded testy, frustrated.

She tried to pull out of his grasp but he wouldn't let her. The roses fell to the floor.

"Isn't it a bit pointless to discuss any of this?" she sliced at him with her cool tone. "You did what you had to do. You obviously accomplished your mission or you wouldn't be here."

"I hurt you." More than he ever wanted. It kept him awake at night. Kept him from finding any semblance of peace. "I never meant to hurt you. It happened, but it didn't mean I wanted it to happen."

"I know." The words fell like ice crystals—splintered facets of fragility waiting to dissolve.

She knew? But wouldn't forgive him?

He almost gave up right then and there, until he noticed her hands. Maybe by instinct, or desperation, he glanced at her hands and felt the first inkling of hope since he'd seen her. Her words might be overly calm and aloof, but her hands, pleating the plain fabric of her skirt, were anything but.

He pulled her closer, willing her to look at him.

"There's something else I needed to tell you." He saw her brace herself as if for a blow and wondered if he was doing the right thing. But if he never once said the words, never once took the risk, neither one of them would ever know what might have been. "I want us to be together, Jane. To start fresh, with the past behind us."

Jane had thought she couldn't hurt anymore, couldn't feel through the numbness that had encased her since she had awakened on a private jet—alone except for one of Lucius's faithful team members who gave her no more information than that she was on her way back home and the effects of the drug given her to make her appear dead would wear off after a few hours.

Well, they hadn't. The coldness had remained. The sensation of things not being quite real had persisted. The feeling of utter hopelessness had weighed down upon her until she had wanted to break with the bending. Until now.

"Don't." She held her hands before her as if to ward off a physical attack. "Just don't…"

His features looked as anguished as she felt. But that wasn't possible. He'd made his choices months ago.

"You lied to me." She hated that it sounded like a whimper, but she knew she couldn't survive hope again. "You used me and let me believe I was going to die."

"I know. I know. Every day I've gone over and over

what other options I had available. What else I could have done.''

"You knew it was Elena behind the attacks."

"I guessed Eustace was involved. But I knew there had to be someone else. When Elena walked through the door so much finally made sense. But all the time I was hoping to get you away before I had to resort to using the drug.''

"Why didn't you let me know?"

"If I had let you know you would never have been as convincing as you were.'' His words fell like leaden weights. "Elena had to believe you were dead. That I would kill you or she would have done it herself. I couldn't risk that. I couldn't risk you.''

She stepped back. This time he released her, letting his arms fall to his sides. Why was he forcing all the pain she'd begun to bury back to the surface? Why couldn't she just hate him and be done with it?

"Jane?" The word sounded like a plea. But this man was not the one who had begged for his life. She was. "You've got to understand that deceiving you, hurting you that way was the hardest thing I've ever done in my life."

Hadn't she known that even then? Known that if he killed her he'd also be killing a part of himself? She'd worried about it then, when she was facing death, but she hadn't thought what acting as if he'd killed her would have cost him. Was costing him if she gauged the deepness of the creases around his eyes, the tension radiating from his body. Is that what he'd meant in saying that if she'd loved him she should have trusted him? Trusted her own realization that he'd never hurt her?

She hadn't let herself see beyond her own feelings of betrayal, of pain, to think that he, too, might be hurting.

Suddenly she felt too tired to deal with any of it. She was on her home turf now. Safe. Secure. Boring, yes, but the intrigues that surfaced at the library involved abusing break time or petty insults exchanged, not lives lost and hearts broken.

She'd had a choice once. Not much of one, but he had given her a choice. Now she had another one. Stay in her safe, sane world, or step out on an impossibly shaky limb with Lucius McConneghy.

"Does it make any difference what you did and why?" she said at last.

The words hung between them until he stepped forward, his hands shoved into his pockets, his expression as intense as it had been on the night they'd first made love. "Yes. It does make a difference. It can—if you'll let it."

"Have you forgotten that I'm still a Sioux Falls librarian and you're from an obscure department in an obscure corner of the Pentagon?"

"Not anymore."

"What do you mean?"

"I quit."

He was doing it all over again, tilting her world on end, one sentence at a time.

She looked at him, really looked at him, wondering if she'd heard him quite right. "What do you mean you quit?"

"I mean I turned in my letter of resignation, cleaned out my desk drawers and walked away."

"Why?"

It was his turn to stare at her, his features softening, the smallest of smiles touching his lips. "I didn't want to make my wife a widow. I didn't want her to deal with the McConneghy tradition even for one day."

"Your wife?" She knew she sounded addle-brained but that wasn't unusual around him.

"I assumed you'd want to get married." He gave a small shrug. "Though I'd be willing to live together. At least until our firstborn is due to arrive. Which I hope happens as soon as we can make it happen."

"Our firstborn?" Now she was downright stuttering.

"Of course." He stepped beside her, reaching out to pull her to him again. "I always thought three was a good number but we can have more or less if you want."

"This isn't real." She could only stare up into those gray eyes she'd once thought cold. "You're not real. I don't know why you're doing this but I want you to stop."

"Not until you say yes." He shook her, ever so gently, as if wakening her from a long sleep. "I want you in my life, Jane. I need you in my life."

"But..."

"But?"

The old Jane might have buckled. Taken what he was offering and been happy. But it wasn't enough. Not any more. Plain, ordinary, everyday Jane she wasn't. Not any more.

"It's not enough," she said, shaking her head.

He looked stunned, but she held her ground. This was too important to give up on. Way too important.

Suddenly he grinned and his voice sounded raw with emotion. "I love you, Jane. I love you until I ache with it. You are the best thing that's ever come into my life and I hurt you. I won't ever forgive myself for that. For what I put you through. But I still think we have a chance. If you'll let us."

Did she dare trust him? Trust his words?

"I love you, Jane Richards. Only you." He said it with the solemnity of a vow and she could feel her heart begin to beat again. "I'll always love you. I want to build a life with you, a good life, with children and cats and dogs and gray hairs and rocking chairs."

She thought he meant it.

He wrapped her in his arms as if afraid she'd bolt. She could hear the beat of his heart beneath her cheek, inhale the scent that was only his. "You're the strongest, bravest, most giving woman I've ever met."

Was he talking about her?

"You're beautiful and kind, your smile lights all the corners of a room and your kisses make my knees weak."

He thought of *her* like that?

"I want to wake up next to you every morning and go to sleep next to you every night."

"And you want to get married?"

"As soon as we can."

It was true then. It really was. She wanted to pinch herself to make sure it was real.

She heard the sound of laughter and hand-clapping coming from behind the nearest stack of books.

"You go, girlfriend," Marion shouted. Followed by Sue. "This is so much more romantic than some dumb princess in some faraway place."

Jane simply looked up into gray eyes. Loving, caring, smiling gray eyes.

"Friends of yours?" he asked.

"Yes."

"Then we'd better ask them to the wedding."

He didn't wait for a response. But she heard more clapping erupt as he bent to kiss her.

Then she knew it was real and that it would last a lifetime.

* * * * *

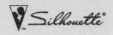

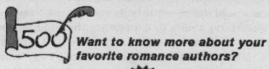

If you enjoyed what you just read,
then we've got an offer you can't resist!

Take 2 bestselling love stories FREE!

Plus get a FREE surprise gift!

///

Clip this page and mail it to Silhouette Reader Service™

IN U.S.A.	IN CANADA
3010 Walden Ave.	P.O. Box 609
P.O. Box 1867	Fort Erie, Ontario
Buffalo, N.Y. 14240-1867	L2A 5X3

YES! Please send me 2 free Silhouette Intimate Moments® novels and my free surprise gift. After receiving them, if I don't wish to receive anymore, I can return the shipping statement marked cancel. If I don't cancel, I will receive 6 brand-new novels every month, before they're available in stores! In the U.S.A., bill me at the bargain price of $4.24 plus 25¢ shipping and handling per book and applicable sales tax, if any*. In Canada, bill me at the bargain price of $4.99 plus 25¢ shipping and handling per book and applicable taxes**. That's the complete price and a savings of at least 10% off the cover prices—what a great deal! I understand that accepting the 2 free books and gift places me under no obligation ever to buy any books. I can always return a shipment and cancel at any time. Even if I never buy another book from Silhouette, the 2 free books and gift are mine to keep forever.

245 SDN DZ9A
345 SDN DZ9C

Name	(PLEASE PRINT)	
Address	Apt.#	
City	State/Prov.	Zip/Postal Code

* Terms and prices subject to change without notice. Sales tax applicable in N.Y.
** Canadian residents will be charged applicable provincial taxes and GST.
All orders subject to approval. Offer limited to one per household and not valid to current Silhouette Intimate Moments® subscribers.
® are registered trademarks owned and used by the trademark owner and or its licensee.

INMOM04   ©2004 Harlequin Enterprises Limited

COMING NEXT MONTH

#1309 IN THE DARK—Heather Graham
Alexandra McCord's life was unraveling. The body she'd discovered had disappeared—and now she was trapped on an island with a hurricane roaring in and someone threatening her life. To make matters worse, the only man she could rely on was the ex-husband she'd never forgotten, David Denhem, who might be her savior—or a killer.

#1310 SHOTGUN HONEYMOON—Terese Ramin
No one had to force Janina Galvez to marry Native American cop Russ Levoie. She'd loved him since his rookie days, but their lives had gone in separate directions. Now his proposal—and protection—seemed like the answer to her prayers. But would he be able to save her from the threat from her past, or would danger overwhelm them both?

#1311 TRIPLE DARE—Candace Irvin
Family Secrets: The Next Generation
Wealthy recluse Darian Sabura had resigned himself to a solitary existence—until he heard violinist Abigail Pembroke's music. Then Abby witnessed a murder, and suddenly it was up to Darian to keep her alive. But would she feel protected—or panicked—when she learned he was empathetic and could literally sense every private thought?

#1312 HEIR TO DANGER—Valerie Parv
Code of the Outback
The Australian outback was about as far as Princess Shara Najran of Q'aresh could go to escape her evil ex-fiancé. With her life at stake, she sought sanctuary in the arms of rugged ranger Tom McCullough. But when her past loomed, threatening Tom's life, would Shara run again to protect the man she loved—or stay and fight for their future?

#1313 BULLETPROOF HEARTS—Brenda Harlen
When D.A. Natalie Vaughn stumbled onto a murder scene, Lieutenant Dylan Creighton knew the sexy prosecutor had just placed herself on a crime kingpin's hit list. And when they were forced to work together to bring him down, their powerful attraction for each other became too irresistible to deny.

#1314 GUARDING LAURA—Susan Vaughan
When it came to guarding Laura Rossiter, government operative Cole Stratton preferred jungle combat to a forced reunion with his old flame. But having someone else protect her from a madman determined to see her dead wasn't an option. Would Cole's nerves of steel see him through the toughest battle of his life—winning Laura's heart?

SIMCNM0704